Praise for *Fervour*

'This is a stylish, puzzling, mystical novel that offers no easy answer to how its characters – or its readers – might react in the wake of destruction. Inviting discussion rather than providing resolution, *Fervour* marks the arrival of an intriguing and intelligent new voice'
Financial Times

'Infused with motifs from Jewish folklore and classic horror films, *Fervour* animates themes of betrayal, belief and the past's long tail'
Observer

'A North London Jewish family, by turns close-knit and dysfunctional, take centre stage in Lloyd's remarkable debut . . . Lloyd has given himself a large canvas, peopled with complex characters, but produced a work of real poignancy'
Mail on Sunday

'In one of the most perceptive of her late essays, "God's Language", Toni Morrison sets out her objective as a novelist: "to construct a work in which religious belief is central to the narrative itself" . . . Not an easy task – but one that Toby Lloyd, in his magnificent, indelible debut novel, *Fervour*, takes on with confidence, and with resounding success . . . Enriching his story with detail and above all heart, Lloyd has crafted a lasting allegory of our dark historical time'
New York Times

'Intriguing, propulsive and profoundly disturbing, this is a fearless look into the dark heart of family politics from a naturally gifted storyteller'
Jonathan Coe, author of *Bournville*

'Darkly comedic in parts, yet deeply disturbing and utterly compelling, *Fervour* is an exceptional debut novel, one that will stay with me'
Jennie Godfrey, author of *The List of Suspicious Things*

Toby Lloyd has published stories and essays in *Carve Magazine*, the *Los Angeles Review of Books* and elsewhere. He earned an MFA in creative writing from NYU and was longlisted for the 2021 V. S. Pritchett Short Story Prize. He lives in London.

Fervour

Toby Lloyd

Sceptre

First published in Great Britain in 2024 by Sceptre
An imprint of Hodder & Stoughton Limited
An Hachette UK company

This paperback edition published in 2025

The authorised representative in the EEA is Hachette Ireland, 8 Castlecourt Centre,
Dublin 15, D15 XTP3, Ireland (email: info@hbgi.ie)

1

A CIP catalogue record for this title is available from the British Library

Paperback ISBN 9781399724654
ebook ISBN 9781399724630

Typeset in Sabon MT Std by Manipal Technologies Limited.

Printed and bound in Great Britain by Clays Ltd, Elcograf S.p.A.

Hodder & Stoughton policy is to use papers that are natural, renewable and
recyclable products and made from wood grown in sustainable forests. The logging
and manufacturing processes are expected to conform to the environmental
regulations of the country of origin.

Hodder & Stoughton Limited
Carmelite House
50 Victoria Embankment
London EC4Y 0DZ

www.sceptrebooks.co.uk

For Zoey

When the Baal Shem Tov was near his death, a student came to him with a written book and said, 'These are your words which I have written down. This is the Torah of Rabbi Israel.'

The Master read what was written, and said, 'Not one word of this is my Torah.'

Hassidic Legend, trans. Meyer Levin

PART ONE
GEHINNOM AND AFTERWARDS

Chapter One

It is told:

Before Yosef died, the three Rosenthal children were summoned in turn to the attic where he'd spent his final decade, a bedroom with an en-suite and adjoining kitchen, all sheeted in a layer of dust; the last cleaner had given notice weeks earlier, and there'd been no need for a replacement. Tovyah, being the youngest, went third. No one said this was going to be the last time he would speak to his grandfather, but he wasn't allowed up before he'd washed his face and changed into a clean shirt. His mother put one hand on his shoulder while she dragged a brush through his knotted hair.

'That hurts,' he said.

'Life hurts,' she replied, and straightened his collar.

He found the old man piled under blankets and propped up by several pillows, his posture not of relaxation but collapse. Zeide's eyes were screwed shut and Tovyah thought he'd fallen asleep. But then Zeide said his name, as though reminding himself what the boy was called.

'I'm here,' Tovyah said.

Blinking a few times, the old man opened his eyes. He wanted to know if his grandson was doing well in school.

Of course! Nineteen out of twenty in his latest maths homework, and no one else got more than fifteen. He left out the part where, after class, Jack Thomas rewarded his success with a Chinese burn.

Zeide coughed, then resumed his perpetual frown. '*Gut.*' Tovyah had grown up terrified of his grandfather. His earliest memory was of firing marbles across the floor with Elsie, ecstatically happy until Zeide thundered down from the attic and screamed at them. 'Five minutes together of peace! What's so hard?' The old man waved his stick in the air, and Tovyah had feared the beak of the eagle-shaped grip would come swooping down towards him.

But illness had transformed the man. These days his hands wobbled and his speech was choked. Looking closely, Tovyah could see a line of red beneath each of his grandfather's faded eyes, almost colourless themselves, like raw egg whites. As for the tautness in his bearing, the sharp edges, the irresistible glowering that could force even his mother into submission – all of that was gone.

Now Zeide's breathing grew hoarse and uneven. Tovyah wondered if it might stop altogether, if he was about to witness the moment the line was crossed. Could the old man die before his eyes? What then? Sam Morris, who on weekends derived great frustration and a little sadistic pleasure from hammering basic Hebrew into kids like Tovyah, was cagey when asked about the afterlife. 'That's not for us to know,' he'd say, before changing the subject.

Zeide's breathing returned to a steady rhythm. Attempting to push himself upright, he beckoned the boy closer. So this was it, the reason he was here. Now he would receive his grandfather's parting gift, the great revelation, something he'd carry with him through the course of his life.

'Don't make me shout,' Zeide warned. Tovyah approached his bed.

Doggedly, the old man rose and sank against the head-board until he reached a stalemate. The effort seemed to do him good. His voice rang out clearer now, more insistent. 'The second son is very special. Abel was the second son, Isaac was the second son, and Jacob was the second son. I was the second son, and you also are the second son. Not Gideon, you.'

Unsure if a response was expected, Tovyah kept his mouth shut. He'd heard this sermon before. Zeide continued. 'Tell me. You believe in God?'

The question struck, a blow from the dark. 'Of course,' Tovyah said. His toes pressed into the carpet.

'No, not *of course*.'

Zeide coughed again and there was silence.

'Let me show you.' With pitiful slowness, the way he now performed every little action, he tugged at the sleeve of his nightshirt. Tovyah wished his grandfather would stop, and not expose that ancient limb.

'You know what this is?' Zeide asked, holding the raised sleeve above the elbow.

Tovyah stared at the white forearm and couldn't speak. The goose flesh, those horrible black marks.

'And you know what it means?'

Tovyah nodded.

'You don't know. It means there are people who think they decide who is human and who is not human.' He paused, scratched his sagging elbow, and went on. 'It has no point, a life without God. What meaning is there? Don't shake your head. What means something to you?'

There was nothing to say.

'You think God cares you don't believe in Him? God laughs.'

Still Tovyah didn't speak. And soon, he didn't have to; Zeide, having expended what small reserves of energy remained, drooped against his pillows. His eyes closed. When he spoke again, he asked his grandson if he had seen Ariel lately. Tovyah was used to this kind of talk, the dropped threads, the questions from nowhere. But he'd never known anyone called Ariel.

His grandfather continued. 'Elsie plays with him sometimes, doesn't she? He's only a little boy. Be gentle.'

'With who?'

'Ariel! Listen. He has colour on his face. Here.'

Zeide was tapping the ridge of his eyebrow, and Tovyah felt his memory prickling. The dimmest of recollections, a shadow at the edge of his mind. On some distant night, he'd been woken by voices from Elsie's room. He'd tiptoed over, wondering who Elsie could be talking to. There was a little light spilling from the open door. And when he peeped through the crack, he saw Elsie's face lit up by her reading lamp. Sitting on the end of the bed, with hands folded in his lap, was a boy his own age. No one he knew. And above his eye was a dark patch, reminding Tovyah of the dappling you get on cows. When he spoke, the language that came out was not English.

Tovyah couldn't be sure if this was a true memory, or something he'd dreamt. It was so watery in his mind. Zeide, meanwhile, was squirming.

'Where am I going?' he said.

Tovyah didn't understand.

'Will they keep me locked up, or set me free?'

The boy lowered his gaze. No answer was required; his grandfather was talking nonsense to himself again.

'Listen!' Zeide said, alert to his grandson's presence once more. 'Watch out for Elsie. And Gideon. The second son protects the others, yes? He carries the torch. Now help me change my pillows. They're scratching. Filthy chicken feathers!' When this was done, he told Tovyah to refill the glass by the side of his bed. For a moment, the boy lingered. Was there nothing more? His grandfather's bent finger and fierce eyes sent him on his way.

Before he reached the kitchen, he was ambushed by his brother and sister on the landing. They led him to Elsie's room, and Gideon shut the door. 'So?'

Tovyah was conflicted. Elsie was his closest ally in the family; the perfect daughter, she always defended his minor lapses to their parents – chocolate and milk within a few hours of Sunday roast, flicking the light one sleepless Sabbath to see where he was peeing. But Gideon made him uncomfortable. His brother was sixteen now, had a man's hard voice, and made a point of standing in front of the bathroom mirror, door wide open, his face slathered in shaving cream. It wasn't just his body that had changed. His interests were evolving too; he no longer participated in the games and fantasies that filled Tovyah and Elsie's free time.

Gideon was speaking again. 'Come on, Tuvs! He told me I was the spitting image of his brother Mendl, who I guess was some kind of war hero, and then he said I was gonna move to Israel. And he basically told Elsie she's a prophet.'

Elsie clicked her tongue. 'He said I hear the voice of God.'

'Same diff. What did you get?'

Tovyah glanced from his brother's face, filled out like risen dough, to his sister's. He wanted to talk to Elsie alone.

'He said the second son is special. You know, like Isaac.'

Gideon waited a moment, expecting more. 'That's it? You got a Torah lesson? I know you're not his favourite, but man, that sucks.'

Elsie looked like she was working something out. 'Did Zeide forget how to count? I'm pretty sure the second child is me.'

Gideon shook his head. 'You're a girl. Girls aren't sons.'

'Don't be so literal.'

If Tovyah mentioned that Zeide had tasked him with protecting the others, he knew he'd be laughed at. Why didn't he get any wondrous predictions about his future, something he could boast about with his brother? Like so much else, it wasn't fair.

'And he showed me his tattoo!' he blurted.

'No way,' Gideon said.

'I swear!'

Gideon laughed. 'Of course he showed you the arm. He's always whipping it out.' He yanked up the sleeve of his shirt, looked down at his own forearm, and gasped in mock horror.

Elsie slapped Gideon's knee. 'It's his first time seeing it.'

'All right, all right, fair enough,' Gideon said, pulling down his sleeve. 'That shit is pretty real. Specially at your age. Was there, like, a reason he showed you?'

Tovyah said Zeide just wanted him to see it.

'You sure he wasn't threatening you?'

'I'm sure.'

'My first time was on holiday. Bournemouth or Cromer or somewhere, one of those little bitch towns on the English coast they used to drag us to. This was before your time, Tuvs. We got undressed on the beach, and I said, "Zeide, you've got a tattoo! Awesome!"'

'I expect he hit you,' Elsie said.

'You're damn right. "Nu, nu," he said. "Zis iz nawt awesome." Thumped me round the back of my head so hard I fell over. Hannah told me he never wanted the tattoo, that bad men put it on him. And for years, I thought the old guy was some kind of gangster.'

Satisfied there was nothing more to wring out of his little brother, Gideon left to cook dinner – something he said Eric and Hannah would be in no mood to do. Calling their parents by name was another thing that made Gideon so different, suddenly. Elsie was less impressed. She said it was pretentious, a word Tovyah didn't know.

Now that the two of them were alone, Elsie studied her younger brother. Her expression softened. 'Did Zeide also tell you he wants to be incinerated?'

Another word Tovyah didn't know. But he was a quick child, and in a flash the meaning came to him. A black gate holding back terrible light, an orange glow, flames. The smell of ashes, like after a barbeque.

Unable to sleep a few nights before, Tovyah had wandered from his room and settled at the top of the stairs. Gripping the banisters, he'd listened to a puzzling conversation his parents were having in the living room below. An argument. According to his mother, Zeide wanted to be cremated. The last few months, she'd gone up to the attic daily, just to sit and hear the old man talk. This in itself was odd; she'd always had a distant, even frosty relationship with her father-in-law. But since she'd got it into her head to write a book about his life story, the two were inseparable. This, Eric did not like.

Nor did he like the idea of cremation. 'Impossible,' he declared. And Tovyah, slinking down several steps to hear better, understood why. The law commands that the dead must be buried. Anything else is a desecration.

'Yes,' Tovyah said now to Elsie, speaking very seriously. 'He doesn't want to be buried under the ground.'

Elsie smiled. 'Who does?'

Tovyah still had the empty glass with him when he left his sister's room. As it turned out, the request for water was the last thing he heard his grandfather say. When he returned to the attic, he found the old man sleeping with his mouth open, teeth bared, and a little drool running down his chin. Snoring uncomfortably, Zeide fought to dislodge something at the back of his throat, while Tovyah crept from the room.

All the next day, nothing happened – no one died. Elsie was noticeably quiet, keeping her door closed throughout the afternoon. At dinner, she bolted her pasta and asked to be excused from the table before either of her siblings had finished. Alone once more, she worked on a long poem for her grandfather. When she read it aloud to the family the following morning, Tovyah thought it was beautiful. Though some passages were hard to understand, the final image imprinted itself with total clarity: a silhouette receding into a dark tunnel, following in the path of a smaller, murkier shape, a boy's shadow. Elsie wanted to chase the figure of her grandfather before he disappeared, but she had to let him go. If she chased him, she was afraid of the face that might turn to meet her.

'I don't like it,' Hannah said. She did not believe in fulsome praise. She believed, without having been told, that her children appreciated her honesty. She believed everyone appreciated her honesty.

'I think it's wonderful,' said Eric, whose preference for his daughter above his other two children was an open secret.

'Tunnel as symbol for death? It's a whopping cliché.'

'She's thirteen! To you it's a cliché, to her it's a discovery.'

Elsie bristled. 'I'm not a child, Dad.'

'Ignore your mother. It's a lovely metaphor. A variation on an ancient trope.'

'But it's not a metaphor,' Elsie said. 'It's a description. A metaphor is something that isn't really happening.'

That evening, when Tovyah's mother pushed open his bedroom door and finally delivered the news, he had an urge to go upstairs and look. He had seen a dead mouse, flattened against the curb with blood pooling round its head, but he'd never seen a dead person. Not even in pictures. 'It's OK if you want to cry,' Hannah said. She was not crying. She kissed her youngest on the top of his head and left the room. Gideon was out with friends at the time, officially playing five-a-side, unofficially doing who knows what. The report of Zeide's death filled Tovyah with a coiled unease. Once, playing a game with Elsie in which they'd imagined themselves arctic explorers, he'd been trapped in his mother's wardrobe. When his sister left the room tittering, he couldn't find the handle to let himself out. Panic-stricken, he threw his shoulder against the door, and cried for help. Nobody came. Again he cried out but still nobody came. Soon his shoulder hurt and his mind spun. He groped among the coats and dresses, felt something rough against his face. When he stopped crying and listened, he couldn't hear a sound. A frightening realisation swept through him: if, for a joke, Elsie had gone out, there was no one in the house. Only Zeide, cocooned in his attic. Eventually, he found the interior handle, just within reach. But if he hadn't? How long would he have spent enclosed in that dark space, bellowing sporadically? Impossible to say. There would have been no way to measure the passing seconds. Just indivisible darkness, folds and folds of limp cloth.

No wonder his grandfather didn't want to be interred: he didn't want to be packed into a small box for eternity, shouting at darkness, slack linen against his face.

*

Although Yosef Rosenthal kept little company in his final years, an impressive crowd met the coffin at the burial ground. All of Eric and Hannah's friends, the adults who populated Tovyah's universe outside of school, showed up. Up front was Sam Morris, his black yarmulke an island on the sea of his bald head, his eyes like a pigeon's, broadcasting disbelief. Behind him walked Ida from the kosher butchers, who sometimes made jokes Tovyah didn't get and that turned his face red. Then came Bryn Cohen and his second wife Clare; the Konigsbergs and all their stocky children; Freddy Marx with the knot of his tie loose as a schoolboy's; Jane and Jonathan Strasfogel, swapping pleasantries with Benny Michaelson, whose father had married out, bestowing on him the humiliation of converting. (Rumours, there were, of adult circumcision.) As they approached the newly dug hole in the ground, Gideon kicked Tovyah's ankle and directed his attention to Ruth and Rebecca Solomon, sometime baby-sitters, and heroines of much nocturnal speculation. They were trailed by unmarried Lotte (let us not forget her in our prayers); all three Shaw sisters; Yehuda with his repulsive face-mole; and enormous Harry Nathan arm-in-arm with slim, six-footed Vera, a couple once described by Hannah as the dish who ran away with the spoon. There were as many faces again that Tovyah didn't recognise. All black-garbed, solemn-eyed, and silent, as if to bid goodbye to a departing era. Was Zeide so important?

Rabbi Grossman, clutching his script in his tiny hands, took a few goes to unclog his throat. In an interval between Hebrew incantations, he praised (in English) Yosef Rosenthal's heroism as a witness and a survivor, a man who refused to give up no matter what, as evidenced by a sight no less miraculous than that of his adult son, and his three beautiful grandchildren.

By the law of averages, none of them had any right to be born. And yet despite tremendous forces of antagonism, here they were today, healthy, united, and loving.

At this moment, Eric placed a hand on each of his son's shoulders, and Tovyah had the strange sense that without their support, Eric would fall down on the spot. He had never seen his father cry before. Looking up at that familiar face, transformed by grief, Tovyah flushed with guilt; he'd thought only Elsie was upset. Soon, he too was crying.

Like any verbal will whose instructions confound its listeners, Yosef's final wishes were simply ignored. Following centuries of custom, Eric decreed that his father would be wrapped in his tallit and buried in East Ham Cemetery next to Janet of beloved memory. Only Elsie objected. As the body was lowered, she stood back, clicking her tongue. And when her mother handed her a small round stone to place on the grave, she stowed it away in her pocket. 'This is all wrong,' she said. Elsie was drawing attention to herself now, but Hannah let it go. 'Funerals do funny things to people,' Eric said later.

Afterwards, the family huddled in the attic and sat shiva along with various honoured guests invited to complete the minyan. There was much weeping and rocking back and forth. All the mirrors in the house were covered with black cloth, and for seven days the portals to those illusory depths were closed.

That was in summer, the last of the century. And so, Yosef Rosenthal, child of the twenties, never made it to the new millennium. He was a Jew born into Warsaw's lower middle class, whose first home was long ago obliterated by ancient hatreds and modern politics well beyond the reach of his imagination. As the course of his life bundled him across first countries then eras, his memories of childhood came to seem no more than a series of pleasant tales, an evening's diversion. Meanwhile, the surviving world made less sense with each passing year, until, by the end, coughing away his last hours in that dusty attic, he hardly believed in it at all.

Chapter Two

Elsie kept hold of the stone her mother had given her on the day of the funeral. Grey with white striations, it had a perfectly formed hole to one side, as though it had been drilled. She took to rolling it between her fingers while she talked, and when she was anxious, she would clasp it to her chest. No one in the family remembered where the stone had come from, and soon they stopped remarking on these new habits.

In the park, one day, Elsie's school friends saw her toying with it for the first time. Everyone noticed, but it was Meredith who commented.

'What's with the rock? That your new boyfriend?'

Meredith had a fat smile that revealed a little too much pink gum. When she found something ridiculous, as she did now, she would shake her frizzy hair and wince. In their circle of friends, Elsie was better-liked and, as both girls knew it, Meredith was always looking for opportunities to bring her down a notch. There were a few of them in the park that day, legs dangling from motionless swings.

Elsie stood up and turned to face the group. 'You can do a lot with a stone,' she said.

'Eww gross,' one of the other girls said. A few of them laughed.

'I wasn't talking about *that*.' Elsie lifted the stone level with her cheeks and crooked her elbow, as if she was about to let fly. Meredith flinched.

'What's the most violent thing everyone's ever done?' Elsie asked. No one answered. Elsie continued, 'If you ever catch a fish, you have to hold it by the tail and smash its brains against a rock.' She tensed her bicep a moment, then, slowly, slowly, lowered her arm. Her father hated all blood sports, and no one had ever taken her fishing.

Afterwards, there were no more jokes. For a brief spell that August, Meredith and a few of the others picked around in the soil of their parents' back gardens, searching for pebbles, and would sometimes choose one to carry around for a bit. But they never really saw the point, and the fad soon died out.

*

Come autumn, some way into the first term of the new academic year, Elsie's English teacher called in Hannah and Eric for a meeting. Ms Varden had concerns about their daughter, which she preferred not to mention over the phone. An unexpected summons. As far as Hannah and Eric knew, Elsie had always been a model pupil.

Mrs Wilson, round-cheeked and heavily pregnant in a loose floral dress, met them at reception, then led them to Ms Varden's room. Wilson was the Head of English, apparently, and would be sitting in on the meeting. 'Just for support.'

Hannah strode into the room first, letting the teacher hold the door. You'd never know this commanding woman, suited and high-heeled, felt anxious about the encounter, for reasons she herself could not name. In the carpark outside the school, she'd had the distinct urge to throw up. Now she took her seat opposite Varden – younger than Wilson, and slightly better dressed – and waited for her husband to follow.

To one side of the room was a row of blue and green lockers that recalled the changing areas at the public swimming pool. Inside those tall metal boxes, no doubt, were textbooks and diaries, a few crinkled love-letters, and perhaps the odd stash of cigarettes. In Hannah's day the school lockers had been grey, and no stickers were permitted on the outside. Even so, she had loved them. Having your own key and a locked door barring access to your possessions gave you a terrific, adult feeling. The tables and chairs were wooden with a dark varnish, and on the walls various posters displayed the talent and creativity of the girls of 4B. But where was Elsie's work? None of the displays bore her name. Was it possible that her projects were not deemed worthy? Hannah's brilliant daughter, whose precocious creativity was maturing under her influence – surely some mistake. Just look at the stuff that had made the cut.

Mrs Wilson asked if anyone would like a cup of tea, or a biscuit maybe. There were no takers.

'Do you sometimes help Elsie with her homework?' Ms Varden asked. 'If she's given an essay to write for history or for English, does she show it to you?' Through the lenses of her glasses, thick and wide, her eyes stretched beyond the limits of her face, an effect both clownish and mildly sinister.

Hannah said, 'Our children are very independent. I hope you don't think they're handing in work that's not their own.'

'Nothing like that.'

Eric shifted in his chair. 'Generally, Elsie shuts herself in her room to do her schoolwork. Her grandfather used to look over her work with her sometimes, especially when she was younger. More on the maths side though – he was good with numbers.'

'He passed away recently, didn't he? Must be tough on Elsie.'

Ms Varden nodded as she spoke, and for a little while after she finished speaking. The Head of Department frowned sympathetically.

'We get by,' Eric said, just as the teacher's head slowed to a stop.

'I'm afraid this isn't going to be easy,' Ms Varden said. 'As you know, I take the girls for English, and lately, well for a while now, some of the things Elsie writes have been . . . what would you say, Maggie?'

'Concerning,' Mrs Wilson suggested.

'Concerning. Yes.'

Hannah asked how so.

'To put it bluntly, Elsie has a violent imagination. This week, for instance, she wrote a story about a young woman whose father, after returning from war, tied her to a fence, bound her hands behind her back, and then set her on fire, while all the neighbours watched from their front gardens.'

Mrs Wilson's eyes widened. There was a brief silence, which Eric broke. 'What was the assignment?'

'To write a story about a family reunion,' Ms Varden replied.

This was not the only example. Another story centred on a girl named Dinah, who fell in love with her own rapist, a foreigner. When her brothers discovered the affair, they approached the boy's parents and proposed a marriage that would unite the two families. Then, having lulled the foreigners into a false state of security, Dinah's brothers slaughtered the lot of them. Mrs Wilson hoped it went without saying that xenophobia was not tolerated at the school. In a third story, Ms Varden carried on, a young man has a premonition of his own death when he sees the ghost of his father.

Hearing these things, Eric wondered how well he knew his daughter. Elsie wrote all that? The same Elsie who insisted on eating her salad with ketchup, who often narrated her actions in scraps of song, *Now I'm going up the stairs / To have a bath and wash my hairs*? The Elsie who only last week cried over a bad roll in family monopoly? The one with the impish over-bite, the little girl whose blue scrunchies found their way to every floor and carpet in the house? That same Elsie was now fantasising about rape, immolation, and mass death?

Hannah had a different question in mind. 'Was it any good?'

'Excuse me?'

'Elsie's story. Were you impressed? Or did it simply get you reaching for the parents' phone number?'

'Literary merit is not really the point here,' Mrs Wilson said.

Hannah begged to differ. If her daughter was just coming up with horrible images, hoping to shock teachers, then that was pornography. But if she was producing something with real power, then wasn't that the aim? Or would she rather the girls wrote stories like the pictures on the wall: garish, saccharine, unserious.

'Perhaps you'd be a better judge of this than me,' Ms Varden said. 'From a purely academic standpoint, I have no worries about your daughter. But where does she get these ideas?'

To Eric and Hannah, that was obvious. They never kept things from their daughter; her own curiosity set the limits. And since Yosef's death, she'd spent more time closed up in her room, fondling that stone, reading. Especially scripture.

The sacrificed child was Jephthah's from the Book of Judges, and Dinah was one of Jacob's daughters.

'It's all in the Tanakh,' Hannah said.

'She means the Old Testament,' Eric said.

'This is not a religious school,' Mrs Wilson put in. 'Here, in our English classes, we focus on secular literature.'

Hannah tried not to smile. 'You must be joking. Secular literature only. What, so no Chaucer, no Milton?'

Confused, Mrs Wilson turned to her younger colleague.

'Elsie told me you were readers,' Ms Varden said.

Hannah laughed. It was obvious now. Elsie had been mocking these absurd ladies.

'I don't see what's funny,' Mrs Wilson said.

How much this moment resembled a dream. The school in which there were no children, the classroom that was also a changing room. Look how they were discussing Elsie, but the Elsie in this dream world was not the same as the one she knew. Elsie was happy, she sang every day of her life. And yet these women, these supposed English teachers who didn't read books, were saying her daughter was broken and needed fixing.

Eric put his hand on Hannah's knee.

'We're very grateful for you calling us in like this,' he said. 'And I can see why Elsie's choice of subjects is worrying you. But I don't think there's anything to get excited about. She misses her grandfather, and she's passionate about scripture. My father was too.'

Ms Varden removed her glasses and, with a licked thumb, peeled an eyelash from one of the lenses. She was quite pretty, really, when you looked at her. Young, too. Twenty-three, twenty-four at the most.

Squinting, the teacher said she was worried about the effect Elsie was having on the other girls. 'They're frightened of her.

I know this must be difficult to hear. But she makes them do things that are against their nature. They misbehave. Sometimes, when they all get together, they can be cruel.'

Earlier that week, a girl in Elsie's form – no need to name names – was found by a prefect crying in the school library, angry red marks along her neck. The prefect took her to Mrs Larsson, her Head of Year, who soon got the story out. It seems the girl had been pressured by her classmates into playing this horrible game, where someone lies prone, and one of her friends pushes down on her neck until she passes out. The game was known, apparently, as 'seeing the other side'. They had lectured the year group, of course, on the dangers of what they'd been doing, and an article was circulated about a student at another school who never came round after blacking out. Anyone who was involved henceforth would be immediately suspended.

'But what does this have to do with Elsie?' Eric asked. 'Or her stories? I thought that's why we're here.'

'What I'm about to say is going to sound a little strange, so bear with me. Sometimes the things Elsie writes come true.'

She'd written a story in which a beloved pet fish was poisoned, and a week later the goldfish at the top of the L building were found belly-up on the surface. It seemed she was getting the other girls to act out her fantasies. And the phrase 'seeing the other side' was used again and again in her stories. Mrs Wilson and Ms Varden could hardly ignore the situation. They wanted Elsie to begin therapy sessions with the school counsellor immediately. They would closely monitor the girl, and hopefully in time she could have back the same liberties as any of her peers.

The clock on the back wall ticked off fifteen, twenty seconds. Hannah dragged her chair forward a few inches.

21

'Let me get this right. Your students are getting up to dangerous activities in their breaks, and on the basis of a single sentence in a short story, you're blaming my daughter? And now you think Elsie and her friends are going to burn one of your girls at the stake? So you want her to go for a cup of hot cocoa with some quack once—'

'Mrs Rosenthal, please—'

'Once a week with some quack, and that's going to fix everything. That's what you're saying here. Yes? I've seen some things, believe me, but never in my life have I encountered ridiculousness, downright—'

'Darling—'

'—downright stupidity on this scale. It's just a shame you weren't around to confiscate the pen from William Shakespeare before the maniac started blinding pensioners. It's a pity you—'

Losing her breath midsentence, Hannah stopped speaking and the outpouring was cut short; whatever climax she was working towards had to be imagined from her warlike expression, her face almost within kissing distance.

'If you can't remain civil, I am going to have to end this meeting,' Mrs Wilson said.

Eric nodded.

In a chastened voice, Ms Varden asked if they would agree to the plan of action. If not, the situation would be discussed by the senior leadership team. They couldn't rule out disciplinary measures.

On the drive home, Eric and Hannah talked it over. Eric agreed the teachers were both fools, and yet the meeting had unsettled him. Didn't those stories worry Hannah? She claimed not. Elsie was a teenager. She was on the cusp of adult life, she was grieving, her body was flooded with hormones, and she was just discovering what sex and death are all about.

'Even a *frummer* kid like you must have gone through something similar. A hysterical teacher is the last thing she needs.'

'True,' Eric conceded, not wholly convinced. He was more annoyed than he let on by Hannah's reference to his teenage years, of which she understood nothing.

'But I don't think the woman's concerns are baseless.'

Something disturbed him that he did not mention to Hannah. Later, much later, he would wonder why he hadn't come out and said it right then. The apparition of the father as a harbinger of death is not a biblical idea. He'd have to look it up when they got back, but he was reasonably sure it came from the writings of the Zohar, the book of splendour, whose pages Jews are forbidden to open before they reach the age of forty. Neither Hannah nor Eric were adherents of Kabbalah, but their bookshelves at home were well stocked, and it was obvious where Elsie had begun her explorations of mystical beliefs. Just then, having indicated late for a right turn, Eric was scolded by a horn-blast, a Volkswagen right up on his bumper. Hannah wound down her window, leaned out, and cried, 'Nazi piece of shit!'

The next day, Elsie was asked by her geography teacher to hand over the stone she held in her left hand while she copied notes from the board. Elsie refused. The teacher insisted, but Elsie remained firm. She wasn't doing anything wrong! The teacher said that a stone could be used as a weapon, to which Elsie asked if the teacher had ever seen what a pair of house keys can do to an eyeball? The whole class laughed then, and Elsie was sent to the Deputy Head's office.

Hearing all this on the phone later, Hannah bit her tongue.

*

In her therapy sessions, Elsie spoke about the stories she'd written and her relationships with the other girls at school. She discussed her imaginary friends, too, including the spirit of her grandfather, and a ghostly little boy called Ariel who was searching for his parents. They talked about her studies, and they talked about bereavement, and they talked about healing. 'There are things that happen, that you don't get over or move past,' the counsellor said. 'And that's OK. They become a part of you, for better *and* for worse.'

On another day, in a different session, she said, 'It's fine to have negative emotions. This isn't about trying to stop you from having normal thoughts and feelings.'

Elsie smirked. 'Who said I want to have normal thoughts and feelings?'

Meanwhile, troubling things kept happening in class. Complaints were made. The report sent home just before half term said that Elsie's progress was 'disappointing', and that Elsie was 'uncooperative'. During her week off, she was sullen at meals, and became protective of her solitude.

After the break, Hannah and Eric were called into the school once more. This time, the Deputy Head was present in the conference and the possibility of expulsion was raised. Elsie's behaviour had reached new lows. She'd stolen another girl's wallet.

Back home that night, Eric gave Elsie a real talking to. She'd had almost two months of counselling, and nothing had improved. She was missing lessons, getting into fights with teachers, losing friends. And now she had broken a written commandment. If she didn't turn a corner soon, Eric told her, then it might be too late. And when she gave the first adolescent shrug he'd ever seen her give, he felt his grip on himself slipping. 'I'm not going to just stand here and watch you fuck up your life.' He had never shouted at one of his children before, let alone sworn at them. Until now, he'd left that privilege to Zeide.

Elsie asked if she could go. Some girls from school were meeting at the cinema in half an hour.

'And you won't be joining them,' Eric said.

'I thought you were worried I was getting anti-social.'

'Don't be clever with me. And can you put that fucking stone away.'

She was rolling it under her chin. She stopped rolling it and held it in her left hand.

Eric opened his palm. 'Actually, you know what, give it here. Now.'

When Elsie shook her head, he grabbed her forearm and wrenched the stone from her grip, surprised by his own violence. The wrist of her left hand was red, and in a moment she was massaging it, like someone newly freed of handcuffs.

She looked at her father with horror and confusion, tears blurring her eyes.

'We only want you to be happy,' Eric said, pocketing the stone.

Minutes later, having retreated to the bathroom, he stood before the mirror; a pair of frightened eyes stared back at him. With his hands clamped onto the towel rack to stop himself shaking, he replayed the conversation in his head, a conversation so like the ones he'd been on the receiving end of throughout his childhood – the ones that were no doubt instrumental in forming his watchful, closed-off, tightly sprung character – and he promised himself that whatever the provocation, he would never lose his temper like that again. Not with his own children.

In his frustration, he hurled Elsie's stone from the bathroom window, and heard it crack against the road outside, then skitter down the street.

Remarkably enough, Eric's dressing-down had the desired effect. The next two weeks saw a steep improvement in the quality of Elsie's work. She began participating in class again, raising her hand to answer questions before she was called on. Her teachers said it was like having the old Elsie back, though no one was so tactless as to say the one from before her grandfather died. She was even getting on better with the other girls; Meredith invited her to come ice skating one weekend, and someone called Pauline asked her teachers if she could sit next to Elsie in science, as everyone else was horrid to her.

Then one night, Hannah got in late and found Eric sitting at the foot of the stairs, the phone nestled in his shoulder and its cord wrapped around his finger. Aside from the light hanging above the downstairs landing, the house was dark. Still buzzing from the meeting she'd had with her agent to discuss her manuscript, and a little tipsy from drinks with a former colleague, she knew at once something had happened. Her husband looked ridiculous, crouched there in the hallway. He hadn't changed out of his suit, still had his shoes on. He hung up on whoever it was without replacing the phone in its cradle, just squeezing the button below the earpiece.

'Where the hell have you been?'

Was Eric drunk? She'd told him that morning she'd be back late. Now she slung her coat over the banister and asked, with deliberate calm, what was going on.

'Elsie's gone! Do you know how many people I've called? I even tried your parents, you can imagine how that went down. She never came home. The boys are clueless. Fat lot of use the school's been. They didn't even notice, can you believe it, no one even *saw* her going. With the fees they charge, you'd think they could post someone at the gate—'

'Slow down. You're not making sense.'

'She's *missing*, Hannah. Don't you understand? It's late, it's dark out, and nobody knows where she is.'

Hannah took this in with a nod. Something kept her from exploding into panic. A small miracle: Hashem had blessed her with the cool lucidity demanded. 'You've called the police?'

'She's fourteen years old for fuck's sake.'

Hannah bent down, cupped her hand around the back of her husband's sodden neck, and pressed her thumb to the base of his skull.

'She'll be back,' she said. And then, as if editing herself, 'We'll find her.'

Chapter Three

I met Tovyah Rosenthal in the Autumn of 2008, on my first day of university. Although I was given the room next door to his, a whole term had to pass before we were friends. Even then it was rocky.

His name was spoken often in freshers' week, on account of his mother, and sometimes you heard people describe him as *not normal*. The other historians resented him; in seminars and tutorials he was both brilliant and a complete jerk. He once told a fellow student that the depths of his stupidity were 'unfathomable' and another that her presentation was 'barely sane'. Outside class, he was a solitary kid. Studious, quiet, unobtrusive. And so, when it became clear he wasn't interested in the social life of the college and couldn't be drawn by bringing up his mother's controversial writings in earshot, the bulk of students might have forgotten Tovyah was there, closed in between walls of books, working towards his inevitable first.

On that first morning, my parents and I arrived later than most. As I walked through the front quad dragging my overstuffed suitcase, new students were already being led to their rooms, or milling about to make small talk, having unpacked as much as an hour ago. My mother, doing the talking for three, spoke too loudly about the beauty of the college and how lucky I was. Though my father said nothing, I thought he was coping admirably; I squeezed his hand as we joined the registration queue. The weather helped. It was a bright day for October and the sun was only half-veiled by clouds. I suspect I knew even then such days might come along three or four times in a lifetime, and this was the first of its kind since I began secondary school, seven years earlier: a day of infinite promise, ferrying this cargo of strangers whose lives were about to collide with my own. I also feared that I was bound to squander it. So far, I'd clung to my parents and spoken to no one my own age.

Amid the bustle of new students, one caught my eye. Hard to say why. He stood with his hands buried in his pockets and gazed up at the bell tower above the great hall, looking bored, even resigned. He was accompanied by a short man, heavy-set and bearded. The father – who surely had work later – sported a three-piece suit the colour of slate, while his son wore trousers that sagged at the heel and a green rain jacket, in pessimistic defiance of the Indian Summer. A third figure, no more than a child, fiddled with the drawstrings of her white hoodie, her face concealed. None of them spoke. After a minute, the man patted the boy heavily on the shoulder, handed him a satchel, and then took the girl by the hand and marched her back towards the front gate. At the exit, she spun round to take a last look at the place, and I saw this was not a child, but a young woman, at least in her twenties, her hand still locked in the man's grip. That's how you walk with a little girl, I thought. Now alone, the boy looped the satchel over the handle of his suitcase. Another moment and one of the second years led him to the room he'd been assigned. At the door to his housing block, he lifted a finger to touch the brickwork then quickly withdrew his hand, as if burnt. I didn't know then that he was reaching out to touch a mezuzah, one of the little boxes fixed at the entrances to Jewish homes, containing a scrap of parchment inscribed with prayers. Such boxes offer divine protection to the house. But on the walls of the college, founded by Christians and now inhabited largely by sceptics like me, there was no mezuzah for him to touch, no seal of God's protection.

Watching him, I found myself engrossed, and it came as a jolt when my father's panicked voice said, 'Sweetie, we're at the front of the queue.'

Soon, the moment came for my own parents to leave. My father reminded me that if I didn't like it, it was only the next three years of my life. My mother, swatting his arm, told me not to work too hard. As a bookish and driven child, not always overburdened with friends, I had looked forward to this moment since I was twelve. And this was their way, I gathered, of wishing me health, happiness, and prosperity. That they had come here together to drop me off, which entailed both taking a day's holiday, was suddenly quite moving.

Newly alone, I decided it was time to start meeting people. I began by knocking on the door next to mine, and a deep voice from within asked what I wanted. When, after a moment's hesitation, I pushed my way in, I was surprised to encounter the same boy I'd seen outside, still wearing his rain jacket. He was kneeling beside a suitcase, now, unloading and piling up books on the floor.

'Tovyah,' he said abruptly, looking up at me. And when I said nothing in response, he added, 'That's my *name*.'

Later, I would conclude that he didn't look much like his famous parent, whose auburn curls and heart-shaped face regularly appeared above printed columns up and down the country. Unlike her, he had straight hair, almost black, and his bony features were sharp and serious. But, standing on the threshold of his room for the first time, I had no idea that his mother was well known.

Having taken out the last of his possessions – there were notably few – he shoved his suitcase under his bed and stood up. I've never seen anyone offer their hand with so much discomfort.

'Never shaken a girl's hand before?' I asked.

'Actually no,' he said.

I decided there was something of the basement-dweller in his pale looks and drooping eyelids. Still, though I would not have described him as handsome, his was a face you noticed: those wide cheekbones, at least, were impressive. As a teenager, impatient for the growth spurt that was ultimately cancelled, not delayed, he discovered that if he angled himself to the mirror just so and pushed his ears out with his fingertips, he looked exactly like a young Franz Kafka.

He told me this that first time we spoke.

'Faces matter,' he went on. 'The early mystics took physiognomy seriously. These were men who believed they'd found the means to ascend to heaven and behold the throne of God. They had to guard their secret knowledge of course – fearing persecution, they were rigorous about who they allowed into their circles. Anyone who wanted to join their ranks had to have, alongside a faultless moral character, the right face.'

He paused, pondered something, then jutted out his chin. 'Do you think I'd have made the cut?'

I faked a laugh, unsure if he was trying to be funny.

'Of course, they wouldn't have looked at you.'

I asked why not.

'Well, for starters you're a woman. And for the mains, you're not Jewish.'

Although he was precisely half-wrong, I didn't correct him. To hear myself referred to as a woman, not a girl, was jarring. Still, it wasn't Tovyah's strange formality I minded. He was so fixed on telling me about himself and his opinions of the college, I'd barely had a chance to speak. And when I said I wanted to arrange my room, he followed me next door. From a cardboard tube I retrieved posters: the first Long Blondes album cover, and a still from *The Virgin Suicides* – Kirsten Dunst sprawled in long grass, possibly dead, otherwise daydreaming. Both had been chosen under my brother's guidance, calculated to produce a favourable impression on my new peers. Which did not work on Tovyah, who told me Eugenides was a hack, and asked if a 'long blonde' was some kind of drink. As I busied myself with unfurling and Blu-Tacking, he continued to regale me. Eventually I told him I would like to make a phone call. And, yes, it was a private call.

I'd been warned there'd be people like this. All the same, it seemed pretty bad luck that he was the first person I'd met, and that we would wake up each day with just a thin wall between us.

If anything, those first impressions understate Tovyah's eccentricity. On day two, when a few of us from the corridor required an afternoon movie to soften the residual pangs of our hangovers, we went round in a circle and made suggestions. The winning film, by an all-but-unanimous vote, was *Mean Girls*. Tovyah, not hungover, was the lone dissenter. 'Let me guess. Beneath their mean exteriors pulse hearts of burnished gold.' His own suggestion was *Hiro-shima, Mon Amour*. When the (presumably dismal) classic of Franco-Japanese cinema was put up for election, Tovyah jabbed his hand into the air, appalled by our philistinism. Then, accepting defeat with minimal grace, he stormed off. I shared the common feeling that he was being a dick, but was struck all the same by his word choice. Hearts that neither pumped, nor beat, but *pulsed*.

Another instance. A common student prank was to drop a penny into a full pint of beer, goading the owner of said pint to drain the glass to save the Queen from drowning. Silly, of course, but the consequences of refusal were real enough – let the penny linger and the drink would soon take on a foul coppery tang – and many of us less experienced drinkers suffered through this spluttering ordeal in the first weeks of term. A variation was to drop a two-pence coin into someone's dessert; the unlucky diner was compelled to eat the dish without using their hands, like a pig at a trough. My friend Jan tried this on Tovyah's apple crumble.

'Go on fresher, lap it up.'

Tovyah fished out the coin and held it for inspection. One side emerged custard-skinned. The reverse was heavily oxi-dised, stippled in green lichen. 'What the hell are you doing? Do you want to poison me?'

Jan shrugged. 'Just a bit of fun.'

'Hilarious. If you ever put a rancid coin in my food again, I'm going straight to the dean.'

'Easy, mate,' Jan said. He made eyes at some of us round the table.

'I could have choked. You could have fucking killed me!'

Tovyah spun many heads in the lunch hall that day and – among those who looked – he did not win friends.

To be fair to him, these were stressful times. At most universities there's an idea you let students have a week to settle in before work starts. It's supposed to help with the homesickness, the abrupt departure from the only world you've ever known. Before I went up, my brother told me freshers' week was the time of his life, then hastily added that I should avoid getting carried away. He didn't want to imagine his little sister spending her time as he had, stumbling between nightclubs and hitting on strangers.

He needn't have worried.

We arrived on the Monday, and on the Tuesday we were invited to drinks with our tutors before formal hall. That summer, the senior academic in the English department had retired. This left Dr Phillips to run the show, a prim medievalist whose research concerned devotional poetry and land taxation in thirteenth-century England, precisely no one's idea of the life and soul of a party. According to Phillips, serving wine at the initial meeting between students and faculty set the wrong tone. Instead, we were greeted with apple juice and biscuits, and assigned our first essay, due the following week: *'We should not condescend those who lived through past eras for their ignorance. They are what we know.' Discuss the novels of Charles Dickens and George Eliot in light of this quotation.* Dr Simms, the college Victorian, asked if we had any questions.

I had one, which remained unvoiced. When exactly did we get our seven days in the shallow end?

Everyone was daunted, but Jan was livid. 'Doesn't she realise that it's supposed to be a *holistic* education. You read the books, sure, but you also have to go out and get smashed.'

He seemed to know what he was talking about, so I nodded. Silently agreeing with people because I assumed they were cleverer than me was a newly acquired habit. If this continues, I thought, I may come to dislike myself. Like Tovyah, Jan had caught my attention the day we arrived. He was unignorably attractive: a natural blonde, and tall enough that he was forever bobbing his head under doorways as he entered rooms. He seemed to know a lot of the other freshers already. I wondered if they'd all been at school together, but on reflection that seemed unlikely.

We weren't alone in being set work so early. Most students had been addressed similarly by their tutors, and you heard a lot of complaints. 'What's the point of having a noughth week if you have to work in it?' Of course, the academics had their rejoinder. Outside the chapel I heard Dr Aylesham, the dean, say: 'This way you get the jump on first week. Don't want to be playing catchup all term now, do we?' It was a total scam. At school, I'd been led to believe when you got to university the academics no longer acted like teachers. Instead, they were merely gatekeepers of the intellect, people who would speak candidly in seminars and, if you earned their trust, take you to exclusive parties, where the boundaries between generations dissolved.

The only student on their side was Tovyah. 'Can you believe people are actually complaining about how much work they have? If all you want to do is scoff pills and get laid, you don't need to enrol in the country's oldest university.'

I suggested that people might want to do the partying *and* the studying. Tovyah considered this. 'But why?' he said, confused. 'Why would anyone want that?'

The Social Committee did its best, despite the workload, to give us a good time. They organised pub crawls, raves, football initiations, and traffic light parties, not to mention the non-drinking options – Jenga club, ice-cream

Wednesdays, friend speed-dating. On the Saturday night, capping everything, was our first bop: a fancy-dress party in the college bar. 'That's where the hooking up will kick off,' Jan predicted. 'One or two marriages might one day trace their origins to this fateful Saturday.' The theme was the Golden Age of Hollywood, and I searched charity shops for a hat like Ingrid Bergman's in *Casablanca*.

When Saturday came around, however, there was an announcement tacked to the cork noticeboard outside the common room. Students huddled. Spotting me outside of the circle, Jan broke the news.

'They cancelled it, they've bloody cancelled it.'

'Cancelled what?' I said.

'We're not getting a freshers' bop! One of the deciding moments in the formation of a year group, and we don't even get one.'

Turned out it was disciplinary. The night before, two students on a freshers' pub crawl fought outside the Gardeners Arms. Both ended the night in a cell, one with two teeth short of a full set. As the dental patient was Vice President of the Junior Common Room and his adversary was Social Sec, it was determined that the incident reflected badly on the whole nature of freshers' week. Hence cancelled bops, cancelled foam parties, even cancelled get-to-know-you Jenga.

Back in my own corridor, I met Tovyah coming out of the kitchen. He was drying a teaspoon with the corner of his shirt. As always, he was both overdressed and a little shabby; his blazer was stained on one lapel and his shirt needed ironing. All his clothes were like that – theoretically smart but worn without care.

'What's all the fuss about?' he asked.

I explained about the fight and the altered schedule.

'That's *it*? Just because of some disco, everyone's rending their hair and their garments?'

'Sorry, they're what now?'

'Rending – traditional response to bereavement. You tear out your hair and you rip your clothes. My grandfather saw it happen in real life, once. A neighbour whose husband was hanged from a lamppost on the street outside her house. She pulled her hair out in fistfuls, he said, and handed him the clumps. Then she tore the skirt of her dress. There he was, younger than us, holding these clumps of hair. What was he meant to do with that?'

Though Tovyah had related the anecdote in the same off-hand manner in which he had told me about ancient mystics and their obsession with faces, he was glaring at me now, and I felt obscurely criticised. I could think of nothing to say in response and left his grim question unanswered.

So, when people in college branded him a weirdo, someone best avoided, I guiltily agreed. No matter the occasion, Tovyah was happier to keep himself to himself, and after the second or third time someone from our corridor asked if he was coming out tonight, only to be rebuffed, we stopped asking. I thought it was to do with not drinking, which in my head was somehow connected to his religious upbringing. But I was doubly mistaken there; even ultra-Orthodox Jews are not prohibited from consuming alcohol – there are certain sages who encourage it – and Tovyah, who was only moderately orthodox, kept a bottle of Glenlivet on the mantelpiece in his room.

Due to conflicting habits (I was an early riser, he was a night owl), we did not run into each other much. We sometimes chatted over coffee in the morning, and occasionally went to hall together. But we were cordial, not close. Nick, my brother, cautioned me that in those first weeks of university life, when the social layout of the college was still taking shape, you had to be careful who you spent time with. I was terrified of not fitting in. There was nothing I wanted less than to befriend a clingy eccentric, someone who might make it difficult for me to get on with everyone else.

Perhaps I needn't have worried. Those first few weeks of term were almost undiluted happiness. I remember smoking from my bedroom, legs dangling over the windowsill, and laughing with friends into the night. The excitement of discovering essays and ideas that might change the way I thought forever. Hurried pencil marks down the side of the page, sometimes accompanied by an exclamation point. Everything seemed charged with potential: the rushed drinks, the clubs, the music, and the mornings swallowed by hangovers. This was it, the great adventure. And here they all were, the people and events that really mattered. Just a few weeks in I had a group of friends more interesting than anyone I had known back home: people with ambition, drive, things to say about the world. If I spoke less when I was around them than I would have liked, it was only because I was still getting used to new social conventions. Later I had my first romantic entanglement. We were totally incompatible, and our relationship burnt itself out within a fortnight. Afterwards I spent two or three days playing the jilted lover, and somewhere, in a battered ring-binder, there exists the awful poetry I felt moved to write.

Tovyah had no place in this new world of mine. I'll never forget his expression the one time he showed up on a night out. As he stood on the edge of the dancefloor, nursing a plastic wine cup and miserable in the coat and scarf he refused to leave in the cloakroom, he summoned me over and asked, genuinely bewildered, 'How is this fun?'

About halfway through term, four of us sat on the benches that overlooked the front quad, smoking. I had only started recently. The summer before I went up, Nick told me I would need an in with people, and smoking was as good as any. 'You're not exactly Little Miss Personality.' I hated him for saying it – Nick had always found acceptance in the main crowd – but I didn't doubt his wisdom. Now here I was on the benches with Jan, Carrie, and Ruby. We swapped stories about tutorials, compared notes on the idiosyncrasies of our lecturers. Jan was the sort of person I had nothing to do with at school – popular, good at sports – but at university we met as equals. He was joint honours English and history so, unlike me, had the chance to observe Tovyah's manner in seminars first-hand. ('Oh, he's a total psycho.') It was well known that Jan and Carrie had hooked up in first week, but they weren't 'a thing', apparently, and Carrie, as I later learned, was pretty much only into women. Carrie studied French and Russian and was tipped for parliament one day.

To be accepted by such people outstripped every social aspiration I'd ever had.

With one caveat: I couldn't really see the point of Ruby. Her face was so symmetrical I didn't quite believe it. And she made a show of complimenting something about every new person she met. (I got 'beautiful fingernails'.) For this, she enjoyed a reputation as charming.

During a lull that fell in the conversation, she asked if anyone had read the piece Hannah Rosenthal had written in *The Spectator*. It was about religious obligations, traditional gender roles, and feminism, apparently. Neither Jan nor I had seen it, but Carrie had. In agreement with Ruby, she found the article problematic and distasteful.

'Can you imagine what it was like growing up with her?' Jan asked. 'I mean the woman's an *actual* fascist.'

I had no idea then why someone would describe Tovyah's mother as a fascist. As I understood it, she was basically a social conservative, a defender of religion and the nuclear family, most of whose pieces seemed to be along the lines of, 'people should believe in God and be nicer to each other'. Someone you could easily dislike but would take hard work to hate. I was not a careful student of current affairs and was yet to read her columns on the topic of Israel.

'I know, I know,' Carrie said. 'Not to mention that whole thing with his sister.'

Everyone nodded; I alone was at a loss. 'What whole thing with his sister?'

Jan said, 'She went missing. As a kid. You don't remember? This was when we were like, nine, or whatever.'

I searched my memory and found nothing. This was to be expected. My parents were deeply protective and would no doubt have shielded me from such news; I only learned the name Jamie Bulger years after the story broke.

'Must have been such a nightmare,' Ruby said. 'She was, what, twelve? Thirteen?'

No one could recall the exact year.

Jan said, 'Do you remember the footage of Hannah Rosenthal telling the nation that Sky Daddy was going to find the poor girl? "Look at Moses, look at Joseph. God does not forget imperilled children." And that's not some mad street lady, that's your mum!'

Carrie observed that kids go missing all the time, and wondered what strings Hannah must have pulled to get that kind of coverage.

'What happened?' I asked. 'Did they find the girl?'

Jan answered, 'Sure, they found her. At the bottom of a ditch.'

'That's revolting,' Carrie said. 'And it's not even true. After a few days she wandered back on her own. I'm sure of it.'

Jan stubbed his cigarette on the arm of the wooden bench. 'You must be mixing her up. I don't want to be dark, but she was def killed. They even arrested some creepy dude she knew. The two of them collected all this weird crap – tarot cards, hexes, voodoo dolls.'

But Carrie wouldn't back down. She knew exactly who she was talking about, Elsie Rosenthal, it was Jan who was getting muddled. There was no 'creepy dude' either, he was just making stuff up now.

Ruby offered a third version. According to her, the girl was still missing, the investigation open. 'What do they call them? Cold cases?'

'The thing I don't understand,' Carrie said, 'is why he makes such a big deal about the whole Jewish thing anyway. At my school, there were loads of Jewish kids, but they didn't go on about it.' Carrie had attended St Paul's Girl's. On a scholarship, she clarified.

I wanted to take the conversation back to his sister, but Jan was speaking again.

'At St Paul's? They were probably all secular. Most Jews are – they're too smart to believe in that bollocks.' He was looking at me now, and I wondered if he'd picked up on something. I was sensitive about my looks, which I considered vaguely Eastern European, and owed more to my paternal grandmother than I would have liked. 'Our friends the Rosenthals, however,' he went on, 'are with the signed-up crazies.'

Jan was the first proper Marxist I'd met, one who could quote from not just the *Communist Manifesto*, but also from latter-day interpreters: Gramsci, Hobsbawm, Stuart Hall. He had a poster of Leon Trotsky above his desk and when I said, isn't that the bloke who was killed by an ice pick, he was unamused. 'He did a bunch of other stuff first.' Jan could often be heard defaming Late Capitalism or the Church, his two great nemeses. Unafraid of being labelled culturally insensitive, he deplored Islam and religious Judaism as well. Whoever was doing it, he'd say, organised faith cults sucked shit.

'Really we should be asking Kate what she thinks,' Carrie said. 'You two are pals, aren't you? Same corridor, no? Or maybe more than just pals . . .'

Although I'd spent a fair amount of time with Jan, I was just getting to know the other two, and was surprised Carrie knew where my room was. I was slow to appreciate the smallness of my new home.

'We're not friends,' I said. 'He just lives next door.'

'But you must know something about him,' Ruby insisted. Everyone was waiting for me to speak again. What could I say? That he drank his coffee sugarless and black, which I found weirdly annoying? That no one came around to our corridor looking for him?

'The main thing about him,' I said, picturing Tovyah under strobe lights, trembling at the volume of the bass, 'is he hates fun. He's got these total Scrooge vibes going on, like he actually enjoys being miserable.'

To my relief, Jan responded with his hard, staccato laugh, and the others followed his lead.

Not needing further encouragement, I went on. 'When I first met him, he didn't even know how to shake my hand.' I mimed it for them, which everyone loved.

Carrie, a little piqued, I thought, at being upstaged, took the discussion back to a more serious assessment of his character. 'Guy has serious anger problems, though. Did you hear he had a fight with Dr Brooks and stormed out of his tutorial?'

I hadn't heard and was eager to learn more. Just then, however, Tovyah himself emerged from the archway that leads up to the library. He walked stiffly as always and didn't so much as glance in our direction. After he'd disappeared through the porters' lodge, everyone bent over laughing again. Not me. In these situations, I'd always been Tovyah.

'Holy shit!' Carrie said. 'Do you think he heard us?'

'So what? We didn't say anything. I only called his mum a fascist. Which, erm, excuse me, *she is.*'

The others continued to laugh, and I made my excuses. If I wasn't Tovyah's friend, who was? For the first time, I wondered if he was lonely. Though pompous, he always took an interest in my studies, and there was kindness in him, often concealed by his strange manners and quick temper. Once I complained of a headache, and half an hour later he brought me ibuprofen. Wondering at the delay, I asked if he had them on him. No, he explained, he'd popped into town.

That evening, when we crossed paths returning to our rooms, he didn't mention what had happened on the quad. I asked how his day was, and he shrugged, then wished me goodnight with his accustomed formality. So, he hadn't heard a thing, thank God. We continued to talk now and then, but as the weeks rushed on my attention was increasingly taken up by my studies, my new friends, and my late nights.

Meanwhile, Tovyah spent his time sequestered in his room; he was so quiet it was hard to tell when he was there and when he was out. Though I felt guilty for what I'd said to Jan and the others, I can't pretend I worried for Tovyah. Not blessed with much in the way of social skills, he would no doubt find some accommodating peers among the misfits of the university soon enough. Nor was I especially curious. My first impressions had now crystallised. He was a coddled, religious boy: shy, knowledgeable, defensive when provoked, but otherwise largely invisible. A boy who had got thus far in life by knuckling down at school, and not causing much harm to anybody. The son every Jewish mother dreams of.

Chapter Four

So things stood until an evening in late November, when with term all but finished, I went to hear Eli Schultz speak about intellectual and artistic responses to the Holocaust. It was not a venue I knew, an address on one of those winding streets that branch off from the high street. My final essay was due in a few days, making it difficult to justify the time away from the library. And yet there I was at dusk, scanning the numbers on the buildings. None of them resembled lecture halls.

I'd admired Schultz's work ever since I read *The Black Light and the White Light* the summer before my A levels. In fact, he was partly responsible for my being here – I wrote about his criticism in my application and was quizzed on his ideas at interview. He was in his eighties then, and who knew how much longer he had. When I chanced to hear he was making a rare appearance to address the Ben-Scholem Society, I had to go. And it was a stroke of luck, really, as the society didn't advertise its speakers; I only knew it was happening thanks to two strangers discussing the event at the table next to mine in Greens the day before.

Having never heard of Emanuel Ben-Scholem, or his society, I had no idea he was a latter-day prophet and founder of a small branch of Hassidism, which I understood was some weird cult thing. I was ignorant of the movement's history, how it evolved from the shtetls of Europe, offering a radically heterodox form of religious observance, one based on ecstatic joyfulness rather than sober prayer. Don't be fooled by the formal attire and unhip facial hair – Hassidic Jews are no puritans. Their worship incorporates singing and dancing. After the prayers are finished and the books closed, obligations of the mind give way to the obligations of the spirit. Chanting and stumbling ensue. Intoxication may not be prerequisite, but it certainly helps.

After locating the correct building, I approached warily. There was not the usual crowd of students outside the venue, finishing cigarettes, locking their bikes against railings. And blocking my path to the door stood a man in black robes and a homburg hat, with his hair curled into ringlets. As I drew near, he said something in what sounded like German.

'Sorry?' I said.

He peered at me through round spectacles and asked if I was Jewish.

'Sort of. I'm here for Professor Schultz's lecture. I'm in the right place, aren't I?'

The man considered, his nose twitching. 'A lecture you want? It's possible.'

I took a step forward and he raised the palm of his right hand. 'But what is this *sort of* business? You mean like a hamster raised by gerbils is sort of a guinea pig?'

'A hamster raised by a . . . what?'

'Jews are Jews,' he said.

It was not a warm night, and I felt my arms coming up in goose-pimples.

'I didn't realise it was restricted entry,' I said.

As I wondered what to do with my thwarted evening, I turned to leave. But the man summoned me back.

'Who mentioned restrictions?'

Stung that I had shown him my back, he stepped away from the door and gestured me on. 'Go up, go up. I expect they're still eating, but you won't disturb anyone.' Before I went in, he muttered the words 'sort of' one more time and shook his head.

The scene upstairs did nothing to settle my nerves. In the wide smoky room, the only lights were candles. The tables were arranged in a horseshoe with diners all the way round, helping themselves from large bowls of limp salads and cold, oily pasta. Some of the younger congregants wore jeans and coloured jumpers, but most dressed like the man outside, and every male head was covered. By now it was abundantly clear; this was no ordinary lecture venue. What had I let myself in for?

*

As a child, I had no idea I was Jewish. My father was born in France, during the war, to a French mother and an English father. Or so he was brought up to believe. There was no French spoken in the house when he was growing up, and rarely any reference to the city of his birth. If he thought this was odd, it could be explained away by his mother's sincere love of England, the country that became a safe haven when she fled mainland Europe, and her consequent desire for her son to be *plus anglais que les anglais*.

It was only after my grandmother died, and my father came into possession of her papers, that he learned he was in fact Lithuanian on both sides. The Englishman he'd called

'Papa' and who had given him his surname (also, by now, long dead), was his mother's second husband. What had happened to his biological father, or any of his extended family, remained a mystery, though one could make certain obvious guesses. The only thing he knew for sure was that they were Jewish, something his mother had concealed from him his entire life. Her maiden name, he discovered, was not Dupont, but Kohn. And among her belongings were a dreidel, a book of Hebrew prayers, and a set of phylacteries, which he could only suppose had belonged to her first husband.

My parents didn't have an ounce of faith to split between them, and the revelation of my father's true ancestry did nothing to change that. But after the discovery, my brother became sufficiently interested in the religion to insist, aged fifteen, on having a belated, Jurassic Park-themed bar mitzvah. (Between Steven Spielberg, Leonard Nimoy, and Stan Lee, my brother never lacked Jewish idols, and was delighted to learn of his new heritage.) We decorated the hall with potted ferns, then sat for dinner at tables named 'TriceraTopol' and 'Menorahsaurus Rex'. Any resemblances to an Orthodox service lay somewhere between superficial and blasphemous.

*

I had not set foot in a synagogue since, and so had no idea how to behave now. Thankfully, a round, motherly woman saw me hovering and asked if I wanted to join her.

'Rabbi Michael is a wonderful man,' she said. 'And they get some terrific after-dinner speakers.'

I asked if Schultz had arrived yet. She pointed me to the far end of the room where an old man sat with his eyes lowered.

Was that the face I knew from the inside flap of dust jackets? He looked exhausted. The curved ridges in his cheeks and his forehead were deep enough to slot a playing card and leave it standing. There was no food in front of him, and he showed little interest in speaking to the people on either side.

Moments later, after a polite but stuttery introduction from the rabbi, Schultz rose from his seat and shuffled to the front of the room. A man with a complexion like a split pomegranate held him by the elbow. Once Schultz opened his mouth, however, he required no more assistance.

'I wish to begin with an old tale. Cast your minds back to the middle of the eighteenth century, what we call the Age of Enlightenment. All over Europe, tremendous advances in natural science, in philosophy, and in political thought were taking place. These were colossal rearrangements in both the human imagination and the social order. Somewhere in the Kingdom of Poland, Israel Baal Shem Tov still numbered among the quick, telling stories by the fire and winning new followers every day. Some men, then, raising their voices over the din of progress, talked of magic and of miracles.

'One evening, two masters were travelling a country road. Their names were Rebbe Elimelekh and Reb Zusia. It was a Friday night much like this one, with a light wind up and a fierce chill in the air, and as the sky darkened, the two men knew they had to find somewhere to rest and observe the Sabbath. Soon they came upon a small inn where they agreed to spend the night, huddled by the stove downstairs. They had no money to pay in exchange for a room but were permitted to stay. This was the antiquated custom of offering shelter to strangers in case they were disguised angels. After the two masters lay down to sleep, silence spread through the village. But in the middle of the night, both woke at the same instant. Rebbe Elimelekh turned to his brother and said he felt an inexpressible terror. Zusia felt it too. "Shall we leave?" asked Elimelekh. "Yes, we must leave this instant," said Zusia. And even though it was a starless night, cold and dangerous, they set out with nothing but the pale moon to see by. What happened next is anybody's guess. But I can tell you where the two men had stopped. A small town in Southern Poland called Oświęcim. Or, as it came to be known to the world some hundred and fifty years later, Auschwitz.'

A few people around the room nodded, indicating that they had heard such accounts. Years hence my friend Jim Baranski would tell me a variation, the tale inverted. Baranski was an oboist and had played across Europe. Once in Vienna, he and his fellow musicians had gone to an old beer hall to celebrate an opening night. This was the late seventies. Amidst the laughter and high-spirited conversation, Baranski was overwhelmed by a sudden pain in his chest, as if pressed in a vice. He was so short of breath, in fact, that he worried he wouldn't be able to perform the following night. He went outside and confided to a friend, not one of the players, but a local woman he'd met the first time he came to Austria. She told him that the bar had been a Nazi stomping ground. Rumour had it there was a sadist who once brought in a Jew and ordered him to lie on the floor so a stool could be placed on his chest. He then invited his friends to climb onto the stool one by one until the Jew was crushed to death.

'What can we make of such a story?' Schultz asked. 'What does it tell us? That to the tzaddik there is no distinction between past and present, that if you see with God's eyes you can look back on the future, and sit with the past before you? Then why could it not be stopped? God knew what was coming. Surely, then, God let it happen. What to do with such a thought? How can we still live as Jews, how can we go on lighting the Sabbath candles, separating *milchedig* from *flayshedig*, circumcising our children?'

Night had fallen. Schultz's ageing face glowed bronze in the smoky light. I looked about me hoping, if I'm honest, to see other non-believers who had come to the lecture but not the dinner. I thought a confederate or two might alleviate my growing unease.

'And yet, the reverse position is equally compelling. It is recorded that in the camps there were those who fasted on Yom Kippur, men and women already living under the tyranny of starvation who still refused their soup rations in order to honour their spiritual commitments, fully aware it would bring their deaths a whole day nearer. Who are we to turn our backs on God, after those human skeletons kept faith?

'We have arrived at a paradox. To live as a Jew is impossible, and not to live as a Jew is equally impossible. Both paths are obscene, both insult the dead. Our subject today is whether it is possible to speak intelligently about the Holocaust. There are men who have claimed, some with great authority, that it is not possible—'

'And women,' muttered my companion, provoking a loud *shhhh* from someone nearby.

'—Theodor Adorno told us that after Auschwitz there could be no poetry. Hell has sprung up on earth, now something must give. So, no more sonnets, no more ballads, no odes, not even elegies for the dead in their graves. How fitting, we might think, how just. And yet the fact remains that much good and even great poetry has been written in the last half century. In English alone there has been Ted Hughes with his strange, mythical imagination, there are the furious songs of John Berryman, and there is the keen intelligence of Elizabeth Bishop. Was Adorno simply wrong?'

Here, Schultz paused and ran his eyes over the listeners, implying that the question was not wholly rhetorical.

'We can go further. The ingenious poet-chemist Primo Levi himself walked out of the camps in '45 and went on to write hundreds of pages about what had happened there – the living corpses, the conveyor belt of slaughter. And even he says that the survivors were not the true witnesses, that the only ones in possession of what really went on, the real horror, are those that left the camps through the chimneys, those that blackened the air and littered the ground with their ashes. The drowned, the starved, the suffocated, and the crushed. The only truthful account, he proclaims, is silence. Another paradox! A lifelong atheist, Levi it seems had an instinct for Talmudic contortions.'

For the first time, Schultz smiled.

'And what am I doing now, you might ask. Have I come to speak or to remain silent? If silent, then why did I come? But if I intend to speak, what can I tell you that Primo Levi cannot, I who was never there?'

With the candle flames and the packed seats, it was growing hot in there, and I felt sweat tickling my neck. Schultz's voice, lightly accented by his native Yiddish, was sharp and clear. He spoke without notes, his eyes now fixed on some high point on the wall behind me, though his fatigued pupils sometimes drifted slowly downwards before snapping back up. A few people fidgeted in groaning seats. Schultz developed his central themes, what he called the 'impossibility of witness', and the simultaneous futility and necessity of remembering, before he built to a soaring climax.

'In the face of evil, our last defence is memory. Orwell knew this. Big Brother's final victory is not the destruction of human sexuality but the obliteration of the past. History itself, sinking down those little memory holes. Shakespeare knew this too. What are the Ghost's last words to Hamlet? He has just revealed that the throne has been usurped by a pitiless fratricide, a dangerous opportunist. A sixteenth-century Hitler, perhaps. And yet the ghost's parting words are not what you might expect: avenge me – slay the usurper, and restore the rightful order. No, he makes a more modest request, far more touching: remember me. Remember me, he says, and then recedes once more into death's dateless night. Remember me. Remember. We must always remember. It is the only defence we have.'

I was enchanted. It didn't matter how much the woman sitting next to me tutted under her breath, or how many restless congregants squeaked in their chairs. This impassioned speech was unlike anything I'd heard in faculty lectures. Schultz did not question what is meant by the term literature anyway, or whether intention was a fallacy. Instead, he delivered nothing short of an exhortation to seek in the wisdom of the dead the means to resist evil. This, it seemed to me, was what it was all about.

Alongside my exaltation, however, a shadow extended. I had come here alone and remained an interloper. I knew no Hebrew and had only the most superficial understanding of Jewish beliefs and customs. My grandmother had no choice but to hide who she was from the world. But at what hidden cost had she swapped Kohn for Dupont?

Our lecturer, of course, had his own story of flight from Europe. He was an only son, whose parents got him out of what was then Czechoslovakia in 1939. After the war, Schultz returned to the country of his birth just once, aged sixteen. When he left, he was ten years old, and now he learned that every one of his classmates, down to the last boy, was dead or missing. An entire cohort of Jewish children, rubbed out by Hitler. Their pale faces could still be seen in a commemorative photograph: a classroom of ghosts arranged in two rows, the taller boys standing at the back, the shorter ones seated in front. And perched in the centre, with moustache and pince-nez, as dignified as he was powerless, the schoolmaster.

Near the end of the evening, Schultz passed on some advice he had been given by his grandmother, more than seventy years earlier, and which he credited with his survival and his long life. 'If you're a Jew,' the ancient woman had said, 'and you're sensible, you do two things. Learn languages and collect passports.'

This was met by murmuring assent. Schultz assured us that his grandmother's wisdom, vital in the thirties, was valid today. 'Life, after all, is still life. And men, I'm afraid, are still only men. To put that into theological terms, the *Mashiach* has yet to come.' This remark, though it sounded quite solemn, provoked warm laughter from the audience. It was only then that I noticed Tovyah on the far side of the room, rocking back on his chair, unsmiling. On his right sat an elderly gentleman whose strong jawline hinted at a face that had once been handsome. I thought I could see a faint resemblance to Tovyah: both had a sharp turn near the bridge of the nose. Untroubled by convention, the old man flouted the Orthodox dress code, wearing instead a loose white kaftan, with his shoulder draped in a blue and white scarf, ornately decorated with frills at the edges. As I looked closer, I saw the garment was damaged, abruptly torn off on one side. Now he bent towards the speaker and rested his hand on Tovyah for support. In response, Tovyah brought all four chair legs to the floor with a clap.

Meanwhile, I'd lost the thread of what Schultz was saying, and now he was winding down. He ended with an apology. He worried that he had failed to express what he had come here to say, but hoped it was worth coming all the same.

'I'll leave you with one last thought,' he said. 'It's an idea I had, possibly quite useless. But worth trying, perhaps. I ask you to find ten names, just ten out of the six million. The lists are widely available. And if each one of us in this room today commits ten names to memory, then that's something. Not a lot, but something. And every now and then, you should recite the names to yourself and ponder what happened to them, the people whose names were stolen and replaced with a number seared into their arms. Those names that were supposed to plunge into oblivion, never to be restored. We must all try to remember. What was Hamlet's response to his father's valediction? Remember thee? Ay thou poor ghost, while memory holds a seat in this distracted globe. Let us always remember, as long as memory holds a seat. *Shabbat shalom.*'

There was a short, startled silence, then a clatter of applause while the rabbi dashed up to help Schultz. Once seated, he angled himself towards the Torah Ark and lowered his head.

The rabbi thanked us all for coming and invited us to stay and enjoy a drink. I was keen to get going anyway when I noticed Tovyah heading to the exit. It seemed odd that he was leaving without the man he'd sat with, but when I looked, there was no one dressed head to foot in white to be seen.

Chapter Five

Outside, members of the congregation hovered, some kitted up in the full regalia, others more casually dressed, smoking. As I passed, they muttered something in my direction. The woman I'd sat next to walked up behind me. 'They're only saying *Gut Shabbos*. It means happy Friday, more or less.' I thanked her and she said she hoped to see me again. The doorman tipped his hat when he spotted me, then called out, 'Sort of!'

As I walked away from the group, I became aware of shouting across the road, just audible over the traffic. Turning my head, I saw a group of men standing outside Wetherspoons, each sporting the acrid yellow of Oxford United, no jumpers despite the weather. 'Hey *yids*,' they called out. 'Fucking yids.' One skipped a few paces forwards, something gripped in his hand, then let loose; a plastic cup came pinwheeling overhead, swerved towards me in the wind, and, as it dipped, I felt a cold spray against my neck. Drying myself with my sleeve, I looked up to see a man darting through traffic.

He stopped about a foot away from me, bent to catch his breath, and said, 'I'm so sorry, love.'

'You're what?'

'You must think we're disgusting. Three–nil tonight, so spirits are down. I guess we had a few too many. Anyway, he never meant to get you.'

'Well he did.'

'That's why I'm apologising, isn't it! And there's no need to look so scared. I'm being nice, now, eh.'

The man was my age or thereabouts, though I suspected not a student at the university. He had a gold stud in his ear and immaculate eyebrows. He asked if he could buy me a drink.

'Please leave me alone,' I said.

'What'd I do?'

I inclined my head towards his friends, who were still hurling abuse.

'Nah, love, nah. You've got it all wrong. They're not shouting at *you*.' He pointed at the crowd outside the synagogue, now some twenty feet away. 'It's that lot winds us up.'

'But I'm one of them,' I said.

The man folded his arms. Then scratched his head. Finally, he burst into laughter. 'You almost had me there, love! All right then, Miss Goldberg, how'd you like to get something to eat?'

After I declined this offer, he followed me to the end of the street, repeating his apology between stabs of laughter.

'Sure you don't want to grab a bite? What about a drink? It'd be a good story for the grandkids.'

I was quite sure, and at the corner he let me be. 'Goodnight, Miss Goldberg!'

It wasn't long before I saw Tovyah, heading back to college. I had to run to catch him and then tap him on the arm to make him stop.

'You didn't want to hang around with the Hassids then?' he said.

So he'd seen me. Was that why he rushed off? I was tempted to recount my interaction outside the synagogue but feared it would come out wrong, like I was somehow boasting. Instead, I asked, just as the United fan had asked me, if Tovyah fancied a drink. 'We'll be passing the King's Arms in a minute.'

I only said it for form's sake, confident he would decline. But after a few moments' internal deliberation, he nodded.

Though the pub was crowded, we nabbed a small table next to some boys in dinner jackets, one of them slugging back his pint in a single, fish-like glug, while his friends cheered. Tovyah raised his eyebrows, and I went to fetch us a pint of ale and a vodka coke.

Until now, our conversations had taken place while we lingered in doorways before returning to work or as we waited for the kettle to boil in our shared kitchen. They were spontaneous and brief. This was different. It was a Friday night, and still early. I could think of several better ways to pass my evening than sitting here with Tovyah Rosenthal.

At least we had something to talk about. 'So the lecture was pretty great, huh?'

'Was it?' Tovyah said. He gulped his beer. 'Can't say it did much for me.'

I was astonished. I didn't think anyone, let alone a religious Jew, could have sat in that room without being powerfully moved. Inspired, even. The way Schultz had sewn history and literature together, blending criticism and belief, seeking in the humanities a profound defence against violent regimes.

Trying not to let Tovyah's coolness affect me, I asked what he didn't like.

'His whole approach is bogus. Oh yes, it sounds all right when he lays it out, all those pretty little sentences, but it doesn't hold up. Learn ten names by heart and whisper them to yourself before you go to sleep. Fucking hell.'

'I think that's a bit unfair.'

'You're going to do it then? Memorise your names?'

I wondered if I could find a list of the Kohns of Vilna. 'Maybe,' I said.

'No you won't,' Tovyah said, flicking his hand at an insect. 'If the names meant something to you, you'd know them already. Meanwhile, there's Schultz acting like a little poetry, some Shakespearian verse, can stand up to guns and bombs. It's just nonsense, nonsense.'

This was how he behaved in tutorials, then, the sneering tone and the barrage of words I'd often heard about but not witnessed.

I started to say something about the power of symbols, but he cut me off.

'Trouble with Eli Schultz is he's a sceptic who wants to believe. He sentimentalises the religion. Look how he talks about the Yom Kippur fasts. All that reverence. Didn't it occur to him that it wasn't pride, not piety, but some more desperate motivation? Those poor creatures, all their hopes ripped away, were trying to save themselves with what, an ancient ritual? A fucking magic trick? Fasting was the only thing they could think of to appease their own monstrous God.'

This was why he'd made no friends on his course, why people like Jan and Carrie despised him. It had very little to do with his mother's Zionist politics, or even his family's religious fundamentalism. Socialising with other students was supposed to provide a welcome contrast to seminars and tutorials; you had drinks, you made dumb jokes, you flirted, and you bitched. But with Tovyah, being in the pub *was* being in a tutorial. This, no one wanted.

Except me, apparently. Encountering Tovyah's combative side, I didn't feel repulsed. In fact, for the first time since we'd met, I wanted to win his respect. This was not at all the timid boy I had taken him to be. For all his oddness, Tovyah had a definite magnetism. Did no one else feel his pull?

He went on. '*Remember, remember, we must always remember!* I can't bear the pseudo-spiritualism. As if all this stirring up the past doesn't come at a price.'

'What do you mean? What price?'

'My grandfather was a survivor. Very religious man. When I was a kid, he said the most appalling things, just to keep me in line.'

'Like what?'

Tovyah shook his head. 'Maybe after a few more drinks.'

A few more drinks? Was this to be a post-synagogue bender?

'And Schultz reminds you of him?'

'No, they're opposites in fact. God, Eli Schultz is a ray of sunshine. Zeide used to say anyone who lost their faith in the camps didn't know their Torah. He said there was nothing Hitler did that wasn't written about thousands of years ago. And he was right! In Leviticus, you know what God told the Israelites would happen if they didn't follow the rules? They'd be given up to their enemies and the ground would open under their feet. And if they survived that, the land itself would turn against them and the crops would fail. Before they died, they would grow so hungry that mothers would eat their own daughters and fathers would eat their sons. Going well beyond Abraham, we would butcher our own children, roast them on an open fire. That was God's promise to our ancestors, the promise we have recited year after year, from Sinai onwards.'

Tovyah scratched a spot on his neck. 'He was no intellectual, my grandfather. His education ended at fourteen and his letters are riddled with basic errors. But he was canny. And he knew more about the Godhead than Eli bloody Schultz. His God was the one who spawned Hitler, Goering, and Goebbels, then turned deaf ears to the cries of Auschwitz.'

I was conscious of other pub-goers listening to our conversation, averting their eyes when I turned to look. *They're not banging on about the Holocaust, are they? On Friday night . . .* I said, 'But surely you don't believe in that kind of a God.'

'Me?' Tovyah said, sitting up on his stool. 'You're asking me?' His face creased with derision, and he leaned towards me, conspiratorially. 'I don't believe in *anything*.'

Now I thought about it, I had never heard Tovyah speak about his religious convictions. But everyone knew about his mother's beliefs – you could read them each week in the papers. And hadn't he reached for the absent mezuzah at the start of term?

He took another swig of beer. He had drained two thirds of his pint in about three sips, spaced out over twenty minutes. After swallowing the dregs, he went up to the bar for a second round. When he came back, he placed another vodka coke next to my first, which was still half full.

Something nagged me. 'What were you doing there tonight then?' I asked.

'It's what I know.' He shrugged at his own feeble reasoning. When he asked why *I* was there, I told him I was interested in Schultz. And for what it's worth, I was Jewish. Sort of.

'You are?' He scrutinised me, as though checking this revelation against my bone structure. 'But not practising. Right?'

'Just my father's side, actually, my mother was raised Catholic. They're both atheists, anyway.'

'Atheists? Lucky lady. And not matrilineal. What the Nazis would have called a *Mischling*. A half-breed.'

It was hard to know if I was being insulted. I didn't appreciate being labelled with Nazi terminology and said so.

'Relax, I'm not saying anything offensive. Proust would have been a *Mischling*. If he'd lived.'

'I've never read Proust,' I said, flatly.

'How's your French? If you can get by with a bilingual dictionary, it's worth struggling through. Otherwise, the Moncrieff translations do the job.'

Tovyah passed his hand over the flame of a tealight, which wobbled and righted itself. He then swung his hand back the other way and grabbed his drink.

I said, 'I've got enough to read for my course, thanks.'

'Come on. You've got to be more curious than that.'

'Why?'

'You seem interesting. The way you sit there listening, taking everything in, not saying much. In the lunch hall, on the quad. Just look at how you showed up tonight – you're *curious*' – the second time he said the word, I noticed the odd way he pronounced it, two squashed syllables, more like *cure us* – 'and you don't fit in with those kids you hang around, Jan Stockwell and his band of morons.'

'Those are my friends. You shouldn't talk like that.'

'Well, they don't talk very nicely about me,' he said. 'My mother who pulls strings, and so on. I thought maybe you were different.'

'You don't know anything about me.'

'Just a hunch,' he said.

He was still fiddling with the candle. After a rapid movement, the gust from his hand extinguished the flame. A plume of thin white smoke rose from the dead wick.

62

'You're very pleased with yourself, aren't you?' I said.

'I wouldn't say so, no.'

Tovyah had a way of shaking his head. Only his chin seemed to move.

A song came on that I recognised but couldn't place, and whoever was in control turned up the volume. My thoughts ran to my A Level year, nights skulking in the smoking area outside clubs, not smoking, watching other people make out under streetlights. It occurred to me that right now, Jan, Carrie, and Ruby were probably ordering a taxi to Park End and I felt no desire to join them. At some point in the last couple of weeks, going big on a Friday had become a tedious ritual, and I could no longer fool myself that I enjoyed doing countless shots or making eyes at strangers in low lighting. I'd been so sure I'd succeeded in escaping the frustrations of school and had found my niche here. But something about the lecture I'd heard, or the vodka that was warming my blood, or Tovyah's unapologetic gaze was forcing me to reconsider. Did I even like my new friends? Rude and unpleasant as he was, at least Tovyah didn't expect you to be anything other than yourself. His bluntness invited a reciprocal candour.

'You don't normally do this sort of thing,' I said. 'You don't hang out much.'

'No.' His chin swung from side to side. 'You don't actually have to, you know.'

The song ended and was replaced by another, loud and unfamiliar.

I had little idea what Tovyah was thinking as he sat there with his shoulders hunched. But I think that's when I twigged that he must be harbouring some tremendous wound. Whatever path had brought him to this point had not been easy; something, somewhere along the line, had gone

63

devastatingly wrong. I remembered what I knew about his sister, and I thought of the girl whose face I saw, half-hidden, the day we arrived.

In an effort to reignite the conversation, I said, 'He sounds like a character, your grandfather.'

'Total shit,' Tovyah said, without missing a beat. 'I know, I know. But you have to understand. My parents were always busy when I was young, even when my mother was jobless she was busy, so he was the one around. And it wasn't just me who was terrified of him. We used to hire women to clean his rooms, and he kept driving them away.'

'Sure, but the things he'd seen . . .'

Tovyah leaned back and clapped his hands together. 'You don't mind stating the fucking obvious, do you.'

At that moment we were interrupted. Someone from the next table was balancing four beers in his outstretched fingers, one of which slipped from his grasp and smashed. Dark liquid spread over the floor and I had to lift my bag onto my lap to keep it dry. His table thought this hysterical.

Tovyah brought his lips to my ear and said, 'It's getting a bit horrible in here.' I agreed. Then he suggested we continue our conversation back at college, over a glass of whisky. Was he flirting? I decided not; by turns he'd been indifferent, antagonistic, and patronising.

On our walk back through town, I lit a cigarette and Tovyah asked if we could swap places – the wind was blowing the smoke in his face, and he found the smell disgusting. I apologised and stubbed it out. Then, as we strolled past the older colleges with their dark windows agape and their pale walls lit from below, Tovyah opened up.

His childhood was idiosyncratic. Although his parents believed in the literal truth of the Old Testament, they were only capriciously observant. While some Jewish customs were honoured in order to affirm their relationship with God, others were denigrated as peasant superstition. So on the one hand, pork and shellfish were prohibited, along with all other forms of *trayf*. Daily prayers were compulsory, as were the convoluted rituals that marked high holy days – unleavened bread for Passover, outdoor meals in the week of Sukkot. On the other hand, after Yosef Rosenthal's death, Eric and Hannah attended Friday services sporadically. They took pride in social and professional advancement and worked right through Sabbath when their careers demanded. God understood, Tovyah's mother explained. Life, for a modern Jew, was difficult.

In short, he said, arrogance and hypocrisy were his parents' defining qualities, and though groundless belief could trump rational thought, worldly ambition usually trumped groundless belief. None of the children were sent to Jewish schools, or even schools with large Jewish populations. They went to whichever school (in budget) was highest in the league tables. All the same, they'd each studied Hebrew, Torah, and Talmud from the age of four.

As for Tovyah, he'd always been, by instinct, an atheist. 'You find yourself living on an obscure rock, hurtling through space at great speed. All around you is a huge expanse of nothing. Even a child knows this. Just look up and there it is.' He'd hidden his views from his parents, of course, who dragged him through a religious upbringing. Until he was seventeen. One day he'd turned around and said: Mum, Dad, there's something I need to tell you. There were many fights and much emotional blackmail. His allowance was stopped. Certain possessions ('My books!') were confiscated. Tovyah was preparing his application to universities at the time – for

English, not history. He was rejected by Oxford and decided to reapply the following year. Desperate as he was to leave his parents' home, he couldn't live with the failure. Academics, he told me, was all he had.

I asked if he got on with his siblings.

'My brother and I don't see eye to eye.'

'You have a sister, too, right?'

By then, I'd learned the full details of Elsie Rosenthal's disappearance. Hers was not a horror story ending; within a few days of leaving home, she was found alive and well. Whether she was abducted or had run away was not clear from the information I found online.

Tovyah stopped walking, and I stopped too. 'Given up pretending, then,' he said.

Later, I got the chance to inspect his room for the first time since freshers. On his mantelpiece sat a square clock, whose hands no longer turned. Unlike the rest of us, he had put up no posters, nor any Polaroids of friends from his schooldays. No smiling picture of the girl he once took to prom. The only things on his shelves were books, mostly hardbacks with their jackets removed, hefty volumes with titles like *How Language Functions*, and *A History of Abstract Thought*. A few of the books were in Hebrew, identified at once by the blocky characters, and there were some collections of English poetry – Larkin, Coleridge, and a translation of the *Aeneid*. The Oxford World Classics edition of the King James Bible squatted on his bedside table, bookmark protruding. On the cover was a detail from the Sistine Chapel, God's face: a white-haired and lushly bearded man stroking his chin.

'Bedtime reading?' I asked.

'Know thine enemy.'

When I opened to the bookmarked page, I saw he was reading (or rather, rereading) the Book of Judges.

We had talked a long time. I sat in his chair, swivelled away from the desk, and Tovyah was on the floor, with his back resting against the side of the bed. With the overhead light on, we were bathed in hospital-ward brightness, despite the hour, and were now on our second or third whiskies. Though mine were diluted with water from the tap over his bedroom sink, I was about as drunk as I'd ever been.

Drunk enough to start talking about my hopes for university. How I felt thwarted at school and saw my life here as a blank canvas; I could fill it however I liked.

'And how's that going for you?'

I said it was early days. 'What about you? Enjoying yourself here?'

He shrugged. 'It's an extraordinary city. If nothing else, you can't deny that.' He asked if I'd been to see the statue of Shelley yet, at University College. When I told him I hadn't, he said he'd take me the following day. 'Shelley saw things as they were,' he said, 'and rendered them more beautiful even than that.' I wasn't entirely sure what he meant, but at that hour, after a few drinks, it seemed a pretty good thing to say.

We were sitting quite close to each other now. I became aware that our feet were touching. After a moment, I drew mine away. Then, interrupting the silence, I said, 'Can I ask you something? Don't you fancy throwing yourself into college life a bit more?'

'How so?'

'Just seems like this could be an opportunity for you to come out of your shell.'

Tovyah winced. 'You're saying I should go to the bops, and get shit-faced, and try to snog someone I've just met?'

'It's what everyone else does.'

Tovyah let his head fall back against his bed. When he spoke again, the words were directed to the ceiling.

'I'm not like everyone else.'

'In what way?'

'In the most important way. People don't like me.'

I knew all too well what it was to be reviled. When I was twelve years old, my first year of secondary school, some of my classmates held me down, tied my shoelaces together then dumped me in a deep puddle that had formed in the playground.

'People like you fine. You haven't tried.'

'What do you know? At the start of term, I went along to the stuff, the freshers' fair, the welcome drinks, all that crap. No one spoke to me. OK, I thought, you're new, it'll take time. Soon everyone was meeting up after lectures, going to each other's rooms, and where was my invite? And then I started to hear the things people said about me. How I was so stuck up, such a freak . . . which of course was nothing compared with what they'd say about my mother, my sister . . .'

It was hard to think of Tovyah, with all his wilful independence, all that disdain, wanting people to ask him to their rooms. And I was sure he got invited as much as anyone else, at least in the beginning. But he kept refusing.

I said, 'I'm sorry if you've had a bad term. But you have to give things another chance. I like you. Doesn't that count for something?'

'Only because you think you're not clever enough to be here. I suppose this insecurity has something to do with your homelife. Or perhaps they bullied the shit out of you at school? Either way you're impressed by my intellect, and you think that if we were closer it might validate your own intelligence, somehow, which, let me assure you, it would not.'

By the end of this little speech, Tovyah had lifted his head up and brought his eyes level with mine. I held his gaze.

'I was trying to be kind.' I slammed my whisky down on the desk and stood up.

'There's no point taking the moral high ground. As you told those bastards on the quad, we're not even friends. Because I don't like fun, right? "Total Scrooge vibes", I think you said?'

I was so angry and drunk that it took me another moment to realise what he was talking about. My face was hot. 'So now you're listening to my private conversations?'

'You're being ridiculous,' he said, a hint of exhaustion in his voice. 'Please just piss off.'

As I left the room, he had one hand on the whisky bottle, the other teasing out the cork stopper. I didn't necessarily mean to slam the door.

*

Over the next few days, Tovyah contrived to not run into me even once. I considered pushing a note under his door or writing him an email, but I decided he had at least as much to be sorry for as I did, and I make a point of only apologising first when I'm unambiguously in the wrong. Else a girl can end up spineless.

And the more I thought, the angrier I was. Who did he think he was to say I craved his validation? Or that I didn't fit in with Jan and Carrie, my actual friends? To hell with Tovyah. And to hell with Marcel Proust.

By the Wednesday, I had completed all my work for the term and the afternoon was wide open. Suddenly a term had gone. There would only be two more and then a year, one third of my university life, was over. How not to waste such increments of time was a major concern. So, feeling more like a tourist than I ever did on arrival, I crossed the Bridge of Sighs, wandered the grounds at Magdalen, and admired Shelley's statue at University College. Cast in marble, the poet reclines on a bronze slab, borne up by two winged lions, while a stone angel weeps beneath him. I left the college laughing. Percy Bysshe Shelley was thrown out of the university for his defence of atheism. Was this how Tovyah viewed himself?

After lunch, I went book shopping. Second term would be our foray into twentieth-century literature, and we were to begin with the daunting works of high modernism: Joyce, Woolf, Pound, and Eliot. Each of us had to pick one of the above to produce two thousand words on over the Christmas break. Having never read any of them, I opted for Woolf on the grounds that she was the only woman.

In Oxfam, after finding copies of *To the Lighthouse* and *The Waves*, my eye was drawn to a large hardback in the memoirs section: *Gehinnom and Afterwards* by Hannah Rosenthal. According to the blurb, it was a biography of her father-in-law, centred around his experiences in Treblinka. The book's cover showed a barbed-wire fence, ten feet high, stretching to the horizon. There were no people in shot, and the land on either side of the fence was barren. Inside the cover was another photo, this time a man late in the winter of his life, his eyes having receded deep into his skull. Evidently the book's subject, Tovyah's grandfather. The face was dimly familiar, and I wondered if it had featured in an advert I'd seen on the Tube or in some literary magazine. The quotation on the back described it as an 'unflinching journey into the dark heart of the last century, a journey all the more remarkable for the author's unwavering belief in humanity, her ability to wrench some scrap of hope, even from the teeth of genocide.'

In the middle of the book, on fat, glossy pages, yet more photographs. First, depictions of life before the invasion. A little girl, six years old, hugging a wooden horse to her chest. Veterans of the Great War in their uniforms. A long-suffering father, eyes pleading as he marshals uncooperative children. A young woman brandishing a copy of Herzl's pamphlet, *Der Judenstaat*. Is she already preparing for the journey east? These were Jews, all of them Jews, those who would leave and those who would remain. Jewish parents and Jewish children, unaware that history was widening its jaws. As I turned the pages, the pictures went from poignant, to heartrending, to obscene.

Including the two Woolfs, my bundle came to £8.50.

Back in college, I googled reviews. Certain critics took issue with Hannah's explicitly religious view of history. Even the title, which conflates the furnaces of the death camps with the ancient Hebrew name for hell, was met with hostility; she was accused variously of aestheticism and obfuscation. In general, believers liked the book and atheists did not. No, that's the wrong word. Believers might have praised the book, but you couldn't like it.

On the Thursday night, I went out with Ruby, Carrie, and Jan — term's last hurrah. Though I was bent on having a good time, the evening was a blowout; boring, loud, repetitive, and inescapably squalid. Standing in a seemingly endless queue for either the bar or the toilet (the lines were indistinguishable), I wondered what portion of life people could spend drinking vodka-Red Bulls from plastic cups. Compared with the Schultz talk – when listening to an old man at a lectern seemed, for the first time ever, *urgent* – this last night on the town was simply time wasted, and I resolved not to repeat it.

Back in college, too drunk and caffeinated to sleep, I was tempted to knock on Tovyah's door. Suddenly, the argument we'd had the other night seemed more like a foolish mis-understanding than a genuine clash of personalities and I wanted things straightened out before I left for the holidays. Thankfully, I lacked the nerve to follow through with the drunken impulse, and so didn't further alienate my neighbour by banging on his door in the small hours.

In the morning, I pressed 'dismiss' rather than 'snooze' when my alarm intruded at eight, and I slept into the afternoon. By the time I'd showered, dressed, and hastily packed, it was one o'clock. Glancing at my phone, I saw that I had several missed calls from my father, who'd been waiting in the car.

'You took your time,' he said, when I emerged at last, and opened the passenger door.

'Sorry, Dad.'

'Long as you've had fun,' he said. 'Now, guess who I've just seen.'

We hung back for a moment and there she was, Hannah Rosenthal, the latest author to join my bookshelf, dressed now in a dark skirt suit, carrying more than her fair share of her son's luggage, and striding quite upright as she came through the gates of the porters' lodge. She was smaller than I expected. Behind her, eyes lowered to the floor, walked Tovyah. He was kicking his feet and looked sick of the world. I waved but he didn't see me.

'Is that her son?' my father said, taking one more glance in the rear-view mirror before moving out into the road. 'Not a happy bunny.' It was true, Tovyah looked awful. His eyes were puffy, and his face drained of colour. At the corner of his mouth was the fresh stamp of a lipstick smile, the consequence of a theatrical reunion with his mother. 'Friend of yours?'

'Jury's out,' I said.

Once home, I unpacked Hannah's book, intending to read the opening paragraph to see if it whetted my appetite. But I found myself unable to take my eyes from the photo on the inside cover. I now knew why the face was so familiar; it was the man who sat next to Tovyah in the lecture. An image search on my laptop revealed that his white robes were *tachrichim*, the traditional garb for a Jewish burial. And his ornate scarf was his tallit, a prayer shawl given to Jewish boys at thirteen, the year they become men. In death, the shawl is wrapped around the body and cut off at one end, to symbolise release from the obligations of the living.

Chapter Six

When Hannah first started talking to Yosef about his experiences during the war, she had no thought of publication. Or so she claimed. Now that Zeide was dying, it was simply important that someone listened while he unburdened himself. Her interest in the story, however, was long standing; it dated right back to her courtship with Eric. They'd met in the drab lobby of a North London hotel, a venue he picked from a choice of three, apparently, though she couldn't see why he liked it; the tables were topped with fake marble, and the striped wallpaper reminded her of hard-boiled sweets. Hannah was then in her mid-twenties, a rising journalist who still got a kick out of seeing her name in print. Eric was the second man that Ziegler, the marriage broker, suggested; the first was a nineteen-year-old yeshiva student called Mordecai, whom she dismissed without meeting. Eric, by contrast, was a barrister of good family, with no skeletons in his closet, and virtually her own age. By skeletons, Ziegler meant broken engagements, and by virtually Hannah's age, he meant thirty-four. So why still single? 'A romantic! Been waiting for the right woman.' Having recently embraced the religion her parents long ago abandoned, Hannah struggled at first with the idea of a marriage broker. But Rabbi Grossman, her newfound spiritual guide, assured her that this was how it's done. She only had to meet the guy. If it was a disaster, no second date.

Eric got there first and did not stand when she arrived. He neither hugged her nor kissed her cheek in greeting. Wouldn't even shake hands. Though Hannah knew such intimacies between unmarried men and women were forbidden, being on the receiving end was another matter. She did not grow up like this. All he did to acknowledge her entrance was sit there and nod. His beard was thick, his features dark and nervous. In his right hand was a glass of water, crammed with ice and garnished with a wheel of lemon. This was the real thing, then, a man who knew no other way of life.

'Had many of these meetings?' Hannah asked as she sat down.

'A few,' he said. 'Your first time?'

'Oh, I've had dozens of these,' she said. Eric looked at her like she was raving mad. Then he saw that she was joking and gave a polite smile.

Catching the eye of a passing waiter, Hannah ordered a glass of white wine. 'A large. Wait, sorry. Make that two.' When Eric said he didn't want one, Hannah said, 'They're for me. As in, both.'

She felt very worldly all of a sudden, thinking how naïve this older man was in matters of the heart. She told him all about herself: the God-free childhood, her studies at university, the career so far. She didn't mention her exes, the last of whom had the nerve to get down on one knee, in Blackpool, on a badly timed weekend break. (It rained throughout. She left him drenched and miserable on the beach at low tide, cradling the gold band.) Eric, having listened patiently to

Hannah's life story, had not touched his wine. Assuring him that she was joking earlier, she encouraged him to take a sip. Which he did. Precisely one small sip, then pushed the glass away.

'I'm no expert,' he said, 'but it tastes a little bitter.'

Tipsy now and irritable, she suggested they move to a livelier bar. Eric said he thought where they were was fine. Their eyes met and he looked away.

She asked if she was boring him.

'Not at all.'

'You don't seem to be having much fun.'

'In fact,' he said, 'the complete opposite. Do you know how extraordinarily beautiful you are?'

As he said it, Eric was transformed into an eleven-year-old boy. How could this man stand up in court, arguing points of law?

'Would you mind if I ask you a personal question?' he said.

'Go ahead. If I don't like it, I won't answer.'

'I want to know what it was like for you as a kid.'

Hannah laughed, not sure if she understood.

'Bacon sandwiches,' he said, 'homework on Saturdays.'

'You mean what was it like growing up without all the rules?'

'Without Judaism.'

Hannah came from a family long-established in this country. Her mother was a doctor, and her father taught chemistry at an independent school in Dulwich. Affluent, liberal, and fully assimilated, they had no need of old-world hocus pocus. As a girl, seeing a congregation filing into the sunlight after mass one Sunday, Hannah asked her father why they never went to church. *Because we're not Christians*, he said. But why don't we go to synagogue? *Because we know better.* She looked back at the line of people breaking up into threes and fours, some walking hand in hand as they made their way towards the broad street. They didn't seem to lack the ordinary faculties.

'It wasn't like anything,' she told Eric. 'Everyone I knew was secular.'

He frowned, then nodded. 'And what brought you to God?'

When asked, she liked to say it began at primary school. A maths lesson, in fact, on symmetry. She'd been given a handheld mirror to learn about reflection. Little Hannah had drawn a shape on squared paper, held the mirror across the page, and watched the lines double. Placed correctly, a mirror could transform a triangle into a square, a square into an oblong, and a splayed hand into a comical undersea creature. The afternoon took a vertiginous turn when Hannah placed two mirrors either side of her pencil, which replicated itself endlessly, tip touching tip and rubber touching rubber. Only later did the enormity of the vision grip her. She told her parents she was terrified of living forever. The thought of all those days, stretching out one after another in an unbroken chain, turned her stomach. *But you won't live forever,* her father said. She was not consoled. The alternative, being hurled into spinning darkness, was no better.

'You were frightened by imponderables,' Eric said. 'And you turned to God for answers.'

'That's not it. The fear, the inescapable terror, that was how I came to understand God. It's like I could feel something otherworldly inside of me. I'm afraid I'm not making much sense.'

'You're making perfect sense. Didn't Moses find God at the top of the mountain, where the ridge of death is all around? Look on his face, we are warned, and you will not be suffered to live.'

Hannah nodded. Perhaps this lawyer was not the dope she took him for.

'Have another sip of wine,' she said. 'It grows on you.'

He sipped and then grimaced. 'You got freaked out as a kid. Then what happened?'

The crisis had come on not long ago, when she was alone in the flat she rented with an old school friend. She'd just thrown out some mouldy bread and put on the radio. Self-recrimination burned within her. What had she done? Nothing terrible. Hers were the usual failings, the run-of-the-mill screwups. Casual lies, selfish impulses, small-time erotic betrayals. A dark stain on the wall caught her attention. And as she contemplated the stain, that bruise on the plaster, she felt she was being watched. How you know you're being followed even before you hear footsteps, the coarse breathing at your shoulder. The difference between being alone and not being alone. Then came a palpable thinning of the air. As she closed her eyes she was aware of a crowding presence, infinitely perceptive; a judgement more intelligent, more penetrating than her own; an eye without dimensions; an ecstatic vision, searingly hot. The dizzying realisation that she and everything else was turning. Forever. How there was no such thing as a secret thought, no dark, unfathomable chamber of the mind, no getting away with it, no silent passions, no forgetting, and no solitude either. Every act of cruelty or kindness is both known and recorded, everything we've ever done weighed in the balance. And we are never, any of us, isolate. Think these thoughts, take them seriously, and you must change your life. That same night, light-headed and fever-bright, she swept out of her front door and bore down the streets in search of a synagogue.

She didn't tell all this to Eric. She finished the second wine and said she was sorry, but she had to go. As she stood up, he asked her for another meeting and to her surprise, she consented. A week later, they went for dinner at a kosher restaurant near Cricklewood. Over starters, she mocked him affectionately, pretending to believe this was his first time in a restaurant. She felt exposed and vulnerable after their last meeting and wanted to put him in his place. When their knees touched under the table, he recoiled. 'You really don't know how to behave with a woman, do you?' she said. To which he replied, 'I was given to believe there's more than one way.'

She continued to make fun of him. She said he was no more than a child, a total innocent. 'Hence the beard, right? You want people to think you're a grown up.'

'Beautiful Hannah,' he said. 'Would you like to know why I wear my beard?'

'Go on.'

'*Bistu zikher?*' Eric said. Hannah stared at him, uncomprehending. '*Mamaloshen.* It means, are you sure?' There was nothing playful in his tone. Hannah said yes, she wanted to know.

'When my father was a teenager, he and his brother both had full beards. *Payot* too, the whole bit. I've seen pictures, my uncle looked like Rasputin. One day, their mother comes home and orders them to shave. Beards, sidelocks, everything. You have to understand, this is completely out of the blue. Mame, they say, what are you talking about? This is crazy. "No discussions, shave! Now! I want two clean faces." I never met my grandmother, but I understand she was feisty, and the boys did as they were told. Only later did they find out why. Earlier that day, my grandmother saw a group of men lined up beside a wall. They were told to remove their hats. Then two Germans, one with scissors, one with a meat cleaver, hacked the facial hair, hacked the *payot*, hacked everything. She watched the blood running through the gutter. Afterwards, they didn't know where to go, looking like they did. They just knelt by the wall, bleeding and crying, covering their faces with their hands.

'So you see, beautiful Hannah. The reason I wear a beard today, is because I can.'

Such stories were the stuff Eric had grown up on, the myths and parables that shaped everything he believed. Hannah stopped making fun. If Eric was overly polite, cautious, and reluctant to assert himself, he had reasons. If he made quick judgements and held them close, he had reasons. And if he readily opened his heart before a lovely, God-fearing Jew, if he asked her to marry him after only a few brief meetings, he had his reasons for that as well. 'At last,' she wrote in the autobiography she published years later, 'I had met a man with greater moral authority than either my parents or my rabbi. What could I say but yes?'

A decade and a half passed before she returned to the story of those two clean-shaven boys, imperilled in Occupied Warsaw. By now she was married with three children. The early promise of her career had come to nothing; breaks fell to rivals and colleagues, and the demands of motherhood continually scuppered her hopes of advancement. Now that Tovyah was almost ready for secondary school, a time she had long anticipated, it seemed too late to rebuild her professional life. She had no steady job, and few prospects. Editors who had once encouraged her now looked embarrassed when they met. 'I'd heard the word, of course,' she later recalled, 'but until then I didn't truly understand what depression was. Now each day rose before me, a wall of hours, impossible to climb over. Three or four times I sat in the window on the second floor of our house and considered hurling myself to the pavement. Just a moment's fall, then whatever's next. But I was scared. Scared because G-d was watching.'

It was during the period of her unemployment that Hannah began to research and write her account of her father-in-law's confinement in Treblinka, entitled *Gehinnom and Afterwards*. The same book that, years hence, Kate would take home after her first term at university.

*

WHEN, SHORTLY AFTER THE DEATH of his wife, my father-in-law came to live with us, I knew only the bones of his story. Born in Poland at precisely the wrong time in the twentieth century (the exact year was unknown, even by Yosef himself), he was among the walking corpses who escaped from Treblinka during the rebellion of 1943. Sheltered by peasants in a dank basement until the end of the war, he did not see the sun for two years straight. When at last the war was over, he emerged from the basement, only to step into the grey dawn of the new Europe that had sprung up behind Stalin's Iron Curtain.

Somehow, between then and now, he'd made his way to England.

Knowing these blunt facts, one could make allowances for behaviour that was otherwise inexcusable. Even so, I found him easier to admire than to love; he was combative, bad tempered with the children, and impossibly stubborn. Before I had any notion of a book, I wanted to hear my father-in-law's story from his own mouth, to fill in all those tantalising blanks, and, hopefully, to come to a better understanding of the grim-faced man who shared our house. It came as no surprise that getting him to tell me this story was one long fight.

'What do you want to know?' he'd ask.

'Anything. Whatever you want to tell me is interesting.'

'I disagree. What's interesting in my life?'

'For a start, you survived.'

'No,' he said, suddenly angry. 'No one survived. I got out.'

*

There ends Hannah's introduction. What follows is an account of her subject's life before the war.

Yosef Rosenthal had the misfortune to be born tone deaf into a family of musicians. Not that he was let off without trying. Along with his siblings, he began lessons on the upright piano aged three, and for years was made to practise every day or no dinner. His eyes stung from reading tiny scores that an aunt had transcribed by hand. He played scales and arpeggios until his fingers were stiff. Counterpoint was virtually impossible – like trying to run in two directions at once. Eventually, he committed swathes of Mendelssohn and Meyerbeer to memory, but the music was only in his hands, not in his head. Definitely not in his heart. As he fumbled his way through recitals for his parents, they groaned and made faces. Afterwards, they asked, 'Yosef, didn't you feel anything as you played the music?'

'Miserable! I felt miserable!'

Over and over, he was baffled at being made to do something that brought so little joy to anybody, and at times drove uncles out of the room with hands over their ears. Poor little Yosef didn't even like *listening* to music. Chopin, Grieg, whatever. All of it was too noisy, just reams of meaningless notes. As he later confided to Hannah, 'I liked the girl who sang in the piano bar in Starówka and kicked her skirt in the air. Now that was music!'

Once he reached his teens, Yosef was finally permitted to abandon his musical studies. He devoted his time to running around with his friends, dreaming about girls. When the extended family asked after him, his parents said it wasn't his fault, there was nothing anyone could do; Yosef was simply born stupid, 'one in whom music goes to die'. At least his slow hands were good for something; with his school years behind him, Yosef was apprenticed to a tailor. It seemed a decent enough path for a *dummkopf*. No one was expecting that within a matter of months Molotov and Ribbentrop would have signed away the fates of an entire nation, Chamberlain's peace would have shattered, the Wehrmacht would have smashed the last of Poland's defences, and the plans of countless families would have gone up in smoke.

Longer than anyone else, Yosef's mother persisted in her belief that the occupying forces would treat them humanely. This was the nation of Bach, Beethoven, Schubert, and Handel. Germans were sophisticated, they spoke languages, revered culture. Nothing like the Poles. In the face of reported beatings and killings, she rationalised, 'It's like with a new boss. They start strict to give everyone a scare, then ease up later.'

When German decrees forced all Jews to relocate to the same corner of Warsaw – supposedly to halt the spread of typhus that was raging through the city – the Rosenthals had no choice but to vacate their modest home. 'At that time,' Yosef explained to Hannah, 'no one talked about anything else. Just typhus. We were more scared of typhus than Germans.' At the worst point in the epidemic, bodies were piled in the street, wrapped in nothing but paper, and left to rot as they awaited transportation to unmarked graves. Even Frau Rosenthal lost hope.

In the ghetto, Yosef and his family were confined to a single room, and Yosef now shared a thin mattress with his brother Mendl, to whom he bore a strong resemblance. (Another mattress was shared by his two sisters, Helly and Tsirl.) So alike were Yosef and Mendl that once Yosef had the misfortune to be taken for his brother by a soldier. He was crossing Chłodna Street, which led from the small ghetto to the large ghetto, where he hoped to trade stolen bric-a-brac for bread and soup. Moving between the ghettoes was always an ordeal. The road intruded into the Aryan Quarter, and before Jews were permitted to cross, they had to wait for patrolling Germans to halt the traffic. At busy hours, hundreds of Jews bunched at either side of the street. To amuse themselves at such times, on-duty Germans pulled musicians from local bars and ordered crippled and elderly Jews to dance to their music. A soldier, who was missing the top half of one ear, spotted Yosef and frogmarched him to an upright piano that had been dragged from across the street and lost its tuning. Once he'd got Yosef seated, he ordered him to play, thinking it was Mendl, the Jew whose artistry he'd rhapsodised about to his friends earlier that day.

Terrified of letting the man down, Yosef attempted a piece he could get through with few mistakes: the slow movement of 'The Moonlight Sonata'. A few bars in, the soldier smashed Yosef's hands with his truncheon, producing a loud, mangled discord. Pain seared through Yosef's fingers.

'Cut the maudlin shit, eh! Give us something exciting, a dance tune!'

The other musicians had stopped playing. Nobody danced. Three soldiers stood round the piano now, waiting for Yosef to resume. Bending to the keys once more, he struck the opening notes of Bach's 'Minuet in G Major', another staple of beginner keyboardists. That bright melody had never sounded more lifeless. Falling harder even than last time, the truncheon crushed his hands against the ivory. His knuckles bled.

'What's wrong with you today?' the man demanded. Yosef said nothing. He heard the sound of a gun cocking, the barrel pressed to his skull. In his ineptitude, he'd enraged the one-eared man, who now shouted incomprehensibly. What could he play? He knew that whatever happened, he would never make the crossing into the large ghetto, would never see his family again. Instead, he would be executed for the crime of humiliating a German, and his body would lie beside the out-of-tune piano for any child to loot until the following morning, when Mendl or his father would collect the remains. Lacking any means of defiance, he let his hands fall to the keys and started to play, he didn't know what, allowing his stubby fingers to chase each other over the keyboard of their own volition. And as the officer grew red in the face, puffing out his cheeks in rage, his two friends laughed and cheered. Yosef kept playing, not turning his head, just staring at the white and black keys bobbing up and down, up and down. When he reached the end of his clownish performance, thumping the major triad he'd started on, he still hadn't been shot.

'What else do you know, Jew?' an amused voice asked.

His oppressor had at last discovered his sense of humour, deciding he liked Yosef's terrible musicianship even more than his brother's immaculate playing. The Germans kept him there for over an hour, calling out 'Bravo, Maestro, Bravo!' while he hammered away ever more madly at the instrument he had hated since childhood.

Chapter Seven

One evening, Hannah paused on her way up to the top of the house to look in on her husband, who was reading in the study. She asked him if he knew who Ariel is.

Eric shrugged. 'You tell me.'

'It's a name your father mentions sometimes, then immediately clams up. He never spoke about him when he was younger?'

'Never.' Eric considered. 'There's an Ariel mentioned in the Dead Sea Scrolls, I believe. A lesser angel?'

'That's not it. He's talking about a human being. A friend from the old country maybe.'

Eric sighed. By now, the interview sessions between Hannah and his father had become an unignorable routine. 'I've been wanting to say something. I'm not sure it's good the way you go up there, stirring up the past.'

'Not good how?'

'When I was a teenager, in the days he started talking about the war, I used to hear him at night, weeping. The sobs came right through the wall. My father, my invincible father! Mame told me it was foxes. And now you're putting him through it all over again.'

'Darling. He never stopped weeping.'

By now Hannah's project had taken possession of her. She woke up, she listened to her tapes, she made notes, she spoke to her father-in-law, then she made more notes. Searching her own conscience, she found it clean. The work needed to be done, and who was better suited than her? She was on God's path.

'Are you saying I should stop?'

'I'm saying you should be careful.' Eric picked a loose fleck of wood from the window frame. 'There are some fields,' he said, 'that should not be churned up.'

*

Survival in the ghetto depended on several things: not starving, not contracting disease, avoiding deportation, and not angering Germans. The safest course was to join the Jewish police, who imposed Nazi will within the ghetto walls. These men were responsible for choosing deportees, and generally found favour with the occupying soldiers. Although Yosef had friends among the police who tried to recruit him, he turned them down. 'If I went with them,' he explained, 'my whole family would turn their backs on me.' He did however sidle up to the authorities in other ways. He earned a reputation for repairing uniforms for soldiers. This work was of course unpaid, but not always unappreciated. A man named Leutnant Heinrich Beck, for instance, took a shine to the boy. Beck had seen his recital on Chłodna Street. 'I like your ugly face,' he told Yosef when they first met. 'You look just like my step-mother.'

Beck treated Yosef to cigarettes and the odd beer for his labour. When Yosef, emboldened by drink, asked for help procuring coloured threads to embroider yarmulkes and other religious garments, the Leutnant said he'd see what he could do. A week later, the officer brought him a box containing various cast-offs and balls of thread. 'Make your Jew hats,' he said. 'And be grateful. I'm risking my life here.' The German laughed. Both knew that the one whose fate was on a knife-edge was Yosef. Just that morning, two young men had accused him of collaboration. It was only after Mendl stepped in that they left Yosef alone. By now, Mendl was a respected member of the Underground; he helped to smuggle ammunition from the city, concealed within bags of flour.

According to official information, the Jews who were trans-ported from the ghetto in packed train carriages were resettled in work camps abroad. No one believed this. Why send the sick and the elderly, why send *infant children* to work camps? A day came when the entire Rosenthal household was selected for deportation. Not daring to go to Beck, Yosef enlisted the help of an old family friend, a carpenter who'd sold his soul by joining the Jewish police. 'You father cuts me dead in the street,' the carpenter said. 'Now you want help?'

'Please.'

'I can probably get you and Mendl taken off the list. Young men are always useful.'

'And my sisters? Helly and Tsirl?'

'Only the young men. That's the best I can do.'

Yosef's mother and father boarded a train the follow-ing day, along with their two daughters. As Frau Rosenthal kissed her sons goodbye, she wished them both long life. Returning to the empty apartment, the two brothers sat in silence. In one corner, Tsirl's clarinet case. Neither Yosef nor Mendl could find anything else to look at.

'We should be on that train,' Mendl said. 'We should have swapped with the girls.'

Yosef said maybe there really were work camps for the Jews. In the East, somewhere, a munitions factory. And his brother said, 'Grow up.'

While preparations for the uprising were under way, Mendl taught Yosef how to make a petrol bomb from a milk bottle, some rubbing alcohol, motor oil, a cloth, and a cigarette lighter. He then pressed a gun into his little brother's hand. Yosef tried to picture himself shooting a man up close. Herr Leutnant, for instance, with a hole punched through the side of his face. He passed the gun back to his brother. Give it to someone who knows how to shoot, he said. The rebellion was pointless, everyone knew it, like ants staging an uprising against children with stomping boots. Mendl was among the first casualties, his body torn by bullets, leaking onto the pavement. Exactly nothing was accomplished – the rebels were slaughtered, order restored, and the survivors loaded onto trains. Leutnant Beck paid Yosef a final visit during the liquidation. 'My friend, did you know what was coming? Be honest, now, I won't tell anyone. No? I don't believe you. You should have been making helmets, eh, not skull caps. And Jews are supposed to be clever!' Before leaving, he thumped Yosef on the back and wished him luck. *Viel Glück*. He would put in a good word for him, he said, with colleagues on the other side.

Hannah asked Yosef what, looking back, he thought the Leutnant meant. Was this one final insult, gallows humour at its cruellest, or was he expressing genuine sympathy? Did he hope you'd survive? Yosef shrugged. 'What does the hope of one Nazi matter? He is dead. He froze to death in Stalingrad, or was killed with machine guns in Normandy, or he got fat, and died with cancer after the war. Who cares? He's dead. Everybody I know, Jews, Germans, Poles, Ukrainians, all dead now. Everybody dead.'

The central chapter of the book, the heart of Hannah's narrative, opens with Yosef's arrival in Treblinka. As the train slowed to a stop, the peasants who lived and worked alongside the factory of death ran parallel to the tracks and gestured to the new inmates by drawing their hands across their throats. If this was a warning, to what end? Even supposing that after months of ghetto-deprivation and then the interminable hours crushed into a cattle car without sleep, without food, without water, if after all that there was a single human being still capable of making a run for it, the question remained: where could you run to?

In the *lager*, Yosef wished he'd worked harder at the piano. 'Some Jews got easy lives for themselves, playing in the band,' he explained to Hannah. While this might have been true, musicianship was no guarantee of safety. Yosef never saw any of his siblings or cousins again, despite their precision on violin, on the keys, and on the clarinet. The monsters put instruments in their hands, they made requests, they clapped and whistled derisively, and then they murdered them, all the same as the non-musical Jews, and burned the corpses afterwards, and sucked the ashes through the chimneys, and watched the drift of the black clouds.

'Here, see this candle,' Yosef said to Hannah, during one of their sessions. 'What burns, the wax or the wick?'

'The wick, surely.'

'The wick doesn't burn. The wax melts and cools it down. By itself, the wick would burn in one minute. Young people don't understand nothing. Too much liquid, flame drowns. Yes? It's the gas that burns.'

'What gas?' Hannah asked.

'From the wax. The wax turns into gas and burns. The package is the fuel. You see? This is the same concept in the *lager*. Burning human beings is tricky. The human liquid, the fat, drowns the fire. Fire dies, you have to start over.'

Yosef was shaking his head. Hannah knew he was trying to tell her something important, but she couldn't see what it was. Not yet.

Music seemed to follow Yosef through life like a bad joke, the one scrap of his world before the war that nothing could shake loose. In Treblinka, he met a cultured man, a great lover of the arts. Unusually for a Jew, he was more comfortable speaking Polish than Yiddish. One day the man was crying into his hands, and Yosef asked him what was wrong. He had not been beaten, he had a good shirt, and there was bread in his pocket. Why was he so upset?

'Listen. Do you hear that?'

A waltz blared from the camp speaker system. Yosef recognised the music, vaguely, but could not have named the composer.

'How could they desecrate immortal Chopin?'

Yosef flared with anger. 'Chopin?' he said. 'That bastard made my fingers bleed when I was six years old!'

When Yosef came across the man again at evening roll call, he was even more miserable. Feeling sorry for this stranger, upset about things that no longer had any meaning, Yosef decided to cheer him up. He offered him a half ration of bread he'd somehow acquired.

The man devoured it in seconds. There was a case for eking it out, but that meant concealing the bread on your person, always dangerous. In the *lager,* there was only one real hiding place: the stomach.

Yosef said, 'My grandfather was a pianist, and once shook hands with Chopin. Take my hand. Go on. Touch my hand, and through me you can reach all the way back to the master.'

It wasn't true. His grandfather did meet a famous composer, once, but it was only Moniuszko, now largely forgotten. It was obvious the man of culture had already succumbed to despair. Yosef had seen enough to know he would soon be a Musselman, one of those empty husks, and before the month was out, he would be incinerated. But that day at least, he didn't only shake Yosef's hand. He brought it to his lips and kissed it, then smoothed down the kisses.

'Listen,' he said. 'I'm getting out of here. There's a plan. Let me tell you.'

Yosef's eyes moved to the watchtower, the barbed wire. 'Don't be stupid. No one gets out.'

Hannah asked her father-in law if the plan came off. Did anyone make it out alive? Yosef only sighed.

'But there *were* escapees,' Hannah said. 'Not many, but some.'

Her father-in-law waved his hands dismissively. 'Fairy stories for children,' he said.

*

A couple of weeks after Eric first confronted Hannah about her interviews, he finished work unexpectedly early and was home at teatime. Wandering up to his room to change out of his suit, he found Elsie at the foot of the stairs to the attic.

She said she was looking for a safety-pin she'd dropped. 'Look, here it is.' She plucked it from the carpet and held it to the light. Muffled voices came from the room above, audible if you strained your ears.

Eric led his daughter to the kitchen downstairs, then shut the door. 'What did you hear?'

'Nothing.'

'Nothing?'

Elsie pointed her big toe and made a figure of eight against the tiles. 'Just some stuff about Zeide's days in Poland.'

'That's not nothing, then.'

'OK. Can I go now?'

'Elsie, listen to me. You must never do that again. Never. When your mother speaks to Zeide, you go nowhere near that room. Go play outside if you like, I don't care, just stay away from the attic.'

'But I already know this stuff. They teach it in school.'

Later, when Eric told Hannah that he was frightened about the effect her work was having on the children, she thought he was overreacting. Elsie would have to learn these things someday. 'We did, didn't we?'

Eric was not appeased. 'But not now, for God's sake. Not like *this*.'

'Not now. So when?'

'Later!'

'And when the time does come, what's the right way for her to learn about the mass extermination of her own family? You think her teachers are equipped to guide her through that?'

In the window, a gibbous moon sat on a bank of cloud. The last of the afternoon light faded from the sky.

'You think it's important for him to tell his story before he dies. I get it. He needs to be heard. But you don't have to write this stuff down. You don't have to put it in *a book and publish*. This is our family. The whole world and his brother do not need to know.'

*

So far, my conversations with Yosef had been tantalising but insubstantial, and the narrative that was taking form was decidedly patchy. He'd given me some interesting details

93

of Warsaw in the thirties, describing the lessons his mother gave, how the house rang out with bungled renditions of Beethoven and Liszt. He told me about the cold nights in the ghetto, the sudden and never-explained disappearance of his uncle, the first of the family to be murdered. Often, he contradicted himself. Sometimes he would say that no one knew anything about the camps, sometimes everybody knew. He described the train journey to *Gehinnom*, the cattle cars stuffed with people, the deaths along the way, the stench of piss and shit dulled only by the cold, how the first thing they did on arrival was toss out the corpses, someone's sister, the old mute whose name nobody knew.

But of his experience of life in the camps, he was reticent.

'Tell me more about the *lager*,' I would say. 'What was it like?'

'I told you hundred times! We were hungry and we were cold. One portion of bread a day is all you got, sometimes two if you could trade for someone. Or steal. We were all thieves. But everybody knows these things. You can watch it on the television.'

'Tell me a story then. Something that happened there.'

'I don't remember. Too much years.'

He said this despite having recounted various illuminating episodes. It was obvious he was hiding, and when I pressed him, he would derail the conversation. I heard that I was bringing up my children all wrong. I let Elsie get away with too much, and I allowed Gideon to be stupid.

One night, I awoke to a crash at the top of the house. I knew at once Yosef had fallen. Eric slept through it, so I crept upstairs to see if my father-in-law was all right. I found him on the floor by his bed, still wrapped in his duvet, groaning softly.

'Yes, yes, stop touching me,' he said. But even once I'd got him back into bed there was a wild terror in his eyes.

'Channah, I had a horrible dream.'

'Tell me.'

'I can't! I don't remember. I only know I was back.'

'Where?'

'Back! *Poyln*.'

'Would you like some water?'

'No, sit down. I want to tell you. Things are coming back now. Things I didn't think about for fifty years.'

I held his hands in mine as he told me the following story.

'There was a little boy. He was very small, and there was a gap in his front teeth. And he had colour on his face.' I asked if he meant the boy was black, but he said no, no. Yosef had been in England for decades and spoke the language fluently, but there were still words he lacked. I realised he was talking about a birthmark.

'The second I see him, I know. This is a boy from *Warszawa*, I saw this boy before. "What's your name, little boy?" I asked him. First Yiddish, then Polish. He didn't speak. I tried French and German too. *Comment tu t'appelles? Name*? Eventually, he answered me. His name was Ariel.'

'What language was this?'

'*Mamaloshen*. Yiddish. I asked if he was scared, and he said yes, very scared. He didn't find his parents. First mother was taken away, then he was split from father at selections. He didn't tell me this, he just said he didn't know where they were. But I knew.'

'And when you say "the selections" you mean—'

'I told you this already. We lined up, and they said you go right, you go left. This one strong, he can work. But that one weak, get rid of him.'

'Yes, but wouldn't a child always be—'

'That's what I'm telling you. Listen! His father was young man, strong, so he could do some work.'

Yosef always told his stories angrily. To say that I was having trouble following, as I did now, was to risk an explosion.

'How come you don't understand?'

'If this boy was selected for extermination—'

'Always children killed at once. They never let them live in the *lager*.'

'Yes, I understand, but why were *you* there? Had you been selected as well?'

'No, I was strong. Wait. You're getting me confused. Why was I there? Yes, you're right, I must have got selected. Maybe it was the time my foot got infection and I couldn't walk so good. I say to the boy, "It's OK. Take my hand. I'll be your daddy now. Come with me, we seek your parents." And he was so trusting, he give me his hand. Children are like dogs, you know that? They decide the moment they see you they like you or they don't like. Maybe it's smell. Adults are different. You meet a man, he say, come on, impress me, then we see if we are friends. But children just know.'

'So where did you take him?'

Yosef didn't answer this question. He was staring into the depths of the room.

'Did you find his parents?'

'You're not *listening*. His mother was in woman's camp. And his father . . . no one got to see their parents again. Do you understand? Not me, not Mendl, not no one.'

'I'm listening. Where did you go?'

Again, Yosef was silent. I squeezed his hand.

'I took him where we had to go. I said, "Don't listen to anything people say. Everyone is scared here. Don't talk

96

to nobody, follow me. Have you said Shema this evening? Let's say it now. Put your hand over your eyes like this." And we said the prayer together. *Shema Yisrael, Adonai Eloheinu Adonai echad . . .*'

With his sight covered by the palm of his right hand the better to concentrate his mind on the unity of God, Yosef recited the whole prayer, the prayer that Jews are commanded to say twice daily, the words with which we greet each morning, that we teach our children to recite before they go to sleep, and that we hope to say as our last words in this life, if our killers give us time to do so. My father-in-law, who had at least a smattering of six languages, spoke the most beautiful Hebrew. He recited like a poet. As those ancient words poured forth, I felt myself in holy company. I hope that lost child felt the same way, all those years ago, stranded in *Gehinnom*.

When he was done, I could see that he was crying. Fat tears slipped from under the hand which he had not removed on the second line of the prayer as custom dictates.

'And what happened then?' I asked.

'What do you think? I let go and he walked into the gas. Ariel was his name.' Yosef finally lifted his hand from his face. His eyes were bloodshot, his nose streaming. 'I didn't see him for fifty years, but I see him now. Right there.'

Yosef wasn't pointing at his temple, the seat of memory, but to some dark place in the room before him. I looked, as though I too might see the terrified little boy among the shadows of that attic. But our ghosts are as private as our dreams, and I saw nothing.

Though I knew he wanted me to leave, I lingered. At this point in his life, Yosef's mind was like a book whose pages kept being torn out by some careless vandal; there was every chance that by the morning, he'd have forgotten this whole incident. If I didn't ask now, I might never find out.

'But what happened to you?' I said. 'Didn't you have to go with him?'

'No, no.'

'How did you get away?'

'Because I wasn't selected. Don't you understand? Never. I was strong and I could work, and they never selected me. In the ghetto I had my family, and there was Leutnant Beck, he looked out for me, and in the *lager* I had nobody. Mendl was lucky, he never saw that place. That's a bad thing to say, but sometimes I think it's true, he was the lucky one. Not me. I watched out. I picked up food. I kept my strength. I did what I was told. You see a little boy all on his own, crying for his parents, and you want to tell him it's OK, everything is OK. Isn't that normal? You would do the same thing, no? So I told him. I told all the little boys they would be OK. I don't want to talk about this any more. Please, Channah, turn that thing off.'

From this talk, Hannah deduced her father-in-law was part of the *Sonderkommando*, a German term meaning 'Special Squad'. Jews assigned to the Squad had the most repellent tasks necessitated by the sick logic of the death camps. They led the other inmates to the gas chambers. Afterwards, it was their responsibility to search the dead for concealed treasures, to rip gold from the mouths of corpses, and then to dispose of the remains. Not that this saved them from the common fate, as they well knew; among their duties as new recruits was to immolate their predecessors.

But there were certain privileges – better food rations, extra shirts, even booze.

'How did you end up in that position?' Hannah asked him. 'Did Beck help you?'

'No more.'

'What happened in the ghetto? For three years you were never deported. Were you a member of the Jewish police?'

'I told you no, never, no.'

'What about the rebellion at Treblinka? That's when you got out, right? Did you take part in organising? Or did you—'

'Enough!'

Hannah assured her father-in-law that she wasn't here to judge him. She only wanted to understand exactly what had happened. He refused to answer any more questions, and it was several days before she got him talking again. Even then, Yosef was wary. He asked Hannah why she had to tape everything.

'YOUR STORY IS IMPORTANT,' I explained. 'I want it recorded.'

Yosef was perplexed. 'You mean you're going to play people these tapes? Who would want to hear an old man talk about his life?'

'I'm going to write it down. In a book.'

'No.'

'No?'

'This is my life, Hannah, it's not your book.'

I had, of course, anticipated this resistance; it was one of my great fears as I set out on the project. And if he'd pushed back at the start, I might have given up. But since then, everything had changed. In the months before we began, I was jobless and depressed. For too long I had endured the daily confrontation with purposelessness. The setting down of Yosef's life had re-energised me. Now I had it, work, real work, the kind I could throw myself into with my entire being. I do not wish to diminish my father-in-law's reservations, or his fears, but I did think at the time – and I still think now – that he was wrong. History, be it yours, mine, or the next person's, belongs to us all. And that's what I told him.

'So you will write the book, even if I say no?'

'I've made up my mind.' Not only that. I had already spoken to my agent, pitched the idea to publishers.

'And the whole world will know what I did?'

'Anyone who reads will understand.'

'You think people are better than they are.'

Cynicism about human nature is a position I have always rejected. Despite everything, I believe, along with Anne Frank, that people are fundamentally good at heart. Life, otherwise, could not be endured. But my father-in-law had been through what he'd been through, and there was no contradicting him.

'And Gideon will read this?' he said.

'He's not old enough.'

'But one day.'

I couldn't lie to him. 'One day, yes, I expect one day he will.'

'And Elsie too?'

'One day Elsie too.'

'And even little Tovyah?'

I nodded. His eyes closed and his face began to quiver as though waiting to receive a blow.

'Make me a promise,' he said. 'When I'm dead, don't stick me in the ground. Please. Set the body on fire. When people read about my life, I want to be dust and ashes. Destroy every piece of me, everything that's left.'

'Eric will insist—'

'Dust and ashes, Channah.'

Chapter Eight

In the Talmudic elaboration of the *Akedah,* the Binding of Isaac, rumour of Isaac's death reaches Sarah before her husband and son return from the sacrifice unscathed. Overcome with grief, Sarah makes the conventional wish, that she herself had perished rather than her little boy. She then travels to Hebron in search of Abraham, planning to rain down all hell upon her child-murdering husband. But look as she might, she can't find him. And so, giving up at last, she returns to her tent in the Negev, where she encounters the same man who told her earlier that her son was dead. It turns out he spoke too soon and wishes to correct his mistake; Isaac is alive and well. *Baruch hashem.*

At which point in the story, Sarah dies.

The day after Elsie vanished, Hannah dialled Rabbi Grossman's number, and this is what he told her.

'Why now?' Rabbi Grossman asked on the phone. 'Why didn't Sarah die when she got news of her bereavement? You may have heard of refeeding syndrome. When a starved person eats too much too quickly, the body can't take it. Insulin levels soar, the heart runs wild. In extreme cases, fatal, instant death. It wasn't grief that killed Sarah, but the resumption of ordinary happiness. Be cautioned, Hannah. Do not lose hope.'

She did her best to take the rabbi's words to heart. She made calls to teachers, to parents of Elsie's friends, to the police and to journalists. Everyone she knew, every professional contact she'd made, everyone was going to hear about this. If necessary, they would scour the earth. To each person she called, she spoke quickly and calmly, giving instructions and making enquiries.

Some time that afternoon, her own phone rang, and she snatched the receiver, eager for news. But it was only Sam Morris, Tovyah's Hebrew teacher. Something had come up – there would be no class that weekend. Bloody fool. A little curtness was required to get him off the line.

Afterwards, she stood at the window, debating whether to put her fist through it. She remembered the rabbi's words and she said her prayers. *Adon 'olam, 'asher malakh, b'ṭerem kol yeṣir niv'ra.*

Next morning, over a breakfast of greyish scrambled eggs congealing on burnt toast, Hannah told her sons that, yes, they would be going to school, just like yesterday, just like the day before that. When Gideon protested, she shouted him down. 'I don't care what people say. Do your work.' Tovyah asked why they were eating a cooked breakfast, it wasn't the weekend. Gideon kicked his shin. The brothers started bickering, and only stopped when their father slammed both fists against the table. Though the food on Eric's plate remained untouched, he stood up now in a single motion, sweeping his chair to the floor with a bang. He did not stop on his way out to right it. For a moment, no one moved. Then, with his father gone, Gideon helped himself to a slice of Eric's toast. Tovyah put his hand on his mother's arm. 'When are we going to find Elsie?' he said.

Eric also ate nothing that night. He didn't get back from work until they were halfway through dinner. When Hannah rose to serve him from the trays kept warm in the oven, he said, 'Sit down, sit down. I'm not hungry.'

But she'd kept a portion back, specially, she said.

'Who asked you?' he said.

Tovyah asked his father why he'd stopped eating.

Eric cleared his throat. 'Sometimes, when you want to focus your mind on God, you need an empty stomach.' He attempted to soften his tone. 'You know. Like Yom Kippur.'

It seemed that along with his daily sustenance, Eric had given up talking to his wife. The last two nights he'd turned in early, then was up and gone before dawn broke. And when they were in the house together, he sought out whatever room she wasn't in. Now was no exception; after refusing dinner, he made himself scarce.

Once she'd dismissed the boys from the table, Hannah went to find her husband. He was in his study, as she'd predicted, hunched over thin lines of Hebrew text, mouthing words under his breath. All he did to acknowledge Hannah's presence behind him was to extract a rolled-up newspaper from his briefcase and hand it to her before he resumed his scrutiny of the page before him.

She didn't have to unroll the paper to know what it was.

TEEN DAUGHTER OF MEMOIRIST GOES MISSING FROM TOP LONDON PRIVATE SCHOOL — POLICE SEARCH RIVERS

- Elsie Rosenthal, aged 14, disappeared from Lady Hilary's School for Girls on Tuesday afternoon around lunchtime, and has not been seen since.
- Mother and author Hannah Rosenthal offers reward for information, and says family put their trust in God to bring back daughter.

It's every mother's worst nightmare. It started off just like any other wet November day . . .

Hannah hated those opening sentences, which she'd only intended as placeholders. But her editor liked them (such cliches were, after all, frictionless), and she'd lacked the energy to argue over prose styles. The important thing was that the message went out.

'Do you want to talk about this?' Hannah asked.

Eric didn't even turn around.

She knew how it must look as she went about her daily rituals still talkative, still busy. A juggernaut, Eric had called her, during their courtship. Once she got going, nothing could stop her.

But had he never heard of a brave face? It wasn't easy, keeping up a front for the boys. Biting down the pain. In bed that night, Eric switched off the lamp while Hannah was still reading. Turning over, he presented her with the wall of his back.

She switched the light back on. 'I'm suffering too.'

Eric lay like a plank, sleepless and unmoving.

'Did you hear? I said I'm suffering.'

'You have a funny way of showing it.'

'You mean because I'm trying to keep it together, you think I don't care?'

'Keep it together! Have you got any idea how inane that sounds?'

'I can't talk if you're being like this.'

Eric said, 'So don't talk.'

Hannah stared at her husband's rounded back. She might have pummelled it with balled fists.

'Is this about the piece? You should be congratulating me.'

'You broke the dry spell. *Mazel tov.*'

'I'm not talking about my career.'

She had insisted on being referred to in the article as a *memoirist*, not a journalist. And at the bottom of the text, it had announced the publication of her first book, due the following year. 'Do you know what their circulation is?'

Eric said nothing.

'Our daughter is missing, this isn't some family secret. The more people know, the better.'

'Great, fine, agreed.' Suddenly hot, he kicked his legs free of the duvet. 'Did you have to use that picture?'

'You want something done, you have to stir people's sympathies.'

The photo showed Elsie on her thirteenth birthday, in front of a cake loaded with candles. Yosef stood behind her, huge and bearlike, with his hands resting on her shoulders. Leaning down, he was kissing the side of her head, and Elsie, distracted from the cake, was smiling up at him. That same picture was sitting in a million households across the country, grease stains from a million breakfasts muddying the image.

'That's a million people who know we're looking.'

Eric sighed. 'You can drop the pretence that everything's going just brilliantly, the boys aren't here.'

'Grossman said—'

'Fuck Grossman.'

Hannah let the words hang for a moment. 'At least I'm doing something,' she said. 'It's only been three days. It's like you've already given up!'

She'd spoken more truly than she intended. Why did she not see it before? Of course. Eric had already lost hope, was even now making a start on the period of mourning. A head-start on a race with no finish. No wonder he couldn't sympathise with Hannah as she endured the lesser torment of not knowing. The knowledge he carried through his waking hours was far worse than any uncertainty. And he was alone with it. Trapped in that bare place, where the darkness was close and heavy. Deep in his soul, he knew what had happened to Elsie. Eric was no more than a boy when, thanks to his father's tales, he got his first graphic lessons in the history of human evil. The early years of their marriage – so much straightforward joy – had deceived her. Now she knew. Her husband had grown up just as his father had wanted: quick to frighten, and without faith in people's basic humanity. What Yosef, with a dry laugh, would have called a realist.

She didn't want to consider the influence the old man had had on Elsie. At times, when she very was young, they'd been like father and daughter.

'Eric,' Hannah said.

He wouldn't look at her. She put her hand to his shoulder and he shrugged it off.

How awful to be divided on this. Something brand new happens, you learn a little more about yourself, about your marriage. 'We're going to find her,' Hannah said. 'She must be—'

'How? By writing more trash for the tabloids? *It was just a normal, piss average day.*'

He'd shocked her into silence. At last, he rolled towards her.

'It was the same thing with Zeide! You should have let him live out those last months without bullying the memories out. It's all just material to you. The career that eats everything.'

'I can't believe I'm hearing this.'

'Open your ears! I've been telling you long enough. You had no business writing that book. Elsie worshipped the man.'

'Zeide needed to talk to someone. He had to unburden himself.'

'You think you're the first person who ever heard those horror stories? For God's sake, Hannah, step outside of yourself for two seconds. Before I met you, the greater part of my life was getting him *to stop* telling those nightmares. Tateh, I'd say, you haven't set foot in Poland for thirty years, do you think we can give it a rest now?'

'What's this got to do with Elsie?'

'Do I need to spell it out? While you were up there, mining for literary gold, she used to sit on the stairs and listen. Whatever he spilled out, she soaked up.'

'If you want to talk about Elsie and your father, let's talk about them. Why did we bury him? Elsie knew he wanted a cremation, everyone knew. Do you remember her face the day of the burial?'

'That subject is closed,' Eric said.

'Oh, so now you're done.'

Hannah considered forcing the argument. Didn't he see that she was blessed with a mind that was meant for more than knockabout journalism? In the pit of unemployment, she'd discovered not just a way out, but her true vocation. *Baruch Hashem*. The book she was writing about her father-in-law was moral work, her contribution to the ongoing effort to ensure that never again . . . And now, if there was anything she could do to bring Elsie home, it would be crazy not to try it. Everything had its purpose.

But she was tired of the old fights, and as she too rolled over, her eyelids dragged shut. She dreamt of Yosef, underground, wrists straining against the lid of his casket.

A sudden movement woke her. The bed shook as Eric convulsed. As she listened, choked little pig noises escaped from her husband. A maternal feeling stirred in her chest. She threaded an arm under his neck and muttered soothing words into his ear, just as she had done on difficult nights with Tovyah, years earlier.

In the morning, Hannah's parents got in touch once more. This was the second time she'd spoken to her father in a week; the preceding silence had lasted years. He said he'd seen the latest news clip, filmed at a careers event at school: Elsie talking about how when she grew up she was going to be a vet. He just wanted to know how everybody was holding up. Was there anything he could do?

'You could try praying,' Hannah said. And to his credit, he said he would do as she wished.

In her mind, she repeated the rabbi's warning. The whiplash reversal could kill. They mustn't, any of them, despair. Day after day, she told herself things would turn around. They had to. They would *because* they had to. Life could not contain that much suffering. It would split her open, from the crown of her head downwards.

On the fifth day Elsie was missing, Hannah got a call from St Edwards, the school Tovyah and Gideon attended. A voice she didn't recognise asked, stammering slightly, if she was free. When Hannah said she could make time if she absolutely had to, the voice asked if she could collect Gideon. Immediately. He'd been suspended. Just an hour earlier, he'd broken another boy's nose.

Hannah, not driving strictly within limits, was there in half an hour. She found Gideon waiting in the Head of Year's office, having been guided by a young teacher whose name she didn't catch. There was a dull, rusty stain on Gideon's shirt the size of a fifty-pence piece, and one of the buttons dangled from its stitching. Next to him stood a nervous, wiry man: the owner of the weak voice she'd heard on the phone.

'I'm afraid the boys can get a bit territorial this time of year.' he said. 'I often find them locking antlers in the autumn, then they calm down over the Christmas break. Normally, we'd have held him until the end of the day, but I thought perhaps he could be some use at home.'

Hannah thanked him distractedly and led Gideon to the car. They drove in silence. Once home, she asked him if what the teacher had told her was true.

'That depends what he said, dunnit.'

'Don't be cute. You've been fighting.'

Gideon shrugged his broad shoulders. He was getting to be a man now.

'And you broke a boy's nose.'

'Dunno about that. You'd have to ask the nurse, won't ya.'

'*Wouldn't you*. You weren't raised in a slum.'

This estuary English was a new affectation of Gideon's. She didn't care for it any more than she cared for playing chauffeur in the middle of the afternoon. They sat in the living room, either side of the squat apothecary table laden with magazines. Gideon's eye darted now and then to the bundle of papers. Hannah had managed to keep the story in the headlines this long, but there was no real news.

'And don't look so self-satisfied,' Hannah said. 'What did you say the boy's name was?'

'Chaz. Charlie.'

'Is he a friend?'

'Not now.'

'No, I suppose you've blown that one. What on Earth made you do it?'

'Said summin' I didn't like.'

'Some*thing*. What was it?'

'Some-THING. OK now? Everyone thinks I'm a spaz if I talk like you and Eric, but fine, whatever. *Something*.'

'Is that why you hit him? Because he called you a spaz?'

'You know why I hit him.'

Gideon gave his mother a look. She understood.

'He said something about Elsie, then.'

'Her and all of us. Something about Jews.'

'And so you smashed his face in.'

Gideon drummed against the table with the index and ring fingers of his right hand. 'I ain't gonna say – I'm *not* going to say sorry, if that's what you're after. I don't regret it.'

'What I'm after is for the clump of cells inside your skull to develop intelligent life. Don't you see what's happened here? Look at me. Look!'

'What?'

'You come across a black-and-white case of anti-Semitism, black and white, and what do you do? You lash out. And so who gets suspended from school? Is it the small-brained bigot, your friend Charlie Goebbels? No, it's my son who gets suspended from school, that's who. What's the point of having a lawyer for a father if you want to behave like a sav-age? Why do we spend all this money on your education? And so now, if you go and tell the headmaster, if you go and tell the police, who will they believe? A fuming, spitting Jew who yells "Anti-Semite! Anti-Semite!" or poor little Charlie Buttermouth, the Gentile with the broken-nose?'

'The police? Who said anything about the police?'

'There are laws about these things, Gideon. This isn't Imperial Russia. Racial and religious discrimination are crimes in this country. I cannot believe a son of mine is so stupid.'

'You're overreacting.'

'Stop grinning. You won one fight, and now you think you're a tough guy. Well done. But this is what you need to understand. Out there, in the big bad world, you will not win the fights. You won't throw the last punch or even the first punch. You will be smashed over the head before you can turn round. If you wake up at all, it will be in a hospital, where you will take your dinners through a straw. The world is stuffed with people bigger, uglier, and dirtier than you will ever be and they will tear you apart. The enemies of the Jews are stronger than us. Always have been. Why do you think for three thousand years, from Moses to Ruth Bader Ginsberg, we have been obsessed with the law? If you want to survive out there, do not trust in your ability to win a fair fight. Believe me, there won't be any fair fights. There won't even be fights.'

Though Gideon had not been subjected to this exact speech before, the gist was familiar. This time, however, he had a ready comeback: 'Not in Israel.'

'Excuse me?'

'In Israel, nobody pushes you around for being a Jew.'

'My son, the genius, meets one poodle of a Nazi thug, and he decides he wants to live in the desert. You don't even like the heat.'

Gideon was lying when he told his mother that Charlie had got his nose broken for an anti-Semitic slur. Or half lying. 'Have you ever noticed how basically all Jews are faggots?'

the boy had said. Any word other than 'faggot' and he might have kept his cool. If only Jews weren't such nebbishes! Look at his brother, thin, jumpy Tovyah, too scared to dive from the high board into the local pool. Top of the class in maths, of course, good with numbers, yes, and good at fuck all else. Even his father was no more than a fat guy with a big voice. Outside this ridiculous house, that man would be the boss of nobody.

And yet, in Israel they had found a way to overcome the Jewish destiny, to say fuck you to the bad genes and the dorkery. They walked tall, they built themselves up strong, and they kicked ass.

'Maybe that's exactly what I want to do, Hannah,' Gideon said. 'Maybe I want to make aliya.'

'Wonderful. You can wear a bulletproof vest on your way to buy groceries.'

Gideon kissed his teeth. 'What's the alternative? It's not like I'm going to write books or become a lawyer.'

But just as Gideon had started to open up, he seemed to have lost his mother's interest. This was not an uncommon frustration for a child of Hannah Rosenthal. Her eyes scanned something through the window over his shoulder.

'Erm, hello? Are you listening? I'm being serious about—'

'Gideon! Shut up a second!' She had raised a finger in warning.

'What?'

Hannah was still staring out of the window. She stood up now to get a better look. Gideon followed the line of her vision and saw the police car that had just slowed to a crawl in the road outside.

'What the hell?' Gideon said. 'When you talked about calling the cops, I thought you were being dramatic.'

Hannah was trembling now. Her breathing was shallow and rapid. The car stopped next to a parking space on the far side of the road. Hannah climbed up onto the back of the sofa and pushed her face to the window to block out her own reflection. But still she couldn't see inside the rear of the car; the glass was dark. All she could make out was the driver, and a second policeman in the passenger seat.

Gideon climbed up to kneel beside. 'Oh my God,' he said. 'Do you think it's . . . ? Oh fuck.'

Far, far too late, Hannah saw that Eric was right. Everything that was happening was her fault. A famous poet once said that to be a writer was to bring ruin to a family; now she understood. She hadn't given Yosef a second life on the page, she'd done the opposite. You fix people in ink and you kill them. Even if they're already dead, you kill them over. They can't move, they can't breathe, they can only lie there stiff, in whatever shape you bent them into. And if there's a chance, they will have their revenge.

As long as she lived, she would never write another book. That was her penance: to renounce the one thing that had given her, for a little while, a sense of purpose.

The door on the driver's side swung open and a man lifted himself from the vehicle.

Feeling her resolve crack, Hannah closed her eyes. She couldn't cope. How would she sit shiva for her own child? How could she wail prayers for her little girl? How could she get through all the years to come, stabbed by every phantom birthday, every milestone that would never happen: graduation, marriage, pregnancy, grandchildren?

In another moment Gideon tapped her shoulder, and his hand sprang into a pointing finger. 'Look!' he gasped.

His voice, though emphatic, was not devoid of joy. Not quite daring to hope, she opened her eyes.

Baruch Hashem. Baruch Hashem. Baruch Hashem. Baruch Hashem.

The policeman had unlocked the back door and pulled it open. And there, with her arms folded and her head slumped against the head rest, was Elsie. She rose from the car as if half asleep. The officer walked behind her, with one hand on her back, as Elsie stumbled towards home.

It was only once she'd got her inside the house that Hannah noticed something was off. There was a line of dried blood behind her ear, and her eyes had taken on the colour of misted glass.

PART TWO

DAUGHTERS OF ENDOR

Chapter Nine

When I returned to Oxford for my second term at university, I found the city transformed by winter. Roofs glittered beneath frost, cars squatted like stumpy white hills on either side of the broad streets. The snowfall in the university parks was thick enough to build not just towering ice-men, but also, for one group of excited children, an igloo; they huddled in the cave, stamping their feet and sounding the echoes. The view from my bedroom was likewise upgraded. The window above my desk now revealed an expanse of frozen lawn. On the horizon, skeletal trees bent under the weight of snow. Squint and you were in St Petersburg. Squint again and you were in Warsaw.

I was both eager and apprehensive to see Tovyah. Reading his mother's book over the winter break had compelled me to reconsider what had taken place between us at the end of the previous term. Historical atrocities, like great art, drag us into the light, where there's no more hiding your moral character. Both serve as a reminder of the most basic human truths, how simple it is to be better to people, and how important. I knew now that I had treated Tovyah badly, whatever the provocation. I pictured his hot face, scorched by rejection. Tovyah who had chosen me alone as his friend, for no reason I could fathom.

A week slipped by without us crossing paths. It was possible he hadn't returned to university at all, that he'd been so depressed and frustrated by his first term that he'd dropped out. Extreme, sure, but Tovyah was capable of extremes. But no, he was here all right, skipping up the steps to the library one morning, boyish in his hurry. And I realised, with some surprise, there was no one I wanted to see more.

My fears that he was giving me a wide berth were soon dispelled. The following Monday, he invited me for lunch with his mother and sister, due in college in less than an hour.

'That's very kind of you to ask. What's the—'

'You coming or not coming?'

'Coming. Definitely coming.'

'Good. You won't get a word in edgeways, the woman's a hurricane. Order whatever, and don't try and pay your share. Smile, stick to non-controversial topics, and it shouldn't be too painful. I'll knock when they arrive.'

He was gone before I could ask my question. A moment later the door swung open and he was back. 'One more thing. Probably won't come up, but if it does, you're not Jewish. Otherwise my darling mother might get ideas.'

'I don't understand why you've invited me.'

Tovyah paused in the doorway. 'Does it matter?' He was speaking more to himself than to me. Then, once more, he was gone.

Parental visits were a common feature of university life. (My own had come twice so far and were now threatening a third weekend appearance.) But as far as I knew, today was the first time any of the Rosenthal clan had come to check in on their youngest son. I did not regret my decision to join them – you want an exciting life, don't turn down lunch with the famous lady and her vanishing daughter – but I was now a bundle of anxiety. As if to make things worse, they arrived early. I barely had time to get ready before I heard a woman's voice, loud and authoritative, in the corridor. Tovyah called my name.

And there she was. Dressed to match the severity of that unlikely winter, she wore a great fur hat and long coat, looking exactly like a Russian princess displaced by revolution. In jeans, puffer jacket, and bobble hat, I felt like an overgrown toddler.

Hannah was still waiting for me to take her hand when, quite needlessly, she told me who she was. I gave her my name in return, explaining that I was her son's friend.

'So I gathered,' she said.

Only now did Elsie appear, stepping out from behind her mother. She had a thin face, like Tovyah's, and the same hooded eyes. In her these cool features cohered to form an unusual beauty, both elfin and childlike. Her brother was not so lucky.

'We haven't heard much about you,' Elsie said. She made it sound as though the family had been insufficiently briefed.

'All right, all right, let's get going,' Tovyah said now. 'Let's not take all day.'

Out in the frosty streets, Hannah told us about their morning, traipsing round colleges. At Balliol, she'd managed to secure a conference with two senior lecturers: a chemist and an economist. Both were confused to learn that Elsie had no obvious interest in their disciplines, and the chemist had the ill manners to talk about Elsie as if she wasn't there. 'Hannah, if your daughter is not doing science A Levels, then why did you ask me to meet her?' She replied that Elsie didn't know what she was interested in; the chemist's job was to tell her about chemistry, the economist's to tell her about economics. Like chastised schoolboys, the academics made half-hearted sales pitches. Unimpressed, Hannah asked for the numbers of faculty members in medicine, philosophy, modern languages, and classics.

As if prewarned, none had answered their phones.

She proceeded to deliver assessments of the colleges so far. St Anne's was too modern, Keeble simply hideous. Hugh's was a hovel. This litany of complaints annoyed Tovyah, who kept trying to meet my eye. Jesus was too churchy, of course, as were Corpus Christi and Trinity. Magdalen was full of starers.

'Starers?' I asked.

'People who leer. One of man's most disgusting habits, don't you think? And it *is* always men.'

Elsie said she liked the look of Merton.

'Don't you start,' Tovyah snapped.

'Perhaps Elsie would be happy at Slackersville,' Hannah said. 'Or do you think she might get bored?'

I couldn't figure out the tense atmosphere. 'Slackersville?'

Tovyah sighed. 'Ignore her. She's being a snob.'

I understood then. Tovyah's mother was deriding our college, which consistently came bottom of the Norrington table, and had thus earned a reputation. That anyone outside the university knew what the Norrington table was, let alone cared, was news to me. Where I came from, Oxford was Oxford.

Hannah spoke again. 'You shouldn't be so touchy, darling. I'm sure your little place is just fine. But you're so hush hush, you've not told us a thing about it. Perhaps your friend here can fill us in. Bridget, was it?'

'Close enough,' I said. 'Kate.'

Hannah's cold eyes fixed me. 'Not as timid as she looks.'

Though the roads had been salted down, the pavements were slick with ice, and more than once I came close to falling. The second time I lost my footing, Elsie took my arm to steady me. Later, as we crossed Woodstock Road, a couple of students pointed at us from up ahead. 'No more apartheid!' one of them yelled. The other shouted, 'From the river to the sea!' then both turned into a café. In another minute we'd reached the restaurant. After taking our seats, Hannah asked if incidents like that happened often.

I looked at Tovyah, waiting for him to answer.

'Back in the street there,' Hannah clarified. 'You know what that was about, don't you? Those people were anti-Semites.'

'Hannah—' Tovyah began.

'The river is the River Jordan, and the sea is the Mediterranean. Those boys want the elimination of the only Jewish state in the world. They want a population of millions thrown out or murdered, the details don't matter. This is the programme they call justice for Palestine.'

'You promised you wouldn't soapbox.'

'I wasn't soapboxing,' Hannah said. '*Kate* here asked a question. I was only giving *Kate* an answer.'

Under his breath, Tovyah muttered, 'No she didn't.' Which was true, I'd not said a word. But, having been schooled by Jan and others, I was no longer ignorant of Hannah Rosenthal's problematic worldview, and I did not intend to remain silent.

'Anti-Zionists,' I said.

'Excuse me?' Hannah asked.

My heart was in my throat. 'Those boys in the street. They weren't anti-Semites, they were anti-Zionists.'

'There's a difference?'

'One is a form of bigotry, the other is a legitimate critique of a political regime.'

No one was more shocked to hear my speech than Tovyah. His chin shook in warning.

Hannah asked if I believed in institutional racism.

'Yes,' I said, cautiously.

'See, I know the terms. And you believe there is such a thing as unconscious bias? That due to our benighted history, someone might – without even knowing it – carry around prejudiced instincts, automatic preferences for members of certain groups over others.'

'That's right.'

'OK.' Hannah nodded. 'For three thousand years people have hated us for being Jews. Every country in Europe has kicked us out. You want the list? We were kicked out of Hungary by Louis One. Kicked out of France by Louis Nine, by Philip Four, and by Charleses Five and Six. In the sixteenth century alone we were kicked out of Milan, Naples, Berlin, and Bratislava. Even in the land of the free, we were kicked out of Tennessee and Kentucky by none other than Ulysses S. Grant, President of the United States. This country too – Edward One, in 1290.'

Hannah wore many rings, and each time the Jews were expelled from another territory, she took one off and placed it on the tablecloth, forming a pattern like the Olympics logo.

'Tell me Kate, why is it goys love putting numbers after their names?'

'Only the kings,' I said.

'And the queens. The goyisher kings and queens.' Hannah was now gathering her rings, without looking down.

'You'll notice I didn't mention him with the moustache. Too many people think our problems began in '33 and ended in '45.'

I pointed out that I never said anti-Semitism was finished.

'Not in so many words. But follow your own argument, Kate. You believe in inherited racism. But you also believe that after three thousand years, none of that slime has stuck to the anti-Zionists, whose sole political aim is to kick us out of yet another country. You think those rowdy boys alone, of all humanity, are free of unconscious bias, perfectly rational in their convictions. Or have I misunderstood? I'll tell you something, those thugs don't care about the Palestinians. Why would they? They don't know the first thing about Arab culture, or the Islamic faith. What they care about is hating Jews.'

My face was on fire. Anything I might have said about illegal settlements, human rights abuse, the dream of Greater Israel, flew straight out of my head.

'That's enough now,' Tovyah cautioned his mother.

Elsie told me not to take it personally. 'She does this to everyone.'

Having had my first taste of what it was like to grow up a Rosenthal, I was relieved that the time had come to order food. In accordance with his mother's taste, Tovyah had brought us to a French bistro. (Presumably they'd been forgiven Charleses Five and Six.) On the table, rather than printed menus, were handwritten sheets detailing today's starters, mains, and desserts, with several items crossed out, and no English translations of the food. Now that the waiter had approached, Hannah looked at me and said, 'You're not picky, are you?'

I shook my head.

Hannah ordered a selection of vegetarian dishes: ratatouille, potatoes dauphinoise, a tomato salad, and (after

checking with the waiter) a couple of soups of the day –
roasted parsnip. Then she ordered drinks. 'I'll have a glass of
the pinot noir, and the children will have water.'

So much for ordering what I'd like.

'Hold on,' Tovyah said, before the waiter could leave.
'Kate might want to have some meat.'

I said I was OK with whatever. For my benefit, Elsie
explained that they couldn't eat animals here, it wasn't kosher.

Tovyah still didn't let the waiter leave. 'Please can we add
one steak tartare to the order?'

Before the man could write this down on his pad, Hannah
grabbed his arm.

'Raw cow? You want to eat raw cow?'

'I can come back in a minute,' the waiter said.

'Why not order up some snails while you're at it? Perhaps
they have some wild toad they can fry in its own grease?'

Smiling uncomfortably, the waiter left us.

Tovyah glared at his mother. 'You're embarrassing yourself. That poor guy!'

'He's a waiter in a French restaurant, darling, he didn't
invent French cooking.'

Looking over her shoulder, she caught our server's eye,
and gestured that we were happy with the order. 'It won't
hurt either of you to lay off the unclean meat for one day.
Now tell us about Merton. Might Elsie be happy there?'

'Please can we not do this,' Tovyah said.

'A simple question.'

'She's not going to Merton. You *know* that. She's not
going anywhere.'

Elsie put her hand on my knee. 'I don't have A Levels.
Funny thing. I revised like mad, and I even went to the exams,
but I just couldn't help talking to the other candidates. The

boy sitting in front of me had a crescent moon tattooed on the back of his neck. So I had to ask him about that, didn't I? Only they don't like talkers in exam rooms.'

The waiter arrived with Hannah's drink and our waters. She sipped, sneered, then told the waiter it would do. When he was gone, she said to Elsie, 'You'll pass next time, love.'

'What, fourth time lucky?' Tovyah said.

Hannah upbraided her son. Why did he have to be so unpleasant all the time?

'The word is *realistic*. Elsie knows I don't mean any harm,' he said.

'A pity,' Elsie said. 'A little harmful intent might make things interesting.'

Ignoring her daughter's interjection, Hannah asked Tovyah a series of questions about life in Oxford. Why hadn't he joined any societies? Did he have an internship lined up for the summer? Right, then, was his career going to organise itself?

With Tovyah and Hannah now going at each other full pelt, I had my first proper chance to observe Elsie. Naturally, I was interested in her. I knew that after running away from home, aged fourteen, she had struggled with her mental health and, now in her twenties, still lived at home. Seeing her up close, I was again confronted by her extraordinary beauty, that rare kind goes well beyond sexual attraction, and in fact approaches the grotesque. Beauty so perfect that it seems more than human. I wondered if there might be a terrible power to a face like Elsie's, how it could move people to do astonishing things.

'Do you believe in telepathy?' she said, breaking my train of thought. 'Hearing what's in other people's heads and so on. It sounds daft, I know, but I think there's something to it.'

'Tell me what I'm thinking right now.'

'You're thinking Tovyah's family is completely unbearable. You've always hated parsnip soup, and you wish you'd never said yes to lunch.'

'Incredible!' I laughed. 'Absolutely, word for word!'

Elsie smiled. 'I told you. And I didn't have to mention the man dressed head to foot in white that looms at the back of your mind.'

At her words, I felt a sudden pulsing in my chest. While the old man I'd seen sitting with Tovyah at the Ben-Scholem Society was by no means a constant presence in my thoughts, he did trouble me from time to time – like a movement on my peripheral vision. How could Elsie know about that? Tovyah must have mentioned something. I wanted to ask her what she'd meant but, just then, our waiter arrived, carrying three plates to an arm, which he dextrously unloaded, muttering the names of dishes. The plates steamed.

'Well kids, eat up,' Hannah said.

Elsie whispered something to her brother.

Living cautiously on my student loan, I never ate in restaurants, and I did not take long to devour my meal. Especially as I now had no door into the conversation that was developing around me, which concerned old squabbles, and distant family friends. Looking up, I realised with alarm that I was finished before anyone else had made a real start. Elsie hadn't eaten a thing.

In the brief lull that descended, she asked why we were not having fizz. Hannah exchanged a look with her son, then said, 'Children shouldn't drink in the afternoon, dear. When you're my age, a glass of red wine doesn't do you much damage.'

'But we're supposed to be celebrating,' Elsie said.

Tovyah wanted to know what the occasion was.

His sister smiled. 'We've got a release date. End of May – Mummy's latest.'

He looked at his mother. 'She can't be serious.'

Hannah shrugged.

'Not satisfied with the last one?' Tovyah said. 'Didn't feel you'd done enough damage as it was?'

'Watch your mouth.'

Resting his elbows on the tablecloth, Tovyah gripped his hands together. 'Well go on then, what's it about?'

'That's confidential. Just a little while longer.'

She forked a mouthful of salad, brought it to her lips.

'Please tell me you haven't exhumed Zeide all over again.'

'Don't be absurd.'

'Fresh fields, then. What corner of our lives have you ransacked now?'

They were no longer having what might be considered a private discussion. In one corner, two of the waiters huddled, debating if it was the moment to step in.

'Darling, you need to take it down a notch.'

'I don't need to do shit. You can't keep pretending what you do doesn't affect the rest of us.'

Hannah drew herself up. 'I won't let you bully me.'

'Bully *you*!'

She turned to me then. 'He used to be such a sweet kid.'

The two waiters had just started walking towards us, and Hannah's raised hand stopped them on the spot. From behind her, a young man in a gingham shirt and a bowtie approached. His red hair was combed over in a side-parting, and his tortoise-shell glasses accentuated his pale complexion. Was this the manager's son, sent in to calm everyone down? He looked like a sixteen-year-old in borrowed clothes, trying to buy booze.

'Mrs Rosenthal?' he said. 'I hate to disturb you when you're with your family, but could you take a moment to sign this?'

He held out a folded napkin. 'My mother and I are huge fans. The biggest.'

'Of course, my darling.' Hannah took the napkin and uncapped a pen. The boy ran his eyes over Elsie as he waited.

'Keep up the good fight!' he said, raising a clenched fist.

While his mother was preoccupied with signing, Tovyah pushed himself away from the table and flung his way out of the door. Before I knew what I was doing, Hannah had dismissed the red-headed boy, and said to me, 'It's OK. You can go after him now. We did so enjoy meeting you, Kate.'

I found Tovyah outside the restaurant, blowing into his hands. Without exchanging a word, we began walking in step. Soon, Tovyah was moving quickly, darting left and right to avoid other pedestrians, and chancing gaps in the traffic to cross the road.

'Slow down!' I said. 'You'll make me slip.'

He slowed. At the university park, we veered right and continued until we reached a building I'd walked past dozens of times without entering. Even by Oxford's standards, it was ornate, with star-shaped windows and pointed arches, and I had often wondered what goes on in this strange place. I followed Tovyah into an enormous hall with a vast sloped ceiling. We wandered between rows of glass cages, each one containing something arcane: dented spearheads, old coins, rusted keys, pottery, taxidermised animals, teeth, bones. This was the Pitt Rivers Museum, then, home of an expansive archaeological and anthropological collection.

Tovyah and I had not spoken since we'd come in. I approached as he stood contemplating an elephant's skull. 'You were right. She's a hurricane.'

'Don't tell me you're a fan,' he said. But he didn't sound angry. In fact, there was humour in his voice.

'Is she always so . . . critical?'

'Believe it or not, I think she was trying to be conciliatory. In her eyes, just coming to see me was magnanimous.'

It seemed that our fight at the end of last term was forgiven. Perhaps that I had opposed his mother, even for a moment, endeared me to him. He spoke now as though to an old friend. I wanted to know why things were so tense between him and Hannah.

'It's not easy having a writer for a mother, you know,' he said. 'All the mess, all the shit of life at home, just sitting on the shelf in Waterstones.'

This was my chance to tell him that I knew the terrible backdrop to his childhood, that I'd read the stories that echoed between those walls. But purchasing and reading his mother's book, which I'd done without a second thought, now seemed intrusive.

'Was it bad then? When her book came out?'

'Oh, Hannah *loved* it. All that attention! You saw how she preened herself just now when that loser wanted her autograph. But for me and my siblings, it was a catastrophe.'

'I thought the book did well,' I said. 'Wasn't having a successful mum a good thing?'

'You went to school, you remember. No such thing as good publicity. In Gideon's class, fuckwits made cracks about showers and ovens. They laughed at how our great-grandmother had probably been gang raped.'

'You're not serious.'

129

'A kid he knew went to Halloween in jack boots and a swastika armband.'

This would have been a few years before Prince Harry appeared on all the front pages, dressed in a similar outfit. What was it with young men and their Nazi fantasies? Purely a desire to shock? Or was there something darker there, an appetite for extreme power, the bestial drive to impose and subjugate. Dreams of banners, dark coats, and a sea of rigid, unwavering hands.

Tovyah had come to a halt in front of a display, and I took up a place next to him. His eyes darted to the information plaque. And as we stood there, surrounded by strange artefacts and remnants of the long dead, something clicked into place.

'There was no one else,' I said. 'Your mother wanted to meet some of your uni friends, and there wasn't anyone else you could ask.'

Tovyah stiffened, and I regretted my words. Why did I have to embarrass him afresh? Resisting the urge to apologise, I told him I was glad to have come.

'The worst bit is,' he said, not looking up from the exhibit, 'I reckon the new one's going to be about me. A second memoir. The great tragedy of having an apostate son.'

Only now did I look into the display case before us: four shrunken heads. On each one, the features of a human face were clearly recognisable, though boiled down to the size of a man's fist, and each head sported a thick mane, like a wooden horse. The eyelids were all fused together, and the lips sewn shut, pierced through with metal shafts.

Chapter Ten

If Hannah Rosenthal *had* written a book about her youngest son, it would no doubt have told the story of his adolescence and their eventual falling out.

Tovyah, of course, was not always the verbal pugilist who arrived at university, cursed and shouted, and made no friends. Growing up, he'd enjoyed a respectful, if not warm, relationship with his parents. As a child, he was known for his meekness, and even as a teenager he was courteous. Always did his homework, always behaved. But over the course of a lifetime's silent acquiescence, something had been gathering within him. Unknown to his family, unknown even to himself, perhaps, he'd been filling with rage, with frothing, teeming, hissing, spitting, ready-to-bubble-over rage.

Principal among Tovyah's frustrations as he entered his final year of school, the year he would sit A Levels in English literature, history, and Latin before leaving secondary education forever, were the two big Gs: Girls and God. The problem being that neither of them existed.

If he'd been raised Catholic, or amongst the Hassidim, the twin absences might have been connected, but in Tovyah's case, it was not his parents' religion that botched his romantic life. It was something else, some defect of character or circumstances. Or both. The poverty of his circumstances was obvious. He was at an all boys' school, surrounded by enemies. Apart from his sister, life was essentially girl-less. As for his character, he was shy, introverted, and without hobbies apart from reading and listening to hopelessly unfashionable music. (Think the B-Minor Mass. Think *Die Winterreise*.) And while he had heard that girls read books too, it obviously wasn't by reading that you met them. He'd been to the libraries. He knew.

There was, in fact, a third problem, more serious than the other two. At that point, Elsie was languishing as an in-patient at St Anthony's, an institution that shared its name with the patron saint of lost things. It was her second stay that year. But he didn't dwell on this problem. He couldn't. Like God's face – look at it directly, and you will not be suffered to live.

Picture Tovyah in his form room, then, a stuffy space at the top of the history block, with old colonial maps and wartime propaganda on the walls. Acne-ridden and skinny, with a badly cut fringe. Most days he got in early and opened a book, passing time until the scheduled day began. To those kids who deigned to acknowledge him, he'd started lying about his virginity. There was that time on the French exchange, the girl from the village who nobody back home could conceivably have met. Gilberte. He told the story often. How she'd led him to her bedroom while her father was cooking, and the smell of onions rose through the house. How she had pulled her shirt over her head without unbuttoning it, revealing her flat chest, almost like a boy's, but with hard red nipples. 'Come,' was all she had said, darkening the vowel to make it rhyme with *l'homme* or the *Somme*. It was one of

132

the few English words she knew. If only he'd stayed another week, he might have taught her a few more . . .

In reality, there was a girl fitting this description, though he hadn't spoken to her. She'd been carrying plastic bags laden with groceries when he saw her from his window, and for one heart-denting moment, their eyes met.

Of course, no one fully believed him about Gilberte, whose name was inspired by Marcel's first crush in the opening volume of *À la recherche du temps perdu*. But, having the credibility of their own bogus stories to protect, none of the other boys expressed their scepticism: an atmosphere of open suspicion suited nobody. Meanwhile, sex – the stuff itself – was life's central mystery. He'd had the mechanics of the process explained, of course, first with the aid of a banana and a condom by Mr Franklin in PSHE, and then in more baroque terms on the bus to games. He'd even heard it, *live sex*, taking place on the far side of a shut door. (Late one afternoon when Gideon brought home one of his 'mates', Tovyah was enlisted to keep watch for their parents' return.) And yet the first-hand experience remained unknowable. The primmest accounts seemed the most accurate: those scenes from black and white movies where two lovers embrace and are then swamped by darkness, an exact depiction of the blissful, shadowy world to which he had never been admitted.

He began to think there was something wrong with him.

'Tovyah,' Gideon assured him, 'there is.'

And then there was the problem of God. God who was everywhere, all places at all times, and yet was also nowhere ever. The constant intrusion of nothingness. Tovyah had to thank Him for every scrap of food that passed his lips but couldn't even say His name! *Baruch ata Adonai* . . . Adonai! My lord! This was the twenty-first century, wasn't it, they lived in liberal, democratic, modern Great Britain. In affluent North London! The indignities of feudalism, of expulsion, of shtetl life, of the Pale of Settlement, were centuries behind them (centuries!) and here they were, behaving like the lowliest, mudlicking serfs, thanking their invisible *Lord* for the food they ate! Who, brought up in this batshit manner, made to wrap tefillin round his wrists and forehead each morning while he repeated words he didn't believe in a language he barely spoke, who, subjected to all this and bearing a name that meant, wait for it, *God is good*, who wouldn't be bursting with perennial rage? What craven, empty-headed, worm of a human being wouldn't have been pushed to the fringes of his sanity by now?

There was only one way to cope. By waiting.

Soon he would finish school, he would be released from that juvenile prison, and he would at last follow his own path. Once he was at university, he would meet like-minded people, *curious* people, and he wouldn't be a freak for knowing and reading too much. Girls would no longer be kept on the far side of a puritanical curtain, and God would no longer be rammed down his throat daily. Only one more year stood between him and this long-awaited departure. He would go to Oxford. Why not? He'd been top of every class he'd been in since he was six years old.

One afternoon, near the start of the school term, Tovyah was asked to stay behind at the end of double English. His teacher, Ms Zhang, was new that year. Young, quick-witted, and more than capable of outstaring the adolescent boys who challenged her authority, she had already established herself as a popular teacher. But free-thinking Tovyah wasn't a fan. For one thing, she got on too well with all the kids he hated.

'When you were packing your bag just now, did I see a copy of *The Trial*?' she asked.

Not since Tovyah was a child had a teacher expressed interest in his reading habits outside school. 'That's right, Miss,' he said.

'You like Kafka then?'

'Yes.'

'What do you like about him?'

How to explain the feelings provoked by those books. Like walking down an unfamiliar road, the streetlights dim overhead. Each house you pass contains other people's lives, behind each door something quietly going on, just out of reach. And these other people's thoughts and habits are like yours, maybe, but also somehow different, not quite comprehensible. You can almost hear the drone of life as you walk, sheer life unfurling on the far side of each curtained window. Smoke rises from a distant chimney and a pair of headlights swing into view at the top of the street. And it seems so simple, suddenly, so easy to knock on someone's door, to say here I am. Let me in.

'I don't know why I like him, Miss. I just do.'

The answer disappointed her. 'We've had three lessons now, and you've not opened your mouth.'

'I guess not,' he said. 'Sorry.'

'And yet the essay you wrote this week was the best in the class. You did write it yourself?'

'Yes, Miss.'

'And now here you are reading Kafka. Can you imagine how frustrating this is for me?'

'Sorry, Miss,' he said again.

'Don't apologise. And stop calling me "Miss" like that. Why don't you speak up in lessons?'

She wasn't so much older than he was, she must remember what it was like to be in a classroom, subject to those subconscious forces that dictate who speaks when, who makes the jokes, who shuts up. Maybe it's different if you're a girl. Or just not a puny boy at an all boys' school. Or just anyone other than Tovyah fucking Rosenthal.

'I guess I don't really have much to say.'

'Rubbish. I can see from every paragraph you write, you have plenty to say. What are you planning to study at university?'

'Law.'

'Please tell me that's not why you're reading *The Trial*? That's a joke, you can laugh. Look, my husband's a solicitor, and he'll say you're better off doing something else first then taking the conversion course. It's more rounded. Have you considered English? You have the aptitude.'

Tovyah saw himself on the mezzanine of some library, light sloping through high windows. In a lecture hall, at the feet of an aging poet. In someone's bedroom, among friends in the small hours, the only hours that had ever really counted.

'No,' he said. 'I hadn't considered it.'

'Why not?'

Tovyah hesitated. Despite the academic success that had been his from a young age, he did not regard teachers as allies. He was wary of them, in fact, considered their interests counter to his own. Was this woman someone he could trust?

'My parents want me to do law,' he said at last.

Ms Zhang considered.

'Tovyah is a Jewish name, isn't it? Are your parents religious?'

'Yes,' he said, then risked his first coy smile. 'Like Kafka's.'

The teacher cocked her head. 'I was supposed to be a doctor,' she said. 'But I fucked that one in the bud, didn't I?

136

Oops!' Before Tovyah left, she had loaded his bag with editions of Shelley's *Selected Poems and Prose*, David Hume's *Natural History of Religion*, and Bruno Schulz's *Street of Crocodiles*.

*

After blazing through Hume in a day and half, Tovyah brought the other two books with him that weekend, as he accompanied his mother on the drive out of London to visit his sister. They arrived just before midday, parked, enquired at reception, and then waited outside.

With its florid arches, its turrets, and the pointed windows spaced along the southern wall, the white building looked just like a castle, sprawling against the late afternoon sky. *The Castle*, another of Kafka's stark titles. *Das Schloss*. An immaculate garden opened before them, trailing off into a carpark and a café. The lawn had been mown in stripes, which reminded Tovyah of football pitches. Of all sports, he hated football most: those foul rainy afternoons, not to mention the chants, the face paint, the crazed tribalism. They were sitting at a bench under a parasol, now, flicking – to have something to do – through a brochure. The people in the photos didn't look like addicts or the mentally ill; they were so well-groomed, so cheerful. Obviously, they were models, but you'd have thought they'd try a bit harder.

'Don't expect too much,' Hannah said. 'It's wonderful that we're seeing her, but she might not be very chatty.'

He thought about the first time he'd been brought to visit his sister. Not this place, but somewhere similar, years ago, when her troubles first became unmanageable. Elsie had refused to speak then, communicated only with wild shrieks. He knew she was putting it on, but all the same he was so frightened, so *disgusted*, that he deliberately closed a door on his finger and burst the nail. Howling with pain, he was taken straight home.

The second son was supposed to protect the others.

'I know how it is,' Tovyah said.

'I'm only telling you. The lady did say, even compared with last time, it might be a shock.'

In another minute Elsie came out, accompanied by a woman with a puffy face. Elsie's head was covered by a light, colourless down; she'd shaved her own scalp with clippers a few weeks earlier. When Hannah asked if she wanted to sit or go for a walk, Elsie said either way was fine, and the woman left them.

They walked. A loose wind brought up goosebumps on Tovyah's arms. Hannah identified chrysanthemums and cosmos to her indifferent children. A young nurse coming the other way greeted Elsie, who seemed not to notice, and kept her gaze lowered. 'This one's pretty,' Tovyah said, mustering enthusiasm. Worried someone would think he was talking about the nurse, he bent down to touch a globe of petals, deep red, and bordered with bright orange. 'What's it called?'

His mother squatted beside him but didn't know the answer.

'Are you done yet?' Elsie said.

As she walked, she kept her arms folded, not letting them swing at her sides. Her steps might have been measured.

You had to wonder what they were doing here. Elsie clearly had no interest in seeing them, answered their questions in monosyllables. Never smiled. His mother would tell him to remain hopeful, parroting that cretin Grossman. 'We must not lose faith. We must not end up with stomachs for which daily bread means death.' But whatever stores of hope

Tovyah once had were fast diminishing. Perhaps Eric had spoken the truth when he lost his temper the other night. 'This is her life now, you realise. No A Levels, no university, no jobs, no husband, no children of her own. Just *this*. Pills, doctors, hospitals.' Tovyah only had to look at her to understand his father's anger. She was so horribly thin; her arms looked like you could snap them in two. And no spark kindled behind her eye. Where had she gone? Where was his sister?

After doubling back on themselves, they arrived at the bench they started from. Hannah said she wanted to have a quick word with the doctors. Now Tovyah and Elsie were alone, perhaps she would come out of herself a little.

'It's good to see you,' Tovyah said. He thought about placing a hand on his sister's shoulder, but no. You couldn't live your life by doing things you'd seen other people do.

Then, as if the hypnotist had clicked his fingers, Elsie returned with a jolt to the present. 'Tuvs, we haven't got long, there's something I need to ask you. Something important.'

'What is it?'

'Promise you won't tell Mummy? Or Dad? Really promise now.'

He promised.

'I need a drink. I know what you're thinking, but it's not like that, I just need a little hipflask of something, just to sip on when it gets too much. No one will know, I can be discreet. You've no idea what it's like. The others, the ones I'm with, they're all nutjobs – I mean not like me, a little bit barmy now and then – they're genuine lunatics, the sort of people who wander the streets screaming. Some of them are quite scary, the things they cry out, the noises they make, you'd think they might get violent. Blindfolded, you wouldn't think it's *people* making those sounds. Sometimes, in the night, you think anything could happen. I'm not explaining it well. I just need a little booster, just to help me through, no one needs to know. Think of it like a safety blanket. Can you do that for me? Tuvs?'

She spoke rapidly and gripped his wrist so hard that when she let go her nails left an impression. Tovyah said he wasn't sure. In another moment, Hannah was back. When they said their goodbyes, he couldn't meet his sister's face.

On the walk to the carpark, Hannah asked Tovyah what he'd talked about with Elsie.

'Just stuff,' he said.

'Think for a moment. Did she say anything that might give us an idea how she's doing?'

Lately, Hannah had taken meticulous notes about Elsie. She carried her Moleskine everywhere and would think nothing of asking strangers on the Tube to lend her a pen. She wrote down the names of drugs and nurses, she sketched the view from the hospital window, she recorded discussions with medical staff. Before she went to bed, she racked her brains for anything that needed setting down before she could abandon herself to sleep. If she could only gather enough information, enough raw data, then she'd be able to cure her daughter. And so, every word, every detail was sacred.

Tovyah said he couldn't think of anything in particular that Elsie had said. It was only small talk.

Hannah didn't press him. 'I do hate leaving her. It must be awful to be surrounded by those people. I know it's not their fault, but still. Dr Howard told me there's been some difficulty with one of the other patients. Apparently, the poor woman keeps telling people she's seen Elsie levitate.'

140

Chapter Eleven

After school and on weekends, Tovyah set to work on his two UCAS applications and his two personal statements. There was the official one, overseen by his father, in which he argued that the rule of law was the first cornerstone of any civilisation. In preparation, Eric had dragged him to Snaresbrook Crown Court, where he'd listened to interminable arguments, quite irrelevant – as far as he could tell – as to whether the defendant was guilty. What struck him was how friendly Eric was with his opponent, and how the two men (prosecution and defence) seemed to agree privately on the facts and even sympathise with each other's predicament.

Then there was Tovyah's second personal statement, the unofficial one, written under the supervision of Ms Zhang, on whom he'd developed an unbearable crush. Alone in her office, with her lithe body so close, it was impossible to think straight. Yet somehow, he'd cobbled together an application, in which he'd discussed the poetics of Shelley's 'universe of things', a world undarkened by any God. Unknown to his parents, it was this second personal statement, the unofficial one, that he submitted to universities.

Meanwhile, he had not been back to visit Elsie at St Anthony's. He'd been planning to, along with Hannah, but one of the nurses had discovered a bottle of cheap gin between Elsie's mattress and the wooden slats. After a heated confrontation, Hannah was called in, and it was agreed Elsie would return to her parents' house for a bit. And then she ran away again. This time, it was a week before she returned.

A month went by, and then a week. Then some days. Finally, one November afternoon, Tovyah came home from school to find an envelope addressed in his name, bearing an Oxford postmark and with a collegiate crest stamped in the corner. The crisp white rectangle lay flat against the wooden floorboards, perfectly framed. Part of him just wanted to let it sit there. But he could not put off knowing long, and within a few seconds he'd bent down, scooped it, and ripped open the envelope. And there it was: he had an interview. An Oxford interview! Here in his hands was the exit visa to another life. All those years not fitting in at school, keeping his head down, studying, they'd not been wasted after all.

It was only fair to tell his parents together – so although Hannah was back at teatime, he held off until his father returned from work, then fetched his mother from the study.

'Well what is it?' Hannah said, as the three of them sat around the kitchen table. 'You look like the dog that broke into the butchers.'

Without speaking, he produced the letter.

His mother was ecstatic. 'This is wonderful! I woke up with a smile on my face this morning, I knew something terrific would happen.'

But Eric, peering at the printed sheet through half-moon spectacles, failed to get caught up in the excitement. 'There's a mistake.'

'What are you talking about?' Hannah said.

'It says here you're interviewing for English Language and Literature. They must be confused, no? Did they mix you up with another student?'

Of course, Tovyah had expected some awkwardness. But he never thought it would totally overshadow his news. Wasn't this what they'd always wanted? Look at Gideon, two years deep into his military service, an occupation his father described as a game of Russian roulette in the desert. Or Elsie, who never finished school. When he'd opened the letter, he believed he would make them proud.

Tovyah said there was no mistake. 'At the last minute I changed my mind. That's not a problem, is it?'

Eric grunted. 'And you didn't mention anything?'

'English, law, who cares? Our boy's going to Oxford University.'

'It's only an interview,' Tovyah said. 'I haven't got in yet.'

'You'll get in all right,' Hannah said.

Eric turned over the letter, as if looking for a watermark. 'I took you to Snaresbrook, showed you behind the scenes. What boy gets such a chance? I can't believe you lied to us.'

'I didn't lie. I forgot to tell you,' Tovyah said.

His father was a solid man then, with an intelligent brow. Round and forceful. His beard was still dark, and his eyes sat close together in a way that hinted at strength of purpose rather than a weak mind. Now he brought his hands together across his belly and sighed. Since the death of Tovyah's grandfather, Eric had seemed to him father, grandfather, and great-grandfather rolled into one, a man who wielded the spectral authority of previous generations. Gideon and Elsie, being older, had it easy. But the years had hardened Eric, who suffered more than anyone from his daughter's breakdown. Now he was no longer someone to indulge his children against his better judgment. And so, with Tovyah, he did not laugh things off or let them go. When, aged fifteen, Tovyah had *unknowingly* eaten pork sausages at another boy's house, Eric had shown him a video of a pig in a slaughterhouse, failing to die.

'Slipped your mind, did it?' Eric said.

'I'm telling you now.'

'Don't get confused. Either you deliberately misled us or you forgot to mention it. Which one?'

Tovyah didn't answer. His silence was understood by both parents as an admission of guilt. Not a faulty memory, then, but a deliberate misleading.

'So you want to study English literature,' Eric said. 'Novels, poetry, all those fantasies. Jane Austen, Thomas Hardy, William Wordsworth . . .' He pronounced them like the names of foreign cities. 'I hope you're prepared to become a schoolteacher.'

'Dad, I—'

'Let me finish. I understand turning away from maths, too abstract, too theoretical, although you've always been good with numbers.'

'What's maths got to do with anything? I gave up maths after GCSE. I haven't—'

'But *English literature*. Why not study the literature of your own people? I would have been thrilled to send you to yeshiva. You could have trained as a rabbi, done something useful with your life. You are a gifted boy, Tovyah, and that comes with a responsibility.'

'Dad, I don't want to become a rabbi. I never—'

'Tovyah, please. You can have your say in a minute. Let's be grown up. When did we force your hand? We always let you follow your own desires. Believe me, I know what it's like to have a father who rules by decree, who instructs with his fists. Maybe we were too lenient. Now you want to go and study Gentile writers? At Oxford University! When did my son become an English snob?'

Until that moment, Eric had always spoken about Oxford with hushed reverence.

'You don't know what you're talking about,' Tovyah said. All his life, he'd tried to be polite to his parents. But after so many years of strain, having seen his brother's self-willed exodus and the destruction of his sister's promise, something finally snapped. 'The Oxford English department is not some Christian boys' club. Ever heard of Isaac Rosenberg? Harold Pinter? Well, guess what, they're on the syllabus. You can do a whole paper on Philip Roth if you like. Nothing but Jews for hundreds of pages. And you know who I wrote about in my personal statement? Franz Kafka.'

Eric might not have been the reader Hannah was, but he was no philistine, and he registered each name in turn. Bringing up Roth was a dangerous move. On the one hand, yes, he was a famous Jew, both tremendously successful and one of the chosen. On the other, he was a shameless non-believer who had exposed his people to ridicule. Officially speaking, Tovyah had never read a Philip Roth novel.

Now the corners of Eric's mouth curled downwards, and his eyes widened. In response to his son's provocative tone, he assumed the same look he had playing chess when he spotted an opportunity several moves ahead. The face made Tovyah squirm. In the last ten years, he'd defeated his father exactly twice, and one of those times he'd been given a handicap. From now on, Eric had said after turning over his own king, we meet as equals.

'It is a misfortune unique to the Jewish father that his son consoles him by citing Franz Kafka as a role model.'

'Very funny. Kafka was a genius. If you'd read him, you'd know.'

'Is that so?'

The look hadn't slipped from Eric's face. He rose heavily from his seat and disappeared from the room. When Tovyah asked his mother where he'd gone, she shrugged. Her eyes drifted to the bureau in the corner, where she stored her notebooks and other writing materials. She'd never told anyone of her silent vow to quit writing the day Elsie was brought home. And it was just as well: after the confetti-strewn success of her first book, which saw her lifted from dull obscurity to the gleaming table of minor fame, she never stood a chance of keeping it.

'You're not serious,' Tovyah said.

'Excuse me?'

'I saw you looking. You're not thinking about writing this down.'

'What have I done now? My eyes move around in my head and I've committed some crime.'

Tovyah gaped.

'I keep notes,' Hannah said. 'It's my job.'

'Not *of this*. I'm at home. You don't have to take notes about *everything*.'

Overhead, there was the sound of plodding steps, then a cupboard popping open and clamping shut. Calling out from halfway down the stairs, Eric picked up the conversation from where it had left off.

'Kafka is a genius, he says. How often have I heard my son speak of the great Franz Kafka, Prague's answer to William Shakespeare. A couple of weeks ago, I asked Rabbi Cohen what Franz Kafka is all about.' By now Eric had re-entered. 'And Rabbi Cohen, he says to me—'

'Not a rabbi,' Tovyah interrupted.

'What's that?'

'Bryn Cohen does hedge funds!'

'Cohen is the name of the priest caste. From the tribe of the Levites. Moses, Aaron. You know this, Tovyah. Don't mimic ignorance.'

'Priest caste? Really? Caste? This isn't the 1700s.'

Eric chuckled. 'Have it your way. I asked hedge-fund manager Cohen about your idol. I wanted to know where I should begin reading if I was to catch up. And you know what he told me?'

'What?'

'He said Franz Kafka was an anti-Semite.'

'Ridiculous. Literally absurd. Kafka was a Jew.'

Now Eric turned to his wife and shrugged. Look how excitable your boy is. You try to have an adult conversation and he gets pink in the face and shouts at you. It was then that Tovyah saw what Eric was holding in his hand: Kafka's *Letters to Milena*, laminated and stamped by Islington Public Library.

'You don't believe a Jew can hate his own people? Read Otto Weininger. Read Karl Marx, who said the only God we worship is money. You think Kafka wrote only nonsense about men turning into bugs? Then you haven't read this.' He held up the book theatrically. For Eric, all the world was a courtroom, and he was forever appealing to the judgement of an invisible jury. Real life jurors, the ones who presided

147

over the fates of his clients, were at best fools and at worst wilfully obstructive. But the jurors of the soul, God's jurors, were infallible. Tovyah shook his head.

'A collection of letters. Written, I might add, to a married woman. A shiksa. Leaving aside the question of adultery, let us read Franz Kafka's idea of a good love letter. And I quote.' A cough preceded the reading. Tovyah could see that the text beside his father's thumb was underlined in black ink. '. . . Sometimes I'd like to cram them all as Jews (including myself) into the drawer of the laundry chest, then wait, then open the drawer a little to see whether all have already suffocated, if not, to close the drawer again and go on like this to the end.' Eric raised his eyes from the page and looked across the table at his son. 'Charming, no?'

'Let me see that,' Tovyah said, snatching at the book. He read the words back to himself. If ever Tovyah had needed proof of Kafka's powers, this was it. The image of an enormous chest, stuffed with the sorts of Jews he had seen only in photos – ghetto Jews, Jews who stared death in the face – was before him, real as his hands. As though Kafka could bypass words altogether and deliver nightmares directly into his readers' minds. What novelist could do *that*?

Tovyah placed the book face down on the table. On the back cover was a picture of his hero with the slicked-back hair, that haunted face inscrutable as ever.

'This was written in the early twenties. I'll say one thing, he was ahead of his time. Back then, Hitler was still a street hoodlum.'

'You can't compare Kafka to Hitler!'

'Why not? His ideas are similar, no?'

'Because Hitler actually did it. I can't believe I have to spell that out.'

'I judge a politician by his actions, by his speeches, by his policies. A writer, I judge by his fantasies. Is that not reasonable?'

'No!'

Tovyah felt the sweat gather on his forehead. So far, not once had Eric raised his voice. As if to make the point, he now spoke more softly than ever.

'What do you think Zeide would have made of you reading Franz Kafka?'

'You can't bring him into everything. It isn't fair.'

'Not fair, eh? I read over drafts and drafts of that application, correcting points of law, and all the while I believed we were on the same side. Turns out I was a schmuck! Is that fair? And now this. Shouting at me in my own house, shouting at your mother. What do you think it does to us to see you idolise a man like Franz Kafka?'

Tovyah looked to his mother, hoping for a spark of sympathy. Her expression, like Eric's, was dark and creased. Studying his mother's face, he saw Elsie. Lately, they were so alike. The eyebrows, the thin lips. The thought of his sister, deposited once more in some miserable institution, stoked his fury. They'd all grown up in this house together. She must have felt what he'd felt.

'I'll tell you something Bryn Cohen didn't mention,' Tovyah said. 'Kafka also wrote a story called "The Judgement". Did you read that one? It's about a father who commands his son to kill himself. And guess what the son does?'

Eric spread out in his chair. 'I expect that the son, being a good Jewish boy, did just as his father told him.' Then he fell about laughing. He was a man who found nobody's jokes as funny as his own.

*

On the morning of his interview, Tovyah woke before dawn. Propelled by nervous energy, he parted the curtains to reveal only darkness, and as he dressed, the sky took on soft grey light. The trains ran without delays and the printed directions were easier to follow than he'd allowed for. So, having been instructed to arrive for ten, he got to the college just after nine. There was his name, misspelt, on a sheet tacked to the central notice board. Apparently, he would have two interviews that day and might be asked to stay overnight for a third. In the room that served as a holding pen for candidates, he met a Scottish girl, who told him all about the architecture of the college, then launched into a farcical account of losing her breakfast on the train down. 'Oh wait, you're supposed to say up, aren't you? One of those silly traditions. Wherever you're coming from, you always come *up* to Oxford.' She made a point of dismissing her chances of getting in, though Tovyah had a feeling she'd do just fine. She was so easy to talk to, he almost didn't notice how pretty she was.

Soon, he was led to an oak-panelled room, where he was greeted by a pair of academics, a man and a woman. The man was middle-aged, well over fifty, and wore a tweed jacket. The woman, strangely small against her large seat, must have been edging thirty. They sat in armchairs, angled towards a leather couch that was the room's focal point. The walls were covered with books, and there was a strong smell of potpourri.

He only had to get through the interviews, then wait out the next nine months, and he was free. He took his seat and the academics leaned forwards, chins on fists. The woman tried several times to retrieve something lost in her tangled hair, while the man uncrossed and recrossed his legs.

Tovyah's heart fluttered. Not since his bar mitzvah, when he'd chanted the Haftorah before a packed congregation, when his mouth had seemed to fill up with foam, had he felt so anxious.

'I understand you read Shelley,' the woman said.

Tovyah was soon laying out why he admired the poet. His intellectual ambition, his refusal to partake of the old certainties, the skill with which he could manipulate the strictures of formal verse to incorporate complex propositions about the nature of reality. The woman responded to his ideas with nodding encouragement. Although she pushed him to refine and clarify some of his answers, she did not belittle him. The distress of a few minutes earlier was all gone. The feeling Tovyah had, discussing this long-dead poet with a genuine scholar who took seriously what he had to say, was not elation or triumph. It was simpler than that. For the first time in ages, he felt like he belonged.

The other academic, the man, had not yet spoken. When a silence fell, he glanced at a sheet of paper resting on the arm of his chair. Even upside-down, the shape of the paragraphs was uncomfortably familiar. Tovyah's personal statement. Please don't read it aloud, he thought.

'You say here that "the modernist enterprise was poisoned by the toxic political ideas that were current at the time." I wanted to ask – what particular toxins did you have in mind?'

Tovyah recalled that one of his interviewers specialised in literature from the turn of the century. He could soon be out of his depth.

'I suppose I meant fascism. Primarily.'

'You suppose. So you're saying that the ideology of Mussolini's thuggish party influenced writers diverse as Joseph Conrad, living in Pimlico, and William Faulkner in Alabama?

Seems a bit odd. What did they care what was going on in Italy?'

Conscious he'd been slouching, Tovyah lurched up. 'More that the ideas that fascists in Italy, in Italy *and* Germany I mean, the ideas they later adopted were already prominent in artistic circles in, erm, Europe generally. And in America.'

The man pushed his glasses back onto the bridge of his nose to read the sheet further. '"In, erm, Europe generally." Can you give me an example?'

The silence coarsened. Tovyah had lost the thread of what was being asked.

'An example of a European country?'

'Ha-ha. No. An example of the ideas that were prominent in artistic circles in Europe. That's what you said isn't it?'

'Anti-Semitism, for one.'

The word, so heavy, slipped out before he realised what he was saying. The regret was instantaneous. Why hadn't he brought up Nietzsche or Darwin? How boring to play the part of the marginalised Jew, offended by men who lived a hundred years ago. Complaining now, as if he wanted special treatment.

His stomach shrank. And with the man's next question, it shrank further.

'You're Hannah Rosenthal's son, aren't you?' he asked. 'I read her book. About your grandfather, isn't it? Quite good, I thought. When it wasn't being mawkish.'

Concentrating on the matter at hand was getting rapidly harder. How was his mother relevant? He wondered if it was against the rules, bringing her up like that, but said nothing. What rules? Eric's voice echoed in his head. *When the person who makes the decision arbitrates the justness of that decision, there is no law. Only the whims of personality. See also Hitler and Stalin. See also papal infallibility.* Now the man exchanged a glance with his colleague, and it was she who took up the line of questions.

'So you're saying anti-Semitism was a constituent part of modernism? I'm not saying you're wrong, just trying to understand your position.'

Tovyah was hot now and wanted to remove his jumper. He needed to focus.

'Not consciously, no, but it keeps coming up. I mean, Pound, Eliot, Lawrence, they all shared the same casual Jew-hatred. Yeats was an admirer of the far right—'

'Hang on, you're being a bit selective there,' the man pounced again. 'It's true, Eliot wrote about "the rat underneath the piles, the Jew underneath the lot," but he was never a fascist. Made great fun of Mosley's Blackshirts in his play *The Rock*. And what about the other writers who don't fit this picture? Auden was a communist, an outspoken opponent of the Nazis. Thomas Mann fled the country to get away from Hitler. Virginia Woolf was married to a Jew. Hence the lupine name, eh? And James Joyce's key novel, the central text of modernism in English, has a *semitic* protagonist.'

Ever since the man had mentioned Hannah, Tovyah found his mind wandering. If only he wasn't such a coward. If only he had the guts to tell his parents that he found their way of life intolerable and then live with the consequences. Instead, he had put up with everything, always pretending to be something he wasn't. Even with his father laughing in his face, he'd stood there and said nothing.

And this, right now, was the way out. Here was the chance to escape both his parents' mad religiosity and the ignorance of his peers. Not fucking it up was imperative. So let the man call Leopold Bloom 'semitic' if that makes him happy. Let him call Leonard Woolf lupine. Let him gleefully quote Eliot's hateful verses.

The woman was speaking again. 'Which is not to mention the writers, especially in Europe, who were Jewish themselves. Proust, for instance, Elias Canetti, Franz Kafka—'

'Kafka was an anti-Semite,' Tovyah broke in. It was the first time he had interrupted either of them.

'He was what?' the man asked.

'An anti-Semite,' Tovyah said again, more confident now.

'You are aware that Kafka was from a Jewish family? His grandfather was a show-shit.' Tovyah had no idea was this last word meant, and the man went on to supply the definition: 'a ritual slaughterer. The man who makes sure everything's kosher, as it were.' At that stupid joke, rage coursed through him. Of course he knew what a shochet was. שׁוֹחֵט. What's more, he knew how the word was pronounced. What did this goy academic know?

'Yes, I know he was Jewish. But all the same he had anti-Semitic views,' Tovyah said. He was surprised by the tone of his own voice. Angry now, practically growling. 'He wrote a letter to a woman, some girlfriend. Marina, or Elena, or something.'

'Milena,' the woman put in.

'Whatever! And in this letter, he says he would like to murder the whole Jewish people, including himself. Did you know that?'

He knew that aggression would not play well. But it felt good to be angry, better at least than bumbling through, restarting each sentence midway. The man looked ready to laugh. The woman rushed in before he could speak.

'I don't recollect the letter you're referring to,' she said, 'but by the sounds of it, I think we can assume Kafka was joking. He had a strange sense of humour, very morbid. It is important to bear in mind that we are reading with post-Holocaust eyes. Such chance comments read very differently to us than they would have done to Kafka's contemporaries. There is little doubt that had he lived to see the rise of Hitler, Kafka would have been appalled. After all, his whole body of work is a condemnation of the abuse of power, is it not?'

Tovyah stalled. The trouble was, he agreed with her. Kafka was no genocidal monster. He was a fantasist of extraordinary gifts, a seer troubled by dark visions. Tovyah had known this all along, and he didn't need some Gentile to explain it to him here, in Oxford, in this medieval college. But he was still burning with indignation. The man scoured his personal statement for the next avenue of discussion.

'It's pronounced *sho-cheyt*,' Tovyah said. Neither of them seemed to know what he was talking about.

In his second interview, he wrestled with an unseen poem and then discussed Shakespeare in terms that afterwards made him sick. At six o'clock, an update was posted on the notice board; Tovyah was not required for anything further. The Scottish girl he'd met earlier stood next to him at the board – she'd been asked to stay overnight for a third interview at another college. 'Hopefully see you next year!' she said as he left.

He didn't stop at the Eagle and Child to buy himself a drink and bask in the atmosphere of literary heritage as he'd planned. He didn't call his parents or his brother to tell them how it had gone. He didn't even swing by University College to check out the statue of Percy Bysshe Shelley that Ms Zhang had urged him to visit.

As he stood on the platform, awaiting the train for London, he made a resolution.

When he let himself into the family home, he was surprised to find both his parents and Elsie waiting to see him. He didn't realise she'd been discharged. There was a cake in the middle of the dining table, and a bottle of sweet sherry with three glasses in a triangle before it. The cake was white, with black frosting on top in the shape of a mortar board.

'What's all this?' he said, shaking off his coat.

'Your mother's idea,' Eric said. 'For the record, I voted against.'

Elsie ran up to her brother, threw her arms around him, and kissed his cheek. 'When did you get so clever?' she asked.

Hannah was working the cork out of the bottle. 'Ignore your father. We're proud of you. All of us.'

Eric held a large bread knife towards Tovyah and clapped him on the shoulder. 'I never said I wasn't proud. Can't I be proud and disappointed at the same time?'

'I don't want any cake,' Tovyah said, refusing the knife.

'You shouldn't bat away an olive branch,' Eric said.

Hannah put the bottle down. 'It probably went better than you think. Some of the worst interviews I've done, I've ended up getting the job.'

She looked at her husband. 'Tell him.'

'Tell him what? I still think he should have gone for law.'

Hannah rolled her eyes. 'We don't know anything yet, so let's hope for the best. There will be plenty of time for commiserations later.'

She nodded at Eric, who cut into the white icing atop the cake and split the mortar board in two. Inside were alternating layers of jam and custard. After commenting on the outrageous price of the cake, he handed the knife to Tovyah. 'Go on, cut a slice.'

Tovyah braced himself. If he didn't do it now, he might never make the leap. He did not cut into the cake. He turned to face his family, crowding in around him. 'I don't believe in God,' he said, just quietly that first time. Everyone had heard. Even so, he said it again, a little louder, 'I don't believe in God anyway.'

His mother took a step towards him. 'Tovyah.'

Tovyah moved away from the table, holding the knife out in front of him.

'Woah,' Elsie said. 'Kid brother thinks he's in a slasher. About to spill some red stuff.'

Eric told him to put the knife down and go to his room.

'But you need to hear this,' Tovyah said.

Elsie's eyes were gleaming. 'What's the truth, kid? I wanna hear it!'

Hannah put a hand on her daughter. 'Shhh, darling.'

'This foolishness stops right now,' Eric said. 'Go upstairs and we'll talk in the morning.'

'Slice him up!' cried Elsie. 'Slice him up!'

'Look at *her*.' Tovyah was pointing the knife at his sister. 'If nothing else gets through to you, just look at her. What God would do that? To a *child*. What sick fuck? There is no Yahweh! Don't you see? It's all bullshit. No Yahweh, no nothing. Just nothing.'

'Tovyah—'

'NOTHING, NOTHING, NOTHING, NOTHING, NOTHING!'

All the next day, Tovyah's throat burned. The thing that cost him most, however, was that he had pronounced God's true

157

name, the ancient Hebrew word that the Orthodox will not write down, let alone speak aloud. Phone calls were made. To friends, to Grossman, to extended family. What do we do with our deviant son? At her most exasperated, Hannah said she was ready to sit shiva.

At length Eric talked her down, and a shaky truce was established.

Back at school, Tovyah was disengaged in English. For a while, Ms Zhang tried to reconnect with him, asking for his opinions in class, offering to lend him books. But he kept pushing her away and before long she gave up. She couldn't stand people who sulked.

The following September, with the agreement of his parents, Tovyah put in an application to study History at a newer, less prestigious Oxford college, whose alumni did not include world famous poets, or disease-conquering scientists. By now he had taken his A Levels and received excellent results, and in December the college wrote to offer him an unconditional place.

This time, there was no bottle of sweet sherry, and no cake.

Chapter Twelve

A couple of weeks after lunching with Tovyah's family in that French bistro, he and I went for coffee at the top of Blackwell's bookshop, where he told me about his first, unsuccessful application to the university. We had just browsed through the poetry section, taking down several volumes before each deciding to buy nothing. I was hard up as ever, and Tovyah thought that pretty much all contemporary writers were simply terrible. As for the older poets, he was in no mood to pay money to replace books his parents had taken from him.

After he'd related the story, I asked if he ever made a formal complaint about the interviewer. He didn't understand.

'The man's behaviour!' I said. It was, at the very least, inappropriate, and I thought you could make a case he was being actively anti-Semitic.

Tovyah flared his nostrils. 'So?'

'What do you mean so? If you'd made a complaint, someone might have done something. They might have changed their decision.'

Now he laughed. 'Haven't you been paying attention? No one gives a fuck about anti-Semitism.'

*

Since I'd met his mother and sister in the first week of term, Tovyah and I had become inseparable. 'How's your weird friend?' people would ask. Having established that we got on, it was difficult to see why we had spent so long circling each other.

We spoke about everything: families, relationships, books. Our long talks were, for me, a second education. For instance, he brought my attention to various strands of esoteric Judaism, from the Merkabah Mystics of the first century right through to the school of Isaac Luria, and modern Hassidism. He taught me about the lineage of False Messiahs – beginning, of course, with Christ – those bearded impostors who claimed to speak with the voice of God. Despite himself, Tovyah loved these stories. His favourite took place during the Napoleonic Wars. A conspiracy of three holy men sought to hasten the end of days by invoking God to take the part of the French emperor, whom they saw as the incarnation of Gog and Magog, the arch-nemeses of light. Once Bonaparte had subdued all the nations of the world, the true Messiah would be forced to make his long-awaited appearance to defeat his great adversary, thus bringing about the final salvation of the Jewish people. According to legend, the plan failed only because Napoleon spoke disparagingly of the Seer of Lublin, leader of the holy men. This hubris led to his defeat, humiliation, and exile.

I asked him if his parents believed this sort of stuff. 'Surely not, right?'

'You'd be surprised. They think everything that happened to my sister is some weird punishment from God.'

'OK, that's also mad. But, sorry for asking, what exactly *has* happened to Elsie?'

I'd been curious about his sister for a while. Though I knew she'd had a difficult life, I was ignorant of the specifics. Now, for the first time, Tovyah sketched a time-line of events.

'She was the brightest kid you could hope to meet,' Tovyah began. 'Then everything somehow went wrong.'

No one ever found out where Elsie went when she disappeared. Or why she'd gone. Was she unhappy? Scared? Did she want adventure? No therapist could get her to open up. Eventually, she was diagnosed with depression, and prescribed 20 mg of fluoxetine.

Later that year, she was expelled from her school for 'anti-social behaviour'. On her charge sheet: destroying another girl's property (she dumped a copy of *Harry Potter and the Chamber of Secrets* in the toilet on the grounds that it was stupid), fighting (she stabbed a girl in the thigh with a pair of compasses) and emotional bullying (everyone, her teacher said, was frightened of her). At fifteen, having been kicked out of two more schools (for stealing and bullying respectively) she tore up a copy of the Hebrew Bible and told her parents she hated God. The following year she kidnapped some chickens from a neighbour's garden and slit their throats. In November, Hannah's first book came out: *Gehinnom and Afterwards*. Elsie wrote a blog post claiming the whole thing had been an invention by her money-grabbing mother and had nothing to do with the true events of her grandfather's life. She wrote that her grandfather had been a sort of wizard, a powerful Kabbalist, who evaded Nazi persecution through ancient mystical techniques. Even now, his spirit outwitted oblivion and could still be seen around the house.

'This would have been 2002*ish*,' Tovyah said, 'when everyone was suddenly into *LiveJournal* and the whole world started vomiting their opinions online.' It hadn't occurred to me that the Rosenthals kept pace with internet trends, but once again,

I'd mischaracterised them. It was easy to forget that Hannah was far more at home in the modern world than she let on; whatever cultural moment this was, she was thriving.

In any case, Elsie's blog was discovered by one of Hannah's detractors and reposted, amplifying the readership and the family's embarrassment a hundredfold.

It was around this time that Eric said to his daughter, before the whole family, 'Who are you? I don't recognise this person.' To which Elsie broke into a laughing fit. Then threw a full wine glass against the wall; a red streak ran to the ceiling. Then she attempted to walk barefoot across the shattered glass, stopping only when her older brother manhandled her out of the room.

At sixteen her anorexia was judged life-threatening, and she was hospitalised. There she attempted to kill herself with a smuggled safety razor. When the family's rabbi visited her bedside, she spat in his face and told him he was a fraud. Remarkably, she managed to sit her GCSEs after she was discharged, but she never attended another school. She was now taking 75 mg of venlafaxine, having given up on both citalopram and sertraline (the former 'didn't do anything,' and the latter made her violently ill).

In the following years, Elsie continued to bounce between her parents' home and psychiatric hospitals. She drank whenever she could break out and find someone to take pity on her. A scrawny teenager with big, dark eyes, she didn't struggle to find them. Her venlafaxine dose was increased to 150 mg. The doctors were quietly optimistic that with the stronger prescription, her moods might start to stabilise. 'Not her life, you understand, just her moods.'

By the time Tovyah had finished this tale, his eyes were shining. I said how sorry I was.

Tovyah scrunched his nose. 'Don't be. It's like Tolstoy says. Each family gets fucked in their own way.'

Just behind the beat, I asked, 'Tolstoy said that?'

There was a pause, then Tovyah said my name.

'Yes?'

'Let's go get something to eat.'

As the term ran by, the weather brightened. I made it my mission to integrate Tovyah into college life, and there was a period when I regularly got him out, if not always to the house parties and social occasions, then at least to pubs and to various cultural events: art shows, film screenings, concerts. Friends of mine remarked: 'He's actually not so bad, when you get to know him.' And: 'Sometimes, he can be quite funny.' I can still picture his face on a certain spring night, when a few of us gathered in the White Horse on the corner of Broad Street. Several beers in, when his eyes were no longer able to hold their focus, he made a pronouncement. 'If every night were like this, then I'd know what the fuss was about.'

'But they could be, Tovyah,' I said, linking my arm in his. Later, I got him to take a drag on my cigarette. He breathed in deeply, managed not to cough or splutter, then exhaled a thick stream of smoke. 'Funny,' he said, 'I thought it would feel more like suffocating.' But did he like it? He smiled. 'Absolutely not.'

I think I was a little in love with him that night. The same way that once, aged five, I told my parents I was going to marry Nick, my older brother.

Then global events intruded on our university lives. That winter, an Israeli operation targeting Hamas military bases and training centres in the Gaza Strip had caused the deaths of some thirteen hundred Palestinians. In March, an official report from the Israel Defense Forces claimed the vast majority of those killed were militants or, in the language of tabloids, terrorists. The claim was disputed by the Palestinian Centre for Human Rights: according to their figures the bulk of the casualties were non-combatants. After a lengthy debate, our Junior Common Room voted by a wide margin to condemn the IDF report and stand with Palestine. Among the speakers who made the case against the Israeli military was Jan, who spoke with controlled passion. 'Thirteen hundred dead. And we're meant to believe none of them were just quietly living their lives?'

Tovyah was not present. Not because he didn't care about the conflict, but because he considered student politics a joke. 'People only go to those meetings for the free pizza,' he said.

I told him that wasn't true. This week especially there'd been an impressive turn out. He nodded. 'Netanyahu will be devastated.'

As a family, the Rosenthals were not impartial. For the last five years, Gideon had been living in Tel Aviv. And though his active military service was complete, he had friends who were involved in the IDF operation, one of whom received a splinter of shrapnel in his right eye and now saw the world as a clutter of indistinct shapes moving through fog. Another friend's daughter attended the kindergarten that was bombed by Islamists. Although no one was harmed, the school being empty at the time of the attack, the parents were understandably terrified. That week, Hannah wrote a piece defending the IDF report and Israel's actions. She cited conversations she'd had with Gideon, told the story of his blinded friend and the bombed-out school. And she quoted the words of one Hamas leader: 'The Zionists have legitimised the killing of their children by killing our children.' Whatever else you want to say about Israel, Hannah argued, no one in charge is calling for the slaughter of Palestinian children.

After reading the piece, Jan was incensed. I ran into him in the university parks, on the way to a lecture, and he grabbed my elbow. 'She's a monster! She basically comes out and says it, Jewish lives matter more than Arab lives.'

I disagreed. All she was saying was that the Israelis have a legitimate reason to feel scared. Jan brought up the figures of Israeli casualties compared with Palestinian casualties, the horrific numbers I was sick of hearing. I tried to explain that I wasn't diminishing Israel's actions, only trying to see where someone like Hannah Rosenthal was coming from.

'But why is your knee-jerk reaction to understand *her*? Why not reserve your sympathy for the victims?'

Jan wasn't the only one who took exception to Hannah Rosenthal's writings that week. Tovyah showed me the envelope someone pushed under his door. In place of an address was the message scrawled in sharpie, *show these to your mum*. Inside the envelope were pictures of Gaza, clipped from the papers.

We were in my room. The window was open and it had just started to rain. I suggested that he should make a report to the dean.

'It's nothing. My mother picked up the phone yesterday, three o'clock in the afternoon. A man said he was going to cut her fucking head off.'

'Seriously? Is she OK?'

'Hannah? She knows the score. You want everyone to like you, don't start talking about Israel–Palestine.'

'Do you think that's what her new book is about?' I asked. 'The conflict?'

'Maybe.'

He did not sound convinced. He was still under the impression that his mother's latest subject was himself. The second son.

*

Although I'd considered it, I'd not been back to the Ben-Scholem Society. I might have gone to keep Tovyah company, but he no longer went. When he announced that he was done with the place, I suggested he might miss some of the regulars. The night of the Schultz lecture, for instance, I'd seen him sitting with an old man, dressed all in white. Who was he?

Tovyah said he had no idea. There was a thing he sometimes did with his face – he narrowed his eyes and drew his mouth into a straight line. Not for the first time, I wondered if it meant he was lying.

'But you must know,' I said. 'He was sitting right next to you. He had his hand on your knee.'

Tovyah gestured dismissively. 'Just some old Jew, steadying himself. You say he was wearing a kittel? But it wasn't a holiday.'

He would not be drawn, and so for now, I dropped the subject.

The more it came up, the more disturbed I felt by my ignorance of Jewish culture, and I began attending services at the liberal synagogue, just out of town. No one minded that I knew no Hebrew and was undecided on the question of God. People dressed casually, although most of the men still wore skull caps. It was there I had my first Seder. We were treated to the story of the Exodus: the baby entrusted to the river, Moses's early years, the burning bush, the Ten

Plagues, the Israelites' escape from Egypt, God as cloud of smoke, God as pillar of fire. I knew the outline, of course, but the details surprised me. For instance, that God hardens Pharaoh's heart against giving into Moses's demands, thus forcing the escalation of divine reprisals. Tovyah was right; the Old Testament Jehovah was no one's cuddly father. I felt great discomfort when we dipped our fingers in wine to dot the rims of our plates with red liquid. Ten spots of blood, one for each blow that was dealt to the Egyptians, culminating with the mass death of firstborn children. The rabbi caught me grimacing. 'To be honest with you,' she said, 'I don't love this bit either.'

I liked the relaxed attitude of the liberal congregation, who gathered in a sweet, homely building with children's drawings taped to the wall. It was much warmer than the Orthodox synagogue, that solemn fortress, still holding out against the upheavals of the twenty-first century. And I liked the female rabbi – she was attentive, patient, knowledgeable. But I wondered if there was something lost by this modern revision of the ancient ceremony. At the Ben-Scholem Society, I'd seen men rocking back and forth while praying in a language that has outlasted the Roman Empire. The evening might as well have taken place in black and white. It might as well have taken place in *oils*. Was it possible those bearded men knew something the friendly, liberal Jews had forgotten?

Before I left, I heard a student in a 'Dark Side of the Moon' T-shirt say, 'In all these years, archaeologists have never found one scrap of evidence the Jews were in Egypt. It's a metaphor. We're all in Egypt, and we all gotta find our way out.' And that was it. To the Orthodox, nothing was just a metaphor; if you put out an empty chair for the prophet Elijah, it's because the prophet Elijah might just show up. I remembered what Tovyah's grandfather said about Leviticus. For Yosef Rosenthal, imprisoned in death's antechamber, Old Testament legends weren't consolation for what was happening to him. They were *corroboration*. Hence the title of Hannah's book, *Gehinnom and Afterwards*. In the biblical Valley of Hinnom, the high priest sacrificed children. In the Warsaw Ghetto, in Treblinka, who can say what horrors went unrecorded?

*

'You want to know the ironic thing? I don't even like Israel.'

Tovyah had just come back from the faculty library, where he'd had an altercation with some students from our college. Cornering him, they'd asked his opinion of his mother's politics. He said it was none of their business. 'I'm not *her*.' They followed up by saying, 'Don't you think that if you remain silent, you're complicit?'

At which point Tovyah told them to go fuck themselves. One of them had trailed him back to college, walking six feet behind the whole way.

Now Tovyah was catching me up. 'I was nine the first time I went. It was very hot and everything tasted of burnt sesame. And as for the ideology . . . The early Zionists, I mean Weizman, Bentwich, those lot, they had two big fears. You know what they were?'

I had a feeling he was about to tell me.

'The first was that the pogroms tearing through the Jews of Eastern Europe – which back then was most of the Jews in the world, remember – were going to get worse not better. They realised, before anyone else, that the violence in Galicia, in Russia, Poland, and Romania, represented an existential threat. One day the Cossacks, the Inquisitors, the

168

sons of Amalek would be coming for us all. That was problem number one.

'Problem number two was assimilation. They looked West and they asked themselves, how can a tiny, secular minority survive without being swallowed up? The Jews of France would become Frenchmen, the Jews of England would become Englishmen, and the Jews of Italy would become Italians.'

I said, 'I know what assimilation means.'

'You have to hand it to them, they read the currents of history, they saw where we were headed. But history still fucked them. Despite all their hustling for a safe haven, the Shoah happened anyway – Ben-Gurion declared his state ten years too late! Auschwitz, Dachau, Sobibor, they were dust heaps. The population Herzl wanted to adopt had been wiped out. What good was Israel now?

'Which brings us to fear number two, assimilation. Well, if you ask me, that's the best thing that could have happened to the Jews.'

Tovyah rarely spoke about current affairs. He'd be more likely to discuss the death of Socrates than, say, the death of Saddam Hussein. I suspect this was a product of his loneliness. With no community, there is no politics.

'All right,' I said, 'so you're not a believer, you're not a Zionist, and you don't go to synagogue. So what does being Jewish mean to you?'

'If I could wash my hands of the whole thing, I would.'

I told him he didn't mean it.

'Don't be sentimental,' he said.

'I'm not being anything. Stop pretending you don't care!'

We parted sourly and for a few days I didn't see him much. When we did cross paths, his manner was uninviting. I worried that in light of recent incidents, the business of introducing Tovyah to the social life of the college had suffered a major setback. Already he had returned to old habits of refusing to spend time with friends of mine, people who, in low moods, he dismissed as trivial or moronic.

Incidentally, one subject Tovyah and I had never broached was sex. Confident he was a virgin, I figured he was pretty much uninterested. Now and then I'd catch him gazing at someone, but it always seemed more like envy for other people's contentment than sexual desire.

Then one Friday, he knocked on my door and asked if I wanted to get dinner in hall. He'd put on his favourite shirt and was unusually upbeat.

'Guess what I'm doing tonight?' he said.

'You're going to listen to a visiting professor discuss mass exterminations.'

'I've got a date.'

I was tempted to ask if it was a man or a woman. Tovyah told me he was meeting the lady at the Gardener's Arms at 7.30 and asked me to wish him luck.

'What's that face for?' Tovyah said. I said it was nothing, just something hard in my food.

Once Tovyah had left me to work my way through a rather sad lasagne, I was joined by Jan.

'Where have you been hiding?' he said, seating himself in the pew opposite. 'I feel like I never see you these days.'

It's true, I hadn't spent as much time with him of late. Although I'd felt the pull of Jan's charm when I first met him, he was a difficult person to get close to. He was always surrounded by other friends, and our conversations rarely went beyond the superficial.

I told him I'd been working too hard.

'That and trailing around Mr Rosenthal, I hear.'

'We're mates. So what?'

'You're not shagging, are you?'

'Jesus, Jan, that's none of your business. And apparently, he's got a hot date tonight.'

'Really? Wow. If I were him, I wouldn't want to show my face in town right now.'

Confused, I asked what he was talking about.

'You mean you don't know? You haven't seen today's *Times*?' I shook my head. 'I won't spoil it for you. But the fascist has really outdone herself this time.'

Intrigued, I made my way after dinner to the common room. In the magazine rack, I found a wrinkled copy of the paper and discovered the news about Hannah Rosenthal's latest book. It seemed the controversy that had flared up over her recent political tirades had done nothing to harm her public profile – the announcement warranted a full feature, apparently, and *The Times* had secured an exclusive preview. I read the article twice through in quick succession. Without serious rival, this was the weirdest thing that had ever happened to someone I knew.

Like Hannah's first, the new book was a memoir. But now, rather than casting her gaze backwards at the trauma of her father-in-law, she had written about her own offspring. Not Tovyah. *Elsie*.

The book's title, the article explained, was once again biblically derived. Let me summarise:

At the end of the First Book of Samuel, King Saul has been deserted by his God. Half-mad and encircled by civil war, the broken king seeks aid from dark powers. He enlists the help of a woman, referred to by theologians as the Witch of Endor, to raise the spirit of Samuel, the king's deceased prophet. The scene is depicted in a nineteenth-century

painting by Nikiforovich Dmitry Martynov, an image repro-
duced alongside the columns of print, and which would later
appear on the book's cover: a woman in a dark cloak, her
face hidden, lifts her hands towards an otherworldly light,
while Saul cowers in the foreground, not daring to look at
the obscene wonders taking place in the shadows. In this
painting, I couldn't help but notice, the dead Samuel appears
draped in a white shroud.

With this story of necromancy in mind, Hannah titled her
second book, a telling of her middle child's life, *Daughters of
Endor*. Yes. Tovyah's mother had written a work of so-called
non-fiction in which she accused Elsie of being a witch, a girl
waylaid by demonic influences. A summoner of the dead.

Already, there was an extract from the first chapter available to read online:

PICTURE A GRAND VICTORIAN HOUSE, somewhere near
the top of a gently sloping hill. The east-facing garden
out front is paved with gravel. Watch the inhabitants come
and go through the bottle-green door, freshly painted that
spring. Each morning the façade catches the light of the rising sun, and often a man can be seen watering the roses and
blinking in the day's first brightness. Passers-by sometimes
reckon they hear him speak words of encouragement to the
budding flowers, but perhaps he is only muttering to himself, as preoccupied people are supposed to do. That would
be Eric, by turns son, husband, and father of the house,
though his time as a son is almost at an end. After midday, when the sun has made its slow journey to the far side,
the French windows at the back gleam. The garden beyond,
with its apple trees and its summer house, suggests an idyllic existence of afternoons passed in tea and conversation.

Most days a silver dish bearing triangles of white sandwiches sits atop a latticed table, and a wireless narrates ball by ball the Test match. Bees hum contentedly, gathering pollen until dusk falls, when the teacups are swept away, and dark cocktails are poured over clicking ice. As the sun sinks behind the edge of the world, the back wall glows amber. And then it's done. Night has fallen. Imagine this home now like a doll's house; the roof lifts off, and each wall peels back to uncover the still lives cloistered within. If you look hard enough, the dolls start to move.

On the top floor, a small man, bent with age, walks restlessly between his bedroom and the pantry. He props himself against the counter, opens cupboards, looks around, gives up, and returns to the chair in which he sits neither fully asleep nor fully awake. His mind is littered with phantoms. Soon he will be dead, and the dynamics of the family will change irreversibly. Directly beneath him a young girl is huddled under the cave of her duvet, leaning on her elbows. Her bedside lamp is on, and she has a book under her chin. She is, as everybody says, the happiest child in the world.

Less than a year from now, that girl will run away. Her face will be paraded on the news. The nation's sympathy will be stirred, and people will assume the worst. She's been murdered. She's been raped. How repulsive, another tragedy of innocence destroyed. But they will be wrong. After four nightmarish days, the girl will be picked up, a hundred miles from home, and driven by police officers back to her parents' house. This too will make the news. A happy ending for once, people will think. Again they are mistaken. The girl who comes back will not be the same girl who vanished.

But we're getting ahead of ourselves. For now, we are simply peering into the doll's house. The girl is still under her duvet, reading. Listen. If you listen carefully and you do not come too close, our mannequins will take on voices as well as movement.

Did Tovyah know what his mother had done? He must. Why hadn't he said anything? I was desperate to talk to him. But when I tried his door, he'd already left for his date. I called his phone and got the voicemail. The message I left went unanswered, as did my texts.

I was still awake, revising an essay due the next day, when at around midnight he burst through my unlocked door. After stumbling a few paces, he managed to right himself without falling over. As he tried to fix his gaze on me, his eyes shone with dark light. I was sitting at my desk, quite still. Before we'd exchanged a word, he seemed to come to a decision, and collapsed onto my bed. Finally, he spoke. Drawing his knees up to his chest, he announced – not that I'd asked – that he was absolutely fine.

'How'd the date go?'

'Date?' He took a moment to consider. 'Total disaster. For some reason I couldn't shut up about Israeli domestic policy. The reality of the threat from neighbouring countries, the inhumane treatment of the occupied people, two-state solutions, one-state solutions, must have bored the shit out of her. Anyway, she left hours ago.'

'So where have you been?'

'Just having a little drink, you see. Just a drink. Well, a few drinks, really, if you're keeping count. I might have another. There's whisky in my room. I've got mugs, too. Do you want one?'

'It's a bit late for me, pal.'

'Killjoy.' He spoke with his face pressed to the pillow, one eye visible.

I said he should go to bed, and he asked me to reconsider having a drink with him. Once more, I refused.

'Fair 'nuff, fair 'nuff. That girl tonight didn't want to have another drink either. Just the one was good. Personally, I disagree, I happen to think one drink is a bit pathetic. But you can't force someone, can you? Got the hint, you know. Just friends, she said. She thought maybe we could be just friends. Are you sure you don't want a drink?'

'You're shitfaced.'

'Maybe you're right. Maybe I am a little . . . inebriated. By the way, do you want to know what my mother's done? It's funny this. It's hilarious. My mother, she's written a book, the fucking crackpot, she's written this book, right, where she says my sister has been possessed! How do you like that? Possessed by a fucking demon!'

His laughter was like a submachine gun. I tried to quieten him.

'I don't want to go on about it, but it's just a bit much, you know. I mean here I am, trying to get away from all that, and look what *she's* up to. It's just a bit fucking much.'

'I'm really sorry, Tovyah.'

'You? What have *you* done?'

Rather than answer, I poured him a glass of water from my sink. I sat down next to him and placed the glass on my bedside table, then stroked the back of his head. I told him it would be all right, that I was here for him. Then my hand was in his and he was massaging my palm with his thumbs. I didn't pull away.

'Kate?' he said.

'Yes?'

'Do you reckon I could sleep here tonight?'

Chapter Thirteen

I was woken by the morning light stabbing through a gap in the curtains. Tovyah lay on the floor, naked apart from his boxers and vest. As he began to stir, he reminded me of a beached fish.

Despite the state he'd been in, sleeping together had been a moderate success. It felt vaguely transgressive to reach up under his shirt, to run my hands over that skinny body. Transgressive and yet familiar. And safe. Eager to satisfy me, he took instruction without self-consciousness. After we had each climaxed, he held me in his arms. Then, in his sleep, he made panicked, whimpering noises. I didn't know when he had made his way to the floor.

With my big toe, I now prodded him awake. Groaning, he pulled on his trousers while still lying there. When he sat up, I could see red lines on the side of his head, imprinted by the ridges of the carpet.

'How did you sleep?' I asked.

'Terribly.'

'You should have stayed up here.'

I pulled the covers off and stood up, towering over him.

'Stop that, don't move. Think I might throw up.'

He bent his head between his knees and grabbed an ankle with each hand, as if prostrating himself before some terrible power. He stayed like that for a minute or two. I watched him suffer, unsure whether to hurry him to the sink or just let him sit there. When the moment of danger passed, he spoke again. 'Fucking bloody piss.'

'It's not a big—'

'I can't believe, I really can't believe her.'

His gangly body unfolded itself. Under his eyes, the skin was pouched and violet.

'Your mother,' I said.

'Of course my mother. Who else? I take it you've seen the news.' He began to stand up, thought better of it, and thumped back to the floor. 'What? Why are you looking at me like that?'

'You really don't remember,' I said.

'Oh God, I wasn't whining on about it, was I?'

'You did a bit. And—'

'I hate being drunk. It's so ugly.'

Some people make too little eye contact and come across as shy or rude. This was not usually Tovyah's problem. When he looked at you, you felt like you were being examined. But now, for once, he was reluctant to meet my eye.

'About last night,' he said.

'You didn't forget everything, then.'

I knew exactly how uncomfortable he was and I was enjoying myself. I raised my eyebrows as I waited for him to respond.

'I just wanted to say I'm sorry.'

'You're *sorry*?'

'If I misled you. I don't know what came over me. I was very drunk. No offence, Kate, I just don't have those sorts of feelings about you.'

It was too early to know how I myself felt about what had happened. Mortified? Triumphant? Interested in a repeat? There would be plenty of time to work it out. For now, I too had slept badly, and decided to take things as they came.

'It's nothing,' I said.

Tovyah started to dress himself, quite uninhibited in my presence. I watched him, amused by his pale body.

'So your mum's written a book about your sister . . . having supernatural powers?'

'You don't know her. Sometimes, I even feel sorry for Eric. When they married, I don't think he had any idea what he was up against.'

Ever the rationalist, Tovyah saw his sister's troubles as a complex web of mental disorders, a product of brain chemistry and the incidents of her life so far. So much bad luck compounded by so much bad parenting. His mother, not believing in luck, interpreted things differently. For Hannah, the unimaginable change in Elsie must have a spiritual dimension. A *meaning*. If something was happening to her daughter and not to someone else's, then it was because that was what God wanted. In *The Times* article, they printed this teaser from the book:

WHEN I LOOKED AT HER then with her hair shaved close to her scalp, her eyes sunken into her face, I couldn't help but think *that isn't my daughter*. Something had taken possession of her. Some imp, some demon, some dybbuk, something that cared nothing for the well-being of my darling Elsie . . .

I asked Tovyah if he was close to his sister growing up. 'She was my best friend,' he said. 'And then she went away.'

No wonder Tovyah had drunk himself senseless and ended up in bed with the nearest available person. I was still having trouble believing his mother's central premise was sincere. Her journalism, though often misguided, was intelligent and well argued. The book she was bringing out now was obviously insane.

'You wouldn't believe what went on in that house,' Tovyah said. 'The things they did to "cure" Elsie.'

'Like what?'

'OK, she goes missing. Hannah rings up everyone she's ever met, asks them if they've seen her. Fair enough. But what does Eric do? He *fasts*. He doesn't eat a thing until Elsie has been found. The crazy bastard went on hunger strike against God.'

'Why? Is that a Talmudic thing?'

'You're not getting it. Where it came from is not the point. A little fast now and then? That's chicken shit.'

He told me a story about a mezuzah, the little box that contains a scrap of parchment and offers protection to Jewish households. Once, Hannah read that if there was a mistake on one of the prayer sheets, the house would by cursed rather than blessed. During one of Elsie's darker spells, she decided to take down the mezuzah above the front door, just to check. And of course, after unscrewing the box and comparing the text with a prayer book, she noticed a discrepancy. Eric! Come now! After a brief consultation, they buried the script with the error and commissioned a scribe to handwrite a new sheet. For a week or more, Hannah genuinely believed this would solve Elsie's problems. Meanwhile, her daughter had just decided that she didn't like her latest medication and had been caught flushing it down the toilet. Eric discovered what she was up to when a clogged drain left a pill swirling in the toilet bowl. And what did Hannah say? They shouldn't tell her off about the pills. That's not the issue.

'Was there any improvement?' I asked. 'I mean after the prayer was corrected.'

'Improvement? Are you listening? I grew up in a mad-house.'

Standing now, Tovyah retched, though nothing came up. He stumbled to the door and pushed his way out. But he did not make it to the bathroom. Early though it was, there was someone in the corridor.

'What the hell are *you* doing here?' I heard Tovyah say.

'Lovely to see you too.'

I knew the voice at once: it was his mother.

She went on, 'They tried to stop me coming in, can you believe. Said I had to wait in the porters' lodge for you to come and meet me. But we tried your phone and no one picked up. "This is a farce," I said, "you know exactly who I am." Then I marched on through.'

'Some nerve, don't you think?'

'Buckets of nerve! As if *I'm* a security risk.'

'I meant you coming here, like nothing's happened.'

In the pause that followed, I snuck closer to the door. I wondered if Hannah realised the room Tovyah was standing outside was not his own.

'It's virtually the end of term,' she said. 'You've had your last tutorial, yes? I was in Reading anyway, and I thought you might want to get away from all the publicity. You can take the train if you'd prefer.'

'There's no need.'

'Right, let's get on, then. I knew you'd see sense.'

'You're not following me. There's no need for me to take the train because *I'm not coming home.*'

Hannah betrayed no emotion in her voice when she spoke again. 'Well, if you've set you heart on staying, I can't prise you away. Though, after what I've seen, I wonder how welcome you are.'

'What's that supposed to mean?'

Hannah had been standing in front of Tovyah's door. She now took a step away, revealing something behind. Whatever it was made Tovyah say, 'I don't believe it.'

'You will,' Hannah said. 'You can go back to your whore now. Ring when you come to your senses.'

In another moment, she was gone, and I emerged from the room to find Tovyah hugging himself, staring at his own door.

'*What* did she call me?' I said.

'It's like the idiots want to prove her right.'

For a moment, I didn't understand what he was talking about. Then I saw it too. His door had been vandalised. On either side were two symbols carved into the wood, bridged by an equals sign cut deep into the central beam. On the door's left panel was a six-pointed star formed of two overlapping triangles: the emblem of King David, ancient symbol of Judaism, and icon of the modern state of Israel. And on the right was two bolts of crossed lightning, a crooked shape understood by children everywhere as a token of monumental human evil.

Chapter Fourteen

Unfair but true, most families celebrate a favoured child, about whom the constellation of parents, grandparents, and lesser siblings revolve. For the Rosenthals, this was Elsie. According to family lore, her first word wasn't mama or dada or even some garbled attempt at Gideon. It was *me*. 'Meeee!' she cried, sometimes joyfully, sometimes baffled, and sometimes with bitter indignation. 'Me me me me me!' And always as loudly as her small lungs could manage. Her parents crowed. Eleven months old, and she had attained self-consciousness. Their baby girl was nothing less than a pint-sized Descartes.

Physically, she took after her mother. She had rigid blonde hair, almost white, which darkened and began to curl in the first years of puberty. Cameras embarrassed her so in photos she never smiled. You can find them online, and in her mother's books. Here she holds a cushion before her face, there she looks away, and in this last one, she scowls. Notice, here and there, the chipped canine, a reminder whenever she looked in the mirror that she once slipped on wet paving slabs beside an outdoor swimming pool. She only realised she was bleeding when she saw a burgundy ribbon twist in the water. Twist, unwind, disperse.

Even her grandfather, not known for friendliness towards children, adored her. 'This one I like,' Yosef would say, affectionately tugging her ear this way and that. 'The boys, I can take or leave.' His death was the first blot on an idyllic childhood. Before then, it was possible for Elsie to believe nothing truly bad would ever happen to her. Nothing worse than a lost footing, an outrageous smack to the face, a broken tooth, and one morning ruined in a summer brimming over with days.

She was about to turn fourteen when she lost him. In her diary, which years afterwards was found and read by her mother as research for *Daughters of Endor*, Elsie wrote, 'How can a person be here and then just not here any more? It doesn't make sense.' The word *sense* was twice underlined. Until that point, she'd kept her diary haphazardly – whole weeks passed undescribed – and always with an eye for harmless comedy, such as the time she saw a dalmatian sneeze in the park; the owner wiped the dog's nose with a handkerchief, cooing 'Bless you, dear, bless you.' During her bereavement, however, Elsie's thoughts darkened:

Stepped on snail at lunch. Fascinating to see the mangled sludge and broken shell up close. Meredith called me disgusting.

Sex ed with Humphries. More like sermon on chastity, but for health reasons, not moral. Didn't mention souls, didn't mention defilement.

Met C again this evening. Wants to go to the next level.

Such fragments were no doubt tantalising for her snooping mother to read as she later investigated all that had gone wrong for Elsie. While most of the names mentioned were known to Hannah, 'C' was a mystery. The initial appears regularly for a few months, and then abruptly drops out of the diary altogether, just around the time her daughter went missing. But however much Hannah begged, threatened, and bribed, Elsie would no more talk about 'C' than she would explain why she had run away in the first place.

So Hannah formed her own conclusion. Without meaningful evidence, she decided that 'C' was *Chaim*, Jane and Jonathon Strasfogel's oldest, expelled from school for smoking pot. Proof or no proof, it killed the friendship between the Rosenthals and the Strasfogels. Unpleasant looks were exchanged in synagogue. Seating plans at weddings were rearranged.

*

Unknown to the rest of the family, Elsie's first romantic adventure began just days after her grandfather had been lowered into the ground, when the full-length mirror in her wardrobe was still draped with black cloth, and the atmosphere of the house was thick with prayers and candlesmoke. He was a sixth former at a nearby college, a boy she'd noticed clattering around the park on his skateboard towards evening, sometimes with friends, mostly alone. They met when she was out walking the neighbour's dog Archie, a lazy dachshund that often dug his heels in and demanded carrying. The boy surprised her near the bandstand by asking if she had a lighter. When she said no, he offered a cigarette.

'But how will we get it lit?' she asked.

He smiled. After producing a Zippo, he flicked open the lid and brought the flame towards her mouth. 'How old are you anyway?' he said.

She went with seventeen. Her name was Emily. His was Carl. He offered his hand. She took it without hesitation. She said, 'Carl? Doesn't inspire much confidence.'

Ignoring this, Carl bent down to fuss over Archie, who rolled onto his back submissively.

Later, the two of them sat on a park bench, listening to the soft rumble of evening traffic. For a few minutes neither had spoken. Taking this as a sign, Carl was about to lean in, when Elsie stuffed a hand into her pocket. Rather than the expected breath mints, however, she produced a smooth grey orb, flattened on one side.

Elsie rolled the stone between her fingers, then tossed it into the air and caught it.

Carl blinked. Why were girls so weird? 'Go on, what's with the rock.'

'It was given to me on the day of a funeral. I was meant to place it beside my grandfather's grave.'

'Don't people normally put flowers on graves?'

'Only plebs,' Elsie said. According to Hannah, *plebs* is what goys called other goys when they considered them inferior. 'It's much better to place a stone.'

'And I'm guessing there's some super interesting reason you didn't?'

Elsie didn't mind Carl's scepticism. In fact, it played into the mood she was trying to create; he was her straight man.

'There shouldn't have been a headstone. My grandfather knew what he wanted – after he died, he was meant to be cremated.'

'So?'

'*So?* Sometimes I get the feeling that he's still here, that he can't move on.'

Elsie laughed inwardly. This was her first time playing the part, and the high camp delighted her.

'Do you want to hold it?' she said, proffering the stone. 'Careful though. It belongs with the dead.'

'Uh-uh,' Carl said. 'You keep it.'

Elsie held the stone to her chest, smiling. She drew nearer. 'I've got to hand it to you. You're one creepy chick.'

Their faces were so close now. He only had to extend his lips, and the first delicate kisses formed themselves. After a time, the kisses grew insistent.

For a few months, they made out in the dark of the cinema, lingered in parks, and (after lengthy negotiations) reached what he authoritatively informed her was third base. Carl taught her to skate (a bit) and let her borrow the 18-rated movies he had on VHS (*The Evil Dead*, *Rosemary's Baby*, *Carrie*). Elsie didn't care much for skating, but she did like the films. So many of them about young women, pushed beyond the reaches of normality. All those outsized emotions, internal forces big enough to topple cities.

Carl also taught her to roll her own joints, and how to shotgun a beer. Later, he encouraged her to snort her first line of fine white powder.

*

Zeide in my dreams with flaming eyes. Told me something important. Forgot what.

C wants to go to the cinema Saturday to see some comedy. Yawn.

Cannot believe Mum is having a go at me for how I behave at school. I'm becoming someone who isn't very nice, she says. And

*after what she put Zeide through! He used to dread her footsteps
on the stairs.*

Alongside more quotidian matters – accounts of how she
filled the days, who she saw when – Elsie's diaries chart the
progress of her spiritual curiosity. She read the old Hassidic
legends in an English translation of Martin Buber's lovingly
curated anthology. She delved into the forbidden books of the
Kabbalah. At just over five foot, she had to carry the folding
steps in from the garden shed to reach the top shelf where
such works as the Book of Raziel and the Zohar were kept,
and then replace the heavy steps while she was still alone and
unwatched. But to Elsie, who smoked her first cigarette at
eleven and would lose her virginity at fourteen, nothing was
so inviting as a locked door, the object lifted beyond reach.

Certain Kabbalistic ideas were recorded in her diary. For
instance, that God had created more worlds before this one
but, being displeased, destroyed them.

> *How similar were those other worlds? Did they have their
> Adam and their Eve? How long did they last? Did they have
> their Hitler? Their Elsie? How do we know God won't destroy
> this one?*

Her imagination was stimulated too by the notion that certain holy men had walked in Heaven while still alive, such
as Israel Baal Shem Tov, who departed from the corporeal
realm to consult the ancient dead, the prophets, and even
God Himself. With alcohol and weed now in her life, Elsie
found that the world, having hardened into concrete reality during the tail-end of childhood, had become malleable
again. Limits receded. Aside from Carl, she cultivated older

friends, and drank more heavily, more desperately than her peers. She experimented. She read crazy books. She reached extraordinary heights.

Not surprising, this being also the time of her first bereavement, she fixated on death. About what comes after, the Hebrew Bible, unlike its Christian counterpart, had little to tell her; even the old Patriarchs, even Abraham, Isaac, and Jacob, simply lived out their hundreds of years and then they died. Having survived their generation and finally given up their ghosts, they were packed into the ground and then heard of no more. Was there this and only this for thousands of years?

In the mystical works that she read in secret, she came upon other ideas. Rumours of the world beyond. Souls that refused to give up on all that was going on in the kingdom of the living. On a day in late October of her fifteenth year, she wrote down the following quotation from A. E. Waite, one of the foremost Gentile scholars of Kabbalah.

> *It is said that some souls go up as of their own free will and by their own high intent, to make a holocaust of themselves, amidst the rejoicing in the Supreme Light which shines forth from the Holy Kings.*

A long, slender question mark trailed down the margin, beside the quotation. A ring encased the word holocaust.

*

Although Carl had introduced Elsie to several adult pleasures, for which she was grateful, he soon grew wearisome. It didn't help that he was always stoned, and most of his stories chronicled some earlier time he'd been stoned, with moderately bad consequences. His only other topics of conversation were telling Elsie which bands to listen to, which bands *not* to listen to, and complaining about not getting more money from his rich asshole parents.

The relationship, though heady in its early days, should have died at the point Elsie knew everything Carl was going to say before he did. It survived in large part because Carl had one more thing to offer that Elsie wanted. A mobile phone.

At Lady Hilary's School for Girls, at the end of the 1990s, a personal phone was both a status symbol and a truly advanced piece of technology. The possibility of carrying your social life with you everywhere was the stuff of science fiction. Tapping out messages with your thumbs at whatever hour! Everyone wanted a phone, and almost nobody had one.

Eric couldn't understand. 'But if none of your friends have one, who are you going to call?'

'Dad, it's not a walkie-talkie. You can call any number you like.'

Though it pained him to say no to his daughter about anything, Eric held firm. 'You can ring up your friends on the landline.'

So when Carl told her that she could have his old phone, 'in a week or two, just when I've sorted out a sim card,' she delayed breaking up with him. 'One or two weeks' became a month, and she still hadn't done it.

'Patience, babe, patience,' he'd say, whenever she pressed him.

The last time they saw each other was shortly before Elsie disappeared. At dusk, she arrived at the bus stop on the corner, their usual place, and Carl wasn't there. Good.

Anticipation was the best part, nothing lived up. Her parents thought she was at Meredith's.

A bundle of tossed napkins swirled by her feet. Shivering, Elsie was beginning to regret tights rather than trousers. At least she looked good. She took out a stick of gum and began to chew. Cool air rushed into her mouth. Then she sat, drew up her knees and bundled herself. After a minute she stood, realising she looked like a child to anyone who passed by. So often her age was misunderstood. She had a woman's body, didn't she? Hers was a different world from the idiots at school. Even Meredith was only copying her, would be just as happy drinking hot chocolate and watching *Neighbours*. Those girls didn't read seriously, or think seriously, or do anything besides what they'd been told. One day they'd come to know what it was to be a human being, answerable to no one but God and your own conscience. She'd just got there first. Why should she have to wait until everyone else caught up?

Overhead, the light of a wandering plane crawled between stars.

Bristling with sudden excitement, Elsie stamped her feet and whooped at the moon. There was nothing she liked better than to be alone, outside, at night. The possibilities! An entire life had been rolled out in front of her. Men looked at her differently these days, even in her school uniform: little sideways glances as they passed her in the street, sometimes a full-blown leer. They made comments too, called out to her from the other side of the road. By her age, Juliet had eloped and then killed herself. How many of the patronising teachers who referred to her as a 'young lady' or 'little madam' knew that? Zeide understood. He'd told her things children don't get told, about the life of shadows, and about Ariel, that tragic little boy, murdered by the Germans. Even now that boy was wandering in search of his lost parents, Zeide said. But her grandfather was gone and there was no one left who took her seriously. Zeide was sealed in a wooden box under six feet of East Ham soil. He was walking in the fields of Heaven.

If she could have just ten more minutes with him! Even five minutes. He wouldn't even have to say anything. Just to be there in the same room, so she could watch his gruff smile breaking at the bottom of his stony face. The light in his eyes.

'Hello stranger.'

The voice came from behind – there was never time to grieve. There was the period of mourning, sure, but what was a week? Carl had come the other way for once, probably trying to catch her off-guard. He was wearing that leather jacket again, with the tear at the elbow. Last time she'd said something nice about it.

'What's this, the only jacket you've got?'

'I keep my good clothes for my other girlfriends.'

They hugged and he kissed the side of her face, just catching the corner of her mouth.

'Did you miss me?' he said. It had only been three days since the last time. Elsie shrugged. Carl bit his lip.

'This is for you.' He retrieved two cans from his jacket pocket and gave one to her. He snapped the lid of his can, and she snapped hers, and the beer frothed over and ran down her hand. When she brought the cold tin to her lips, her mouth filled with bitter fizziness. Why did boys pretend to like beer? They were obviously lying. The buzz only kicked in some way through the second can: the first was just legwork.

'Foster's is my favourite,' Carl said. 'King of beers, hands down.' He took a hefty gulp, then pulled a face. 'Do you like it?'

'I'm pretty sure Budweiser is the king of beers,' she said.

'Why do you have to be like that?'

'Like what?'

'Antagonising! You're always antagonising. You're never just chill.'

'If I was just chill, you'd hate it.'

He laughed. 'Yeah, maybe. Maybe.'

He slid his arm around her waist as they walked towards the park. For a minute, neither of them spoke. Carl's words had restored the discomfort of their first meeting, when, after the initial spark had drawn them together, they struggled to find anything to say.

'I've been thinking about something,' he said now. 'Are you in love with me yet? Don't laugh, man! You've seen movies. Man takes a girl around, gives her a good time, then like twenty minutes later she's fallen in love. Thirty minutes tops.'

'It's movies. Time is sped up.'

'I know, I know. But what I'm saying is, I probably could say it back to you. If I had a chance to think about it, you know, get myself ready. That's why I was asking.'

No one had said anything like this to her before. It was a shame Carl was so inescapably Carl. 'You wanted to know if you should start getting ready.'

'Zactly!'

At the foot of the road a pair of headlights appeared, two round yellow eyes. The car slowed, and for a tense moment Elsie feared it was someone she knew. But a sharp wolf-whistle followed by a roar of cruel laughter cancelled that idea. She felt Carl wilt beside her, and only when the car was speeding out of earshot did he call out, 'Fuckers!'

They had stopped walking, and Carl turned to face Elsie. 'It's 'cos you're so fit. I bet you get cars slowing down all the time.'

'Only when I'm next to some loser.'

'See! There you go again. More antagonising. More *animosity*. I was trying to say something nice.'

'Why are you talking like that?' Elise said. 'Did you buy a thesaurus?'

'No! I'm smart, man. I'm just as smart as you, actually. I don't know why you're always getting at me.'

Across the road, a fox leapt over the fence, and disappeared under a gateway to a private garden. Another car rolled by, slower this time, as though the driver was straining to read a street sign.

Elsie hadn't spoken for some minutes. Carl tried again. 'You want a fag? We've gone off all wrong. Let's start over. There's this thing I want us to discuss. For real now. I've got this idea.'

She accepted the cigarette and slapped away his attempt to light it. Was this boy really in love with her? It hadn't taken her long to conquer him.

'Go on,' she said.

Carl grinned. 'You'll need this,' he said, putting something into her free hand. It was a little tatty; the battery pack was secured in place with masking tape, and when she pressed the buttons, they clicked under her thumbs.

But then the small square of the screen glowed with life.

'You wanna keep it,' Carl said, 'you'll give me something in return. Fair's fair.'

Elsie asked what he wanted.

'Something you've been hanging onto.'

At last, Carl had said something that surprised her. 'You want my grandfather's stone? I can't, my dad threw it—'

'No, babe. Something else. Something only you can give.'

*

The day she disappeared, Elsie got in some time before morning registration at 8.30; in the register she was marked present, with no red dot for lateness. Fellow students and teachers confirmed that she attended her first four lessons. At mid-morning break Elsie told Meredith she felt ill and was going to the nurse's office. When she returned to her form room, she announced that the nurse had called her mother, who was going to collect her. This was a lie; Hannah received no call. And the nurse, embroiled in her own domestic crisis (her fiancé, it turned out, was already married), didn't get to work until past midday. The door to her office remained locked all morning, and in the afternoon, students clotted outside to find out if it was true you could hear sobs from within.

When break was finished and the rest of her form headed to the C-block for double French, Elsie went to the bathrooms in the long corridor, where she would hide for the next hour and a half. Inside her stall she changed out of her uniform and into a skirt and jacket that she took from her mother's wardrobe. Although Hannah Rosenthal was at that time in her forties and had given birth to three children, she kept a slim figure, and the clothes fitted happily on her adolescent daughter. At Lady Hilary's, sixth formers were given special privileges, which included the freedom to leave the school grounds during lunch break so long as they signed themselves out at the entrance lodge. Another privilege was to dress in skirt suits of their own choosing, rather than the drab uniform of the younger girls. Elsie only had to stride past the new security man, dressed not in the striped shirt and shapeless green blazer she'd walked in with, but in her mother's dark jacket. She could sign alongside someone else's name, and she'd be free to slip out into the sun-dappled streets.

Carl's parents had flown to Italy for a week leaving their son with money and car keys. Elsie now rehearsed the plan. He would meet her round the corner from school, then they'd drive to the coast and check in at The Union, have sparkling wine brought up to the room. At midnight, they'd rip off their clothes and run into the sea. Then: two whole days of leisure, dodging about like a wild young couple on the run from the law and their families. Belmondo and Seberg in *À bout de souffle*. There was no need, really, for Elsie to leave everyone in the dark – it would have been easy to come up with an alibi. But she wanted to make her parents suffer, just a little. They were so hard on her these days. And why bother disappearing if no one wonders where on Earth you are? The phrase appealed to her. Where – *on Earth* – she was.

Other girls came and went from adjacent stalls. She heard them peeing and flushing then chatting to one another across the blare of the hand-dryers about homework and boys and the teachers they did and didn't like, making plans for their evenings, laughing, giggling, whispering, looking forward to the auditions for that term's play, or to Saturday's netball practice. Those girls lingered for a moment to check their hair in the wide mirror over the sinks and smiled or frowned at their own reflections, and then walked back out into the cosy, humdrum life that was all around them. And none realised what was right in front of their faces, that they were prisoners by their own consent. Until lately, Elsie had lived as they did, appeared like the others. No more. Now she was making a clean break from the humdrum, she was leaving cosiness behind altogether. She'd been one girl when she walked through the school gates that day, and she would be another when she walked out.

None of her friends knew what she had in mind. Not even Meredith, who believed she was in on all Elsie's secrets. She would howl during her interview with the police, swearing blind she didn't know a thing. The two of them were planning to spend an afternoon together that coming weekend; Meredith's mother was going to drop them off at the ice-rink in Queensway at eleven thirty!

The rest of the morning swept by. Classes were taught, detentions handed out, quarrels started and made up. Shortly before one, the smooth progress of Elsie's breakout ran up against a snag. A text from Carl informed her that his parents' flight had been cancelled, and rather than wait for the next one, they'd decided to come straight home from Heathrow and fly out the following week. This way they got lucrative compensation. She texted straight back.

You're joking?

A minute later, a response came buzzing through.

no, babe. sorry. ill make it up.

meet u tonite usual place? 8?

No doubt the excuse was a cover-up; here was a failure of nerves, last-minute cowardice. Or worse, he'd got what he'd wanted, and was now done. She pictured his long, dog-like face, panting over her. What an idiot she'd been! Too late, she saw it plainly. Carl was an animal, always had been. And yet she'd let him enter. God had seen it all, from the first kisses to the final, shallow breath, and now she was stained. All that awful stickiness. She wanted to tear her own skin off, strip by strip. How could she just go home to her parents now?

A few stalls down, she could hear another girl sniffle and then loudly blow her nose.

At ten past one, the bells rang up and down the long corridor. Elsie waited for a few minutes to pass, allowing the rest of the school to busy itself with queueing for lunch, or to start up their breaktime clubs and societies. Then she left the toilets, walked with practised indifference round the back of the main-hall and past the bike sheds. At the entrance lodge, she picked an older girl's name at random, then smiled at the attendant and bit her lower lip. He wished her good afternoon and told her not to get into any trouble.

It was all caught on the school's CCTV. Roughly ten seconds of blizzardy footage were shown on the news the following evening. A figure, half-silhouetted in the weak light. She walks up to the lodge, pauses for a moment, and then moves on, disappearing off the left-hand side of the frame. A few moments after she walks off screen, a crow perched on the roof of the lodge takes wing.

Chapter Fifteen

THE GIRL WHO CAME BACK was not the same girl who went missing.

When the police dropped her to our door, Elsie was swamped in someone else's jumper, with its knitted sleeves coming unravelled at the ends. They said they'd found her on the Norfolk coast, hiking the coastal trail. Her face was cut in several places, her hair was sopping, and streaks of mud lined her neck. I had the strange sensation that she shouldn't be in here, that I was now looking at a wild creature, hauled into domesticity by strong-armed men.

'Darling,' I said, 'let's get you cleaned up.'

Cold, hungry, and obviously confused, she ignored me. She went straight up to her grandfather's old room and started opening cupboards. 'Who moved all my things around?' she said to no one. 'Who came up without asking?'

I ran her a bath which, at length, I persuaded her to take.

I'd asked Gideon to call his father, but he said that when he tried the number was busy. As I dialled Eric's chambers, it struck me how awful it was that he should still be living under the most painful of uncertainties. After a few rings, a female voice came through the phone. I was in luck. The receptionist informed me that Eric wasn't due in court for another hour and was around to take the call. Not having planned what I would say when I heard his voice, I was overcome with excitement and simply blurted the name: 'Elsie.'

From the other end of the line came a sharp intake of breath, then two flat monosyllables, 'She's dead.'

'No! Thank G-d, she's in the bath!'

There was then a silence that went on far too long. As I held the phone to my ear, the image of the Talmudic Sarah, killed by good news, flashed before me. I saw a white-haired woman, mad with grief, eyes rolled back in her skull, limbs spasming.

'My love? Are you there?'

The silence lasted a few more seconds before it was finally driven out by waves of laughter. Miraculous, self-generating laughter, the kind that might never run dry.

'What do we need? Beef! The prodigal daughter is returned, so we must ready the fatted calf, yes? And champagne! We shall have gallons of champagne! We shall have oceans of champagne!'

We lit many candles that night, and all three children were up past their bedtimes. Even Tovyah had a small glass of Laurent Perrier. It should have been one of the happiest evenings of our life. And yet it was as though a pall hung over us; the dining room was a sealed coffin. Around the table, we hardly spoke. Afterwards, as I cleared the plates, I saw that Elsie had spent a long time cutting up her meat into smaller and smaller pieces, then left most of it untasted.

*

Elsie's reabsorption into family life was not easy. Gideon, always competitive, was enraged to see his sister unpunished. He began staying out, sometimes past midnight, and soon made a daily habit of asking for money. 'For what?' his mother would ask. 'For *stuff*!' Tovyah, never the most robust child, was often found sulking about the house, teary-eyed. And as for Elsie herself, she was distant. 'She had come back, yes,' her mother wrote, 'but not fully. Some part of her was still out there, still wandering the coastline.' Eric took a couple of weeks off to put in time with the family. But as he failed to reach his daughter, he grew bad-tempered, hissing at his sons on the smallest provocation (a muddy shoeprint on the landing, a Sabbath candle extinguished by mistake). His presence dampened the mood of the house, and Hannah was not sorry when he decided to go back to the office early.

Though it was obvious *something* was wrong with the girl, the idea that Elsie had an eating disorder only came up when it was suggested by Ms Varden. The phone call was supposed to be about Elsie's attitude to learning (she often sat in class with her head slumped on her desk), but here they were, talking about anorexia.

'Based on what?' Hannah asked.

'Her figure.'

Though she couldn't deny how skinny the girl was, Hannah refused to accept the inference. 'Look at her classmates, they're all like that. Twigs and string!' She thought about the night Elsie returned. How, after all that manic roving, she had diced up her beef and left it to be thrown out cold in the morning.

One time. Anyone can be off their food one time.

Soon enough, Hannah's certainty fractured. One school day, she took a break from the piece she was drafting about dog-whistle anti-Semitism to clean out her daughter's room. Elsie had been such a tidy kid growing up, a girl who folded her own laundry, and had to have everything, all her things, just so. Suddenly, she was a slob. The room put Hannah in mind of a busy street after winds have played havoc with the bins. Elsie no longer made her bed, left the duvet bunched in the middle. Lidless pens on the floor, used underwear too.

Eric, working from home that day, was less disturbed by the state of Elsie's room. When Hannah called him in to take a look, he shrugged. 'You remember the one about the boy who falls in the river?' he asked.

'Remind me.'

'Mother cries out, "God, God, have mercy on my boy, he can't swim!" And sure enough, the boy washes up on the bank. Wet-through, spluttering, a little frightened, but alive. The mother addresses God once more. "What happened to his hat?"'

'Yes, very good.'

She didn't laugh.

'Hannah, you see what I'm saying. It's possible to look a gift horse in the mouth.'

'I got that.'

After shrugging again, Eric returned to his books.

How could he be so blasé? Something was happening to their daughter. It had begun in the summer, around the time of Yosef's death, and it wasn't over, even now. Elsie's room had filled with words: books everywhere, and countless pages of her own writing. There were at least three languages on display: English, Hebrew, and Latin. Was it all schoolwork? The English was mostly poems and fantasies. As she gathered pages together, Hannah skimmed one of the stories, something about a house with a hidden room, a chamber no one knew was there. A little spooky, but mercifully free of domestic violence and sexual assault. When she moved the bed to hoover, she found discarded scraps. Bits of sweetcorn, dried up pasta shells, breadcrumbs, a few grains of hardened rice, and numerous shrivelled peas all heaped in a dusty nook. So then. Varden wasn't imagining things.

She confronted Elsie the moment she got in from school. But rather than sheepish or apologetic, her daughter was indignant.

'What were you doing in my room?'

'If you don't fulfil your responsibilities, there are consequences. You have to keep your room clean. And more important than your bedroom your body. You *have* to eat properly, darling, that's not optional.'

'I eat all the time. Literally every day. Three times every day we sit down at a table and we eat.'

'Darling, I found your little hiding place, OK, so no more lies.'

'You shouldn't sneak, Channah.'

The words did not sound like Elsie's. Even the way she held herself was somehow off.

After hearing about the discarded food, Eric grounded his daughter. She was already on a tight leash; her whereabouts had to be accounted for at all times. Hannah met her after school, and each day they rode the Tube home together. And now, for a week, she would not make plans with friends with or without the supervision of other parents. She would come home straight from school, she would do her homework on the kitchen table, under *his* eyes if necessary, they would have dinner together – and for God's sake, she would eat – then she'd go up to her room.

'I eat fine. You wanna know what hunger is, try living on one portion of bread a day, sometimes two if you can steal.'

Eric felt the breath leave his body. 'What kind of sick joke is that?'

'Who's joking, Eric?'

Until that moment, Elsie had always called him Dad, sometimes Daddy. Tovyah, following Gideon, had lately abandoned the habit, but not Elsie. He had prayed to God on this very subject. Indulge a father. Whatever the boys do, let her call me 'Dad' as long as I live. *Baruch Hashem*.

'That's two weeks! Two weeks you see no one, you do nothing.'

'Whatever. But if you're in the business of grounding people, maybe you should talk to Mr Pink Triangle.'

She was referring to an incident that had everyone worked up. The week before, Alan Carmichael, father of Elsie's friend Meredith, called wanting to speak to Eric. He said Gideon had been at theirs on the pretext of working on his English coursework with Phil, Meredith's older brother.

'Judy came up the stairs with a tray full of snacks, and when she went in, nobody was studying.'

Eric knew his oldest son better than to be shocked by this. 'I presume they were playing violent computer games. Yes? We don't have them at home, so when he's over at his friend's . . . They call them beat-em-ups, I believe. Or was it the shoot-em-ups?'

Alan paused. 'I think you should have a word with Gideon when he gets back. I'm sure he's a little embarrassed, and he might like to hear that his parents will love him regardless.'

Eric had sufficient imagination to fill in the blanks. Still, he asked, 'What should I talk to my son about?'

There was a soft groan as Alan fumbled for the right words. 'I mean his sexuality. You knew, right? With Phil, we clocked it years ago. Probably before he did.'

'I don't think I've met Philip,' Eric said. 'My work keeps me away a lot.'

There was a pause.

'Don't tell me you didn't know?'

Eric had no idea what he was going to say to his son. The possibility that Gideon – or any of his children – might be gay, had never occurred to him. They weren't that type of family. When Gideon arrived home, Eric led him to the garden for a glass of Talisker.

'You'll never believe what Alan Carmichael told me on the phone just now.'

'It's not true,' Gideon said at once.

A tree swayed in the wind. Somewhere a cat yowled.

'But I didn't tell you what he said yet.'

'I know what you're talking about. No one needs this. Don't be weird, Eric.'

And that was it, conversation closed. Gideon remained ungrounded, and neither of them ever mentioned it again. 'Don't Ask, Don't Tell' became unofficial policy within the Rosenthal household, just as the US military was having second thoughts. That is, until Elsie provocatively suggested that Gideon should be grounded, for the crime of making out with a member of his own sex.

*

I WAS NOW IN THE habit of inspecting her living quarters daily. I got to know how the sun moved through the room: wide-angled in the morning, narrowly intense by late afternoon. One day I opened the door and the bed was made; the clothes sat folded in neat bundles inside the wardrobe. Progress! The sense of dread that had fluttered behind curtains was dispelled. Then, emptying out her drawers,

I found chickpeas rolling around at the back. My heart thumped. I held one to the light, pinched between thumb and forefinger. This tiny ball of protein and carbohydrate was an index of what was taking place in my daughter's soul. But what was it telling me?

Again she brought it up with Elsie, who insisted that it wasn't what it looked like. From somewhere came the intuition that her daughter wasn't lying. You don't get through sixteen years of motherhood, you don't get to the bottom of a thousand petty scraps between warring siblings, without developing an internal polygraph.

'This isn't about your weight?'

'No.'

'Then what's going on?'

She wouldn't say. It was the same with her disappearance. You only had to ask the question and the shutters slammed down; she told no one why or where she had gone. Other than to repeat, with a coquettish half-smile, she'd been looking for God.

'But sweetheart, Hashem is everywhere,' her father had said, in the days when he still had patience. 'You know that.'

'Oh, yes, I know that *now*.'

The fortnight of being grounded was extended by another week. Eric took to watching his daughter at mealtimes. One night she ate half her dinner and said she was full.

'Uh-uh,' Eric said. 'You'll be excused when you finish.'

Elsie dipped her spoon into her bowl, filled it, tipped half the broth away, then slowly brought the spoon to her mouth. After she swallowed, she bared her teeth. 'That's it,' Eric said. 'Thank you.' She carried on, moving with maximum possible slowness. Between each mouthful, she cast resentful looks, first at her father, then her mother. Both boys pretended not to watch. When she was done, she pushed the empty bowl to the centre of the table and let out a low growl, a sound like a hurt dog. She stood. In a moment, she fell forwards, as though kicked in the back, her palms smacked against the dinner table, her head went down, and she was overtaken by violent, full-throated heaves, disgorging all that she'd been forced to swallow, splattering across the table.

Afterwards she looked up. 'Happy?'

She scurried off upstairs, wiping her mouth with the back of her hand.

Once the boys had also been sent upstairs, Hannah told her husband that she never wanted him to do that again. 'Long as she's eating *something*, she won't starve.'

'This isn't normal,' Eric said. 'I don't know who she is any more.'

It was hot in the living room and, leaning from the sofa, Hannah twisted shut the valve on the radiator, until the faint hiss died.

'There are cases,' Eric went on. 'People have accidents and afterwards they're not the same people. Maybe there's no physical damage to the brain, nothing that comes up on a scan, but something slips out of place and no one knows how to put it back. A lifelong vegetarian takes up hunting, the shyest boy in class becomes the bully.'

Hannah glared. 'But there wasn't any accident.'

There was an obvious caveat that went unspoken: no accident *they knew of*. Four whole days of Elsie's life were unaccounted for. Hannah's mind filled with possibilities, all the dreadful things that might have happened to her daughter. There were sick people in this world. You only had to turn on the news and there they were.

'Come here, my love,' Eric said, opening his arms to her.

Shrugging off her husband's embrace, Hannah went out for a walk. When Eric spoke to God, he liked to be in his study, crowded by holy books. But then Eric had excellent Hebrew and could read the debates of ancient rabbis as easily as the morning paper. When Hannah spoke to God, she went outside. She had to be away from everyone, far from the domestic clutter, and pacing beneath an open sky.

Not for the first time, she asked Him what was going on with Elsie. What was she supposed to do?

Then she waited, listening to silence. That was how God spoke. His voice was a colossal, unarguable silence. And in His silence, God told Hannah strange truths about her daughter. Truths that from any other mouth, she wouldn't have believed.

When she searched Elsie's room the following morning, she found nothing, just as expected. She then went upstairs to Zeide's old dwelling. By tacit agreement, no one had used the attic for anything since Yosef's death. But as soon as she opened the door, she knew Elsie had been here. It had that lived-in smell. She found half an apple on the bookcase, something mushed into the carpet that might have once been tuna-mayo. Under the bed was an empty vodka bottle and, on the chair in the corner, a stack of Hebrew texts. They were not texts Hannah immediately recognised.

When they next spoke, Hannah asked Elsie to show her arms. 'Come on, roll up your sleeves.'

'Channah, no.'

'Can you please roll up your sleeves? Two seconds. I just want to see something.'

'There are people out there who think they decide who is human and who is not human. My arms are my arms.'

Elsie's voice was changed utterly. It was suddenly deeper, more rasping, and strangely accented.

For a moment, they just looked at each other. Then Hannah made a sudden grab for her daughter's arm. She held her at the elbow. Elsie, scratching at her mother's face with her free hand, tried to liberate herself.

'Get off you bitch!'

Hannah clung on. She pushed up her daughter's sleeve. It was exactly as God had told her. There, all along the back of Elsie's arm, were raised horizontal lines. The lines at the top were older, already half buried in the skin, but towards the wrist, the gashes were still pink.

And if she had understood Him correctly about this . . .

'You don't understand anything,' Elsie said. 'It helps focus my mind.'

'On what? What the hell do you need to focus on so much that you'd mutilate yourself?'

'On God.'

There was no tone of mockery in her daughter's voice.

'Is that what the not eating is about too?' Hannah said. 'A fast?'

'I already told you, the food is not for me.'

'Then who? I'm sick of these riddles.'

Elsie shook her head.

'Darling, please. Let me help you.'

'Help? You think you can help?'

'Give me a chance. Open up.'

'Do you never feel trapped in your own body? That your ribcage is a set of iron bars, tighter than any prison? That your soul is not supposed to be closed up in this tiny cage of flesh and bone? That your brain, you *mind*, is banging itself bloody against your skull—'

'All right, enough.'

Elsie's shoulders were hunched over; she had the posture of an old man. Hannah remembered being taught, as a child, that you could look *at* someone, or you could look *through* them, but looking through them was considered rude. In the same way, she knew now that she could either speak to Elsie, or she could try speaking through her.

She aimed her voice at whatever was inside her daughter. 'What do you want?' she said.

Elsie closed her eyes. 'I want out.'

'Out?'

'You uncovered me, Channah. Now set me free.'

'And how do I do that?'

Elsie's misty eyes opened and fixed on her mother. 'You know how.'

*

The old tales warn of the dangers of overreaching. In the grip of despair, Hannah read that a disciple of the Baal Shem Tov once entreated his master to summon an angel down to bring the two men closer to God. Unable to put off his disciple, the Rabbi Israel attempted the conjuring against his better judgement. But something went wrong. No Angel of Light illuminated the path to God. Instead, the two men had called forth the Angel of Death. The master understood. They had displeased Heaven and were now being punished for their hubris. Frightened and remorseful, he instructed his disciple to sit up with him through the night. Only by incessant prayer could they hold off Death's clutches. And so, they kept their vigil through the dark hours, and no harm came to them. Then, just as dawn approached, the disciple let his mind slip and collapsed in a swoon. The master wept over the body of his departed friend, whose heart inside his chest had burnt to a crisp.

*

When God told Hannah that her daughter was summoning the spirits of the dead, it resonated. As far back as last summer, she had seen things out of the corner of her eye, movements in the shadows. The unmoored soul, still earthbound, was a grotesque thought, yes, but not ridiculous. Who could say what such a thing would look like? She knew that the house was now in some sense ruled by Yosef's shade. Look how everybody was acting. She and Eric hadn't made love in months. The children had abandoned their play. Even outsiders picked up on something; people didn't want to visit the house any more, invitations were rejected or ignored. And everything – Elsie's disappearance, Gideon's confusion, Tovyah's misery – everything stemmed back to her father-in-law's death.

At first, she did not tell her husband what she'd discovered. She told no one. Instead, she took notes, wrote down everything that happened, just as she'd seen it, so she wouldn't later question her own sanity.

But after she found the mystical texts in Yosef's old room, after she'd seen those awful marks on Elsie's arm, after she'd heard *that voice* coming out of Elsie's mouth, she had no choice. If Eric thought she was crazy, so be it.

They talked in the conservatory, after dark, while the children were asleep. Hannah spoke quickly, trying to get it all out before she had second thoughts. Then she waited for Eric to respond.

For a while, his mouth remained closed. He cleared his throat. Then, at last: 'I wonder if we should move.'

'Excuse me?'

'You're right about the atmosphere around here, and to be honest, I've been thinking about upping sticks for a while. With my father gone, who needs such a big place? The five of us rattle in this old house.'

'Did you hear a single word I said?'

Eric paused again. 'Hannah, my love, the Zohar, the Book of Raziel, that's not kid's stuff, sure. And that's a conversation to be had.'

'But?'

'But raising the dead? I don't think I can go with you on this.'

This was the response Hannah had expected. Even so, it smarted. 'If you'd been there. If you'd heard that voice . . .'

'If. In this life, we might all be in the same theatre, but we get different seats.'

'Oh fuck off with the rabbinical shit.'

'Darling, please—'

Sometimes, Hannah wondered how strong Eric's faith was. The unseen world was as real to her as the skin on her hands. Yosef had been the same way. Up in that attic, she could see it all play out in the drift of his eyes, the wonder and terror of existence. Elsie too, she'd seen things. But Eric, for all his learning, was a not a man with wonder in his eyes.

The following week, Hannah was asked to attend yet another meeting with Ms Varden. Both the Head of English, and the Vice Principal were also in attendance. The usual classroom was being used for some after-school club, apparently, and this time they were squashed into a little office that branched off from the reception room.

There's an idea that relationships are built with familiarity. But every time Hannah met with Elsie's English teacher, she came away liking her even less than before. On the most recent occasion, Ms Varden had informed her she'd been reading up on her Bible stories. In particular, she'd read the tale of Jephthah's daughter with great interest, knowing that the story had captivated Elsie so. (Hannah had to correct her: there is no tale of Jephthah's daughter. The girl isn't even named! The story is about *him*.) Still, Ms Varden wanted to know what it might reveal about Elsie that she was drawn to this narrative?

The meeting had proceeded frostily.

Now, a few weeks later, the Vice Principal asked if Elsie was 'acting up' at home. Hannah asked what acting up meant.

'Could be a lot of different things. Disobedience, rudeness, bad temper, low moods, physical aggression . . .'

Hannah said she hadn't noticed anything.

The teachers rehashed the old material. Elsie was showing extreme levels of defiance in all her classes now. She might do her homework (with Eric's breath on her neck, she had no choice) but in school, she refused her work. She was often late for lessons, and sometimes acted as though under the influence of alcohol.

'All this, we know,' Hannah said. 'Why today's meeting? What's new?'

Ms Varden took it upon herself to answer. 'One of her classmates, a friend of Elsie's—'

'So she does still have friends.'

'One or two. The friend told me that Elsie has been talking about bringing a new human being into the world. Several of our girls are very upset.'

'Human *creature*,' said the Vice Principal. 'I think the phrase was a human creature. Building a new human creature from nothing.'

The three teachers nodded, significantly.

'What are you getting at?' Hannah said.

Ms Varden shifted in her chair. 'Do you think Elsie could be . . . sexually active?'

'I beg your pardon?'

'Mrs Rosenthal, please remain calm.'

'What gives you the right to make such accusations? She's a *child*!'

'I'm not accusing *her* of anything. We're only trying to be supportive. She might have done tests. If she were pregnant, I can only imagine how terrifying that would be for her. And it might explain a few things.'

'It explains nothing,' Hannah said, finally. She would not sit and listen to these women call her daughter a harlot. They knew nothing. Just as Eric knew nothing. She was in this thing alone.

*

THE GOLEM MYTH ORIGINATED IN Kabbalistic thinking, particularly in the ideas found in *Sepher Yetzirah*, or the Book of Formation. This short, urtext of Jewish mysticism gives an account of the world's creation, more technical than the one in Genesis. In this account, God built the world not from matter, but from mere letters and numerals.

Ten are the numbers, as are the Sephiroth, and twenty-two the letters, these are the Foundation of all things.

Intrepid scholars reasoned that if Hebrew was the raw material from which God made everything else, then the language must still contain, concealed within, the power of creation. Here is the testimony of a fifteenth-century tzaddik who discovered his own light source: 'I had put out the candle, but still light illumined the room, sufficient that I could continue my reading, though there was no source from which this light might issue forth. I looked down at my own navel and saw that I was myself the source from which the light did issue forth.' In time, students of the Kabbalah went further. Surely, the right combination of letters could create not just a magic light source, but a living creature. With enough study and dedication, the Kabbalist might even bring forth a motherless human being.

Now, thanks to her forbidden reading, Elsie had become interested in these ideas. One night I found her crashing about in the attic room. I told her to go to bed, but she insisted she had something to show me. When I looked into her eyes, her swollen pupils eclipsed her blue irises. 'Look!' she said. 'Look!' To humour her, I glanced round the room, and saw nothing.

'You really don't see him?'

'See who, sweetheart?'

'You find a little boy, all on his own, you want to tell him everything will be OK. Isn't that normal?'

'It's OK,' I said. 'He'll find his way.'

She wanted to sleep in her grandfather's room that night. Against my better judgement, I let her.

The only person Hannah felt she could discuss things with was Grossman, a strong-hearted man who took things as they came. She wanted him to talk to Elsie, to make her realise the dangers of the path she was on. The rabbi, who long ago taught Hannah to live in harmony with God's laws, had been a looming presence for her children all their lives. If anyone could get through to Elsie, it was him.

Fortunately, an opportunity presented itself with the invite to Noah Morris's bris.

A year earlier, Sam (Elsie's former Hebrew teacher) had finally given up on the crush that had ruined his twenties, disavowing his love for Ida from the kosher butchers in order to marry an American woman named Edith, his second cousin on his mother's side, who wanted to move to the UK. 'Marry in the family,' Eric had said, 'and you don't have to pay the broker.'

'Marry in the family,' Gideon warned his little brother, 'and the kids come out with extra fingers.'

And just last week, Sam Morris, unbearably *frum*, was pleased to announce the birth of his first son and to invite everyone to the circumcision. It was at this event that Elsie would talk to Grossman. He would reach into her heart and pull out what was rotten.

When the appointed morning came, the sky was overcast, with some hope of sunshine later on. After a rushed breakfast, the boys shuffled into their places in the back of the car, and Eric fiddled with wrapping paper, Sellotape, and a Babygro in the driver's seat. Elsie had not come downstairs. Hannah came out of the house alone and told Eric to wait in the car while she went to fetch their daughter. Upstairs, she asked Elsie what this was about.

'It's not about anything. I'm just not going.'

The girl wasn't even dressed, was still wearing her loose nightgown.

'Elsie, you're coming to the bris. This is not a choice here. When you're eighteen, you can leave home if you like—'

'Don't worry, I will.'

'—you can leave home and you can make your own rules. You never have to see me or your father again if you don't want to. That's your decision. Until then, you do what we say. That's the deal. I pay for your things, I cook your meals, I put you through school, and on a day like this, you do as I say. When you're my age and you've got kids of your own, I think you'll see I was pretty fair. Elsie? You're not moving.'

'Amends must be made,' she said.

Hannah had no idea what this meant. 'I'm counting down from ten. Nine. Eight.'

'Look, punish me if you like, do your thing. I don't need to go and see some kid's dick get cut off.'

'That's a disgusting thing to say. You should be ashamed.'

'Why? I didn't cut anybody's dick off.'

Hannah did not report this conversation to her husband. When Tovyah's unbroken voice piped up from the back of the car, asking where his sister was, Hannah just said she wasn't coming. Why not? 'She isn't well.'

As quietly as he could, Eric asked Hannah if she was sure about leaving Elsie on her own for the morning.

'We can't keep her under lock and key forever,' Hannah said.

By the time they got home, there was a burning smell all through the house. Hannah rushed inside. The French windows that opened onto the back garden were exposed. While they were out, Elsie had ripped the curtains from the rail, soaked them in brandy, dragged them onto the patio, and set them alight.

Elsie was in Zeide's old room when Hannah found her. 'Now everyone can see in,' she said. 'Isn't that what you wanted?'

*

The final proof Hannah needed that her daughter was practising black magic came in December, just before the children had broken up for the holidays.

ELSIE HAD ALWAYS LOVED ANIMALS. A trip to London zoo
could only end after bribing her to leave, and with promises
to return the following week. No sooner had she learned
to talk than she begged for pets. She wanted all sorts: dogs,
cats, rabbits, chickens, goldfish. Once, she presented us
with an advert for tortoises. Although we allowed her to walk
the neighbours' dog, this was as far as I would go. I am not
an animal person. 'You look into a cat's eyes,' I explained,
'and you can't see what it's thinking.' To which Elsie, aged
eleven, replied, 'When you look into *my* eyes, do you know
what *I'm* thinking?'

Back then, the truthful answer would have been 'yes'.

Now, she seemed to be keeping some wild creature in her
room, probably a mouse; something was consuming the little scraps of food she secreted in nooks and crannies. But
search as I would, I could never find it.

Sometimes, at dusk, I thought I could hear it scratching
at the walls.

On the second or third night of Chanukah that year, we
sat at dinner, blundering through a disastrous evening.
Yosef's old menorah stood in the middle of the table,
shedding light that bordered on the miraculous. Tipped
with gold, the candelabrum once belonged to his grandparents, and was stolen by Germans during the war, only
to be repossessed by its rightful owner in the early fifties.
Precisely how this happened, none of us knew. But rather
than discussing the Maccabee rebellion and wondering at
the vicissitudes of history, how the city of Jerusalem had

itself passed in and out of Jewish hands so many times over the centuries, my children were squabbling. Gideon especially was in a foul mood. When Tovyah asked him timidly enough to pass the gravy, he snapped, 'Get it yourself.'

'Gidi, Gidi, this is a holy night,' Eric said. After rebuking his son, he asked him how everything was going with school.

'The same old boring crap.'

My husband was unfazed. 'Tell me about the boring crap, then. You'd be amazed how interested I can get.'

'Today we done English, so that was—'

'Today we *had* English.'

'—some crappy poems about like, finding your identity or whatever. And then we done history, so—'

'Had history! Is it so hard to say we *had* history?'

'OK, we *had* history. So Nazis, Nazis, Nazis, Nazis. Just like being at home.'

My son's face was half in shadow as he spoke. What I could see of his expression, I did not like. Though G-d knows he had his faults, he was not ordinarily a cruel boy.

'That's not a nice thing to say to your father.'

'Why does everyone around here think I'm stupid? That's *why* I said it.'

'Gideon! What's got into you?'

He glanced at Elsie. 'Ask her.' Then he stormed from the room.

Elsie said, 'I have literally no idea what that means.'

One family member down, we ate in silence. Until Eric said, 'Would anyone like to hear the story of this menorah?'

'We know, dear. Zeide brought it over from Poland.'

'Well, yes, that's one version,' Eric said. He waited a moment, milking the pause. 'But did you never think it was strange he should get it back? Of all the Judaica plundered from Europe in those dark years . . . I mean, sure, we've all heard about the claims, the lawsuits, but how would a young guy like Zeide, with no money, no education, no papers, how would he go about it?'

Elsie was stroking the base of the menorah with her forefinger. 'It's a fake?' she said.

'No, darling. Your father is amusing himself.'

'Just hypothetically,' Eric went on, 'run it through. Zeide wanted one thing that belonged to his family, just one thing from the old days that he could show off on the table each year. So he finds a nice piece in a junk shop that looks about the right age and he tells everyone a story.'

'You have no evidence for that,' I said. 'It's total speculation.'

'You're right. No more evidence than you have for its authenticity. What are the known facts? There is a nine-pronged candelabra in our house that used to belong to my father. Possibly an antique, possibly not. Whatever you believe about it beyond that is a matter of faith.'

'Zeide never lied,' Elsie said.

'Exactly,' Eric replied. 'We don't know anything for certain. So isn't it better to believe what seems good and true than to run to wild conclusions?'

I knew my husband was baiting me. I refused to rise to it and began collecting dishes.

Later that evening, I went up to Gideon's room, where he was swinging his fists at the small punching bag that hung beside his bed.

'What happened tonight?'

Without turning to face me, without even lowering his guard, he said, 'It's Phil. He doesn't want to . . . be my friend any more.'

Taking a step towards my son, I massaged his knotted shoulder blades. No wonder he was miserable; he was sixteen years old and had suffered a falling out. Kids at that age are so dramatic, they think every friendship is meant to last until death, and so every quarrel is a catastrophe. Still, though I knew that his feelings were a touch ridiculous, for now he was hurting. Together we breathed slowly. Finally, he relaxed his muscles, and lowered his fists.

'Why do I have to have a psycho for a sister?'

'Darling, don't call her that.'

'It's what she is! Even Tovyah's probably figured it out by now. Why do we tiptoe around everything?'

'Lower your voice.'

'Who turned Phil against me, huh? That scheming little bitch, Meredith!'

'Language, Gideon. I know you're upset, but—'

'You're bloody right I'm upset.' He delivered a right hook to the bag. 'Wanna know why the brat's holding a grudge? She's terrified of Elsie. According to Meredith, she's got them all convinced she can control them with her Jew magic. And who gets fucked over?'

'Meredith said that? About Jew magic.'

'I don't blame them, to be honest. She's a creepy kid. What other girl her age spends her whole time tripping balls in graveyards?'

'Gideon, if Elsie's own friends are using anti-Semitic taunts, then that's something we need to address. I promise—'

'Mother! For G-d's sake, forget anti-Semitism for two seconds and listen to me. There are other things in the world that need our attention besides people hating Jews. Elsie gets high, like, all the time.'

'What are you talking about?'

'You haven't found any of her little baggies? Why don't we go to Zeide's room, right now. I'll show you her stash.'

'Gideon, you're scaring me.'

'Good! Your daughter is bonkers, your family is a mess. Right now, being scared is the correct response. Being scared makes sense. Come with me. Let's go right now.'

Of my three children, Gideon is the most sanguine, and to see him in this mood was unprecedented. At the words 'Jew magic', I was put in mind of Israel Baal Shem Tov's errant disciple, overtaken by death in the vigour of his youth, his heart burnt up inside his own chest. What was now happening to my daughter? I pictured Elsie with the works of the Kabbalah spread on her desk, vodka sloshing through her blood. Perhaps something harder.

Upstairs, Gideon barged the door. Elsie, who was bent over on the daybed, leapt to her feet.

'Get out!' she screamed. 'Get out now!'

It was too late. On the bed next to her was a small creature, no bigger than a badger, hairless, with sad, grey flesh. It looked a sickly thing, a runt, something that was born dying. Frightened by our intrusion, it scuttled off and was out the window, but not before I'd seen the teeth. The green eyes, and those little teeth.

'Ariel!' Elsie cried, running to the window. A low howl sounded from the street. She leaned out, cried again, then turned to look at me. 'What have you done?'

It was then I noticed the state she was in. Her shirt was unbuttoned, and she wore no bra. Once again, Elsie screamed for everyone to get out. Nobody moved.

Those little teeth were squared off, just like a tiny human being.

PART THREE
FERVOUR

Chapter Sixteen

Everyone in college was talking about Hannah's book. Know-it-alls criticised her literary style, calling it dated, cold, even heartless, while moralists decried the callous use of her own family as subject matter. Certain Jewish kids, (the quietly observant, the ones who practised a sort of reverential agnosticism), feared she was bringing the religion into disrepute. No one – Gentile or Jew – was indifferent. On every corridor, you heard snippets of conversation.

'They're totally gonna make a film of it.'

'Chronically underfund mental health services, now here we are.'

'Like *The Exorcist*, but Jewish.'

'If you read it, you're only feeding the machine.'

'You're implicated.'

'Do you know what the advance was? I heard six figures.'

'Half a million, easy.'

'Whatever. *I'm* going to read it.'

The University Wiccan Society denounced the book as culturally insensitive, making plans to stand outside Blackwell's and distribute leaflets the day of release. A friend of Jan's agreed to review the book for *Cherwell*, which ensured there would be at least one advance copy doing the rounds in college. Selfishly, I anticipated the publication of Hannah's latest as keenly as anyone. When you drive past an upturned car, you don't look away. Especially when you know the passengers.

For Tovyah, publication day was a source of genuine dread.

I knocked for him on the first morning of the new term, soon as I'd unpacked. We hadn't spoken over the break and I was, for obvious reasons, apprehensive. The door eased open, and every version of the conversation I'd drafted in my head now evaporated.

Tovyah stared at me through the crack. 'Oh, it's you.'

His eyes were a little red and his hair shone with grease.

'I see they've cleaned up the door,' I said.

It was an imperfect job. The two upper panels were darker than the rest. It seemed as though after sanding down the vandal's work and applying wood filler, the repairman had gone to work with the wrong shade of paint. By the time he realised the error, he decided to keep going rather than start over. And so, even with the graffiti gone, the door stood out from those either side, as if marked.

Tovyah was not impressed. 'They should have ripped it off its hinges and used it for firewood.'

'Aren't you going to invite me in?' I said.

'As you like.'

Although he offered me a cup of tea, he didn't seem over-joyed to see me. He poured old dregs down his sink, hastily rinsed two mugs, and flicked on the kettle. The smell of burnt toast filled the room, and I got the impression he hadn't gone out, other than for essentials, in weeks.

'So they let you stay in the end?'

Tovyah nodded. College was 'very understanding' about his situation (he said it with air quotes), and had allowed him to keep his room for a fraction of termly rent.

I asked if he was talking to his family at all.

'Only Elsie. Any lingering fondness I once had for my parents is now truly dead.'

'And your brother?'

'He's on the other side of the world.'

I'd often wondered how this third Rosenthal sibling compared to the two I'd met. Tovyah insisted that Gideon was 'dull witted', and a 'sanctimonious shit'. Still, the fact that he got on with those most unusual of parents and had migrated across continents made me want to meet him.

I asked how Elsie was.

Tovyah folded his arms. 'How do you think? My mother is a butcher. She slits the throat, hoists from the legs, and drains to the last drop.'

The kettle steamed. Tovyah placed two mugs on top of his fridge and poured in boiling water, spilling some under his trembling grip.

'You never answered my texts,' I said.

'What?'

'Over the break. You've been ignoring me.'

'I've had a lot on my mind. I'd have thought that was obvious.'

Having added milk and sugar, Tovyah handed me a mug. I sipped too early and burnt the roof of my mouth. What would happen if I touched him now? If I put a hand on his chest, for instance.

'Did they find the vandal?' I asked. 'People seem pretty worked up about the whole thing.'

There were posters in the entrance lodge, asking witnesses to come forward, and there'd been a mass email dumped in our inboxes.

'You think they're taking it seriously? Wake up. A whole month later, and who's been punished?'

Over the holidays, there'd been much speculation about the culprit. Few people actually saw the graffiti before it was painted over, which explains why many seemed to think the hooked cross had stood all on its own, the signature of a neo-Nazi. Jan and a few other self-identified members of the anti-Zionist left fell under suspicion, as did Tovyah himself. An attention-seeking stunt, people said. To make everyone feel sorry for him.

'Even you must see it now,' he said. 'The one thing my mother is dead right about.'

'What is?'

Rather than answer the question, he told a story.

When Gideon finished his military service, he did what a lot of Israelis do. He went backpacking. Finally, a little freedom! He went right through Asia, then swung north and headed to Europe. Did a lot of couch surfing, a lot of staying in hostels. Gideon's a moron – he'll tell you he drank at a hundred bars in a hundred nights – but fair enough, he can take care of himself. He travelled everywhere on his UK passport. And everywhere he introduced himself as British. Not, Israeli, not even English, but *British*.

Why? People hate Brits abroad, it's true. But people fucking despise Israelis.

Anyway, the trip's going well. He's having the time of his life, whatever. And on his way back to Tel Aviv, he stops in Istanbul, where he's put up by these middle-aged folks. Very sweet couple, they make him breakfast, cook him dinner, give him lifts. In short, the perfect hosts. Slightly odd dynamic between them, though. Because the man's a constant stream of opinions, but his wife's a mouse. And the man says to Gideon, very proud, she only speaks when she has something important to say. When that woman opens her mouth, listen.

The last night of Gideon's stay, some friends of the couple come over. Everyone's having coffee and chatting. And Gideon's kind of the guest of honour. People are curious to meet him and ask about his travels.

You went to Kathmandu? someone says. What were the Nepalis like?

And Gideon says the Nepalis were very nice.

And his host says, yes, yes, I know several Nepalis. Very good people.

And someone else asks Gideon, did you ever go to Hungary? My cousin lives there.

Yes, Gideon says, Budapest. Three nights.

And what were the Hungarians like?

Lovely. Really liked the Hungarians.

And Gideon's host says, let me tell you something about Hungarians. Some of the best people in the world.

And this goes on some time. Countries Gideon's never visited get discussed. The Poles are terrific, the Japanese are wonderful, the Sudanese are extraordinary. The Belgians too. And the French and the Libyans and the Dutch. And Gideon says something like, it's only governments that cause wars and famine and poverty. Any country you go to, the ordinary people are wonderful. They're friendly and nice and just want to live in peace with their neighbours.

Everyone round the table is filled with a love of their fellow man. At this point the host's wife speaks for the first time all evening. *Except the Jews*, she says. And everyone agrees. *The Jews are dogs.*

Although the story ended with a clear punchline, I had no idea if I was supposed to laugh – Tovyah had spoken with no mischief in his voice, as though just laying down facts. Then *he* laughed, and his features took on a sudden lightness. For the first time that day, I felt like he didn't somehow hate me.

At last, I relaxed. 'Let's get out of here,' I said. 'I've missed you.'

'And go where?'

I wanted to suggest dinner, or cocktails on Little Clarendon Street, but the romantic overtones gave me pause. Instead, I mentioned that some friends were meeting in the Royal Oak for lunch in an hour's time.

Tovyah asked which people, and I rattled off some names.

'Jan Stockwell? You're not serious.'

'He's a good guy.'

'Give me a break. These people aren't worth your time, Kate. Last term I heard Jan call David Hume a white supremacist! The libraries in this city have collections as good as any. The whole history of human thought is sitting on the shelves, waiting for us to take down the books and peer into the minds of bygone generations. And all anyone does is sling around buzzwords. *Banish Hume! Tear up the Great Western Canon!* You'd think the academics would clamp down on it, but they encourage this drivel, give it good marks. When my grandfather was our age, there were plenty of thugs around telling you very loudly not to read Plato, Aristotle, Voltaire . . .'

I tried to say something about glib Nazi comparison, but Tovyah wasn't having it.

'Oh no, no no, not you too. Carving a swastika, *that's* glib.'

'I'm on your side!'

There was a fierceness to him then, his whole body was tensed. 'I bet you never did learn your ten names,' he said.

'My what?'

'The Eli Schultz thing. Ten victims, learn their names.'

'I thought you said it was pointless.'

'You never listen. I said if you cared, you'd already know them.'

I had not learned my names. In fact, not long after the lecture, I'd forgotten all about it. 'You can do ten?' I said.

'Mendl Rosenthal' – he began counting on his fingers – 'Helly Rosenthal, Tsirl Rosenthal, Avram Rosen—You want just *ten*? I can do ten without changing surnames.'

His eyes were burning. I rested my hands on his shoulders. Our eyes met. I tried to kiss him, but he pushed me away.

'And they put a swastika on my door!'

Later that week, I was in the faculty library, hunting down the one reference copy of some textbook on literary theory I needed to consult for my latest essay. I'd arrived early; on two previous occasions the copy had been removed from the stacks by another student before I could get to it. This time, there it was among the rows of other serious-minded books, perfectly ordered. Thankful not to be met by a gap-tooth in the shelf, I took it down.

As I held it in my hands, I became aware of a boy standing close behind me. He asked, with barely concealed frustration, how long I'd be needing the book I was holding.

'You're the one!' I said, turning around.

'Do I know you?'

His long fringe hung down over one side of his face. As he brushed it aside with slender fingers, he took me in properly, and, seeming to realise how rude he'd just been, smiled in apology.

'We've been squabbling over this book all week,' I said.

He was still grinning. 'So we meet at last.'

We agreed to find two seats next to each other and swap notes. At the end of a three-hour session, he pressed a post-it onto the desk in front of me. *'Do you have a phone number or what?'*

*

IT IS TOLD: IN EDEN, Adam received from the angel Raziel a secret doctrine containing hidden truths about the origins of the universe, the nature of the Godhead, the scheme of providence, and the existence of the soul beyond death. Possession of such mystical knowledge placed him above the lesser divinities, above the seraphim and cherubim, and above the morning star. The Doctrine was lost in the Fall but restored to Adam after another great angel took pity on him weeping. Adam handed on this Secret Doctrine to Seth, his third born, who in turn chose a successor to be the guardian of Kabbalah. Thus the Doctrine was handed on by each successive generation, always concealed from the majority. On Mount Sinai, along with the Decalogue, Moses received the Secret Doctrine, and shared it with chosen disciples. This ancient wisdom eventually passed from oral culture into writing. First in the Book of Enoch, then in *Sepher Yetzirah*, the Book of Formation, and finally in the Zohar, the Book of Splendour, the greatest wonder of Kabbalism.

Our own copy was presented to my husband on his fortieth birthday, the recommended age to begin Kabbalistic study. An amusing gift, it had stood more or less unopened on our top shelf ever since. Or so we thought. At some point, when our backs were turned, little hands reached up for the ancient text; Elsie alone had turned those thin pages in the depths of night, had peered into the dark centre of the Kabbalistic labyrinth. This is what she was reading when her English teacher first called us in for an emergency meeting. 'Your daughter has done a terrible thing,' she said. Taking her inspiration from the legend of Jephthah, Elsie had written a story in which her ambitious parents make of their daughter a human sacrifice.

*

Surely, I was not the only student at college who developed a sudden interest in Kabbalah amidst the furore over Hannah Rosenthal's forthcoming book. There was something kooky about looking into it, however, and I didn't want to be seen calling up dusty volumes from the stacks of the Bodleian library, like someone out of an M. R. James story.

So, my research began online. I learned that at one and a quarter million words, the writings of the Zohar cycle stretch to as many pages as Marcel Proust's many-volumed novel. But unlike *In Search of Lost Time*, it has never been translated into English in its entirety. Understandable, then, that the book has spawned countless legends, often based on little familiarity with the actual text. While no more, as far as I could tell, than an expansive gloss on the writings of the Old Testament, the Zohar has throughout the ages been mistaken for something more sinister: a book of spells. In medieval Europe, practitioners of witchcraft saw the Jewish mystics as powerful magi. Such rumours led A. E. Waite to begin his work on Kabbalah with an exasperated injunction: 'I should wish to exclude from the auditorium those who understand *Scientifica Kabbalistica* as an art of making, consecrating and using talismans and amulets, as a magical mystery concerning the power of Divine Names, or as a source and authentication of Grimoires and Ceremonial Rituals of Evocation.'

Hannah Rosenthal would no doubt have been kicked out of Waite's auditorium. 'I'm not claiming the book we had on our shelves was written by angels and only copied by men. But when I run my eyes over even a few lines, a certain shiver runs down my spine.'

Daughters of Endor was published in third week.

The book's thesis can be summarised as follows. After the trauma of losing her grandfather, with whom she had always been close, Elsie attempted to discover ancient techniques for communing with the dead. Inspired by Biblical narratives, old legends, and fanatical religious zeal, her enquiries led her, via a premature sexual awakening, to the deepest mysteries of the Kabbalah, where she was soon lost among shadows. At some point the girl's soul was overpowered by a demonic spirit, posing as the restless ghost of her grandfather in order to lead her astray. This spirit was an enemy the family has been battling ever since.

Tovyah couldn't get through it, literally hurled the book across his room in disgust – I heard it thump against my wall.

Others had less difficulty finishing. The following evaluation comes from the review that appeared in the *Oxford Student*: 'Oscar Wilde famously pronounced that there is no such thing as a moral or immoral book, only books that are well written and those that are badly written. Hannah Rosenthal's latest offering gives the lie to Wilde's epigram; despite the black magic of the author's prose, *Daughters of Endor* is a profoundly immoral work . . .' Flowery though it is, the evaluation is not wide of the mark. The terrible thing about Hannah's book was just how readable it was.

Sales figures bore this out. It raced to the top of bestseller charts, and we soon saw copies everywhere: glaring out of shop windows, resting next to cups of coffee, folded open in someone's lap.

Given how indignant people were about Hannah's idea of motherhood, the week of release might have been a good time for Tovyah to win allies around college. The sympathy vote was his for the taking. But he continued to see the worst in his peers and seemed to find their attacks on his mother no less irritating than the book itself. 'I wish everyone would just shut up about it,' he would say. 'You don't hear me taking aim at *their* parents.'

It didn't help that pictures of Tovyah and his siblings featured on glossy paper in the book's central pages. I was outraged. 'Doesn't she need your consent for that?' I asked.

'Please. The great Hannah Rosenthal does not know the meaning of the word consent.'

'So you should do something!'

'What, I should call up a lawyer and sue my own mother? How would that help?'

Now Tovyah's face was well known outside of college as well as in. One time, we were in Sainsbury's together, grabbing essentials, when a stranger in dungarees approached. She said it really sucked, what his mother had done.

'And you are?' Tovyah said.

'Just a well-wisher.' The girl started to back away.

Tovyah sneered. 'And why exactly should I care what you think?'

Such incidents made him so angry that I wondered if there was more going on than he acknowledged. When I'd seen him interact with his mother, he was hostile, certainly, but far from indifferent to her attention. Was he disappointed, after all, that the book she'd written was not about *him*? One thing I knew; there was more than one outsized ego in Tovyah's family, and it seemed the fight for parental approval stretched a long way back.

As for me, I read the book in a single afternoon, stopping only to make myself a cup of tea. I was intrigued by the mention of Yosef's spirit, impostor or otherwise. Not that I believed in chain-rattling ghosts, or that I'd seen anything back in November that ought to shake up one's understanding of life here on Earth: the dead are dead. But it did make me sit up. People have always seen things. Shapes in the mirror, noises in an empty house. Studying Middle English, I was fascinated by Margery Kempe (the only woman on a roster of fourteenth-century men), who, while convalescing after the birth of her first child, was hounded by devils at the end of the bed. You could be a rationalist, I thought, and still believe her experience tells us something about the act of giving birth in the pre-modern age, or what it has always meant to be a new mother.

What's more, Elsie had alluded to that white-robed figure in the lecture hall, and Tovyah had been tight-lipped when I asked him about it. The whole strange episode made me unfashionably sympathetic to Hannah. Whatever else you wanted to say about her, she had been through a hell of a lot since her daughter had first disappeared. Who can say what grotesque visions the overwrought mind conjures up?

Tovyah, of course, was less forgiving. We went for a long walk together a few days after the book came out, first crossing through Jericho, then walking along the canal path. It was one of those lazy Saturdays in Oxford when the whole student population seems to be leaning out of windows, calling to friends across the quad, or else sitting in fields, encircled by lager cans and jugs of Pimm's, eating hummus with breadsticks, and talking over the tinny music that plays from somebody's iPod.

As we watched punters ease along the waterway, he dominated the conversation. He listed inaccuracies in his mother's book, both large and small, and refuted many of her interpretations. There was no way, for instance, that Elsie was actually reading the Zohar at thirteen. 'It's in Aramaic!'

Tovyah gesticulated as he walked, his hands springing open to make his points. I had to ask him to lower his voice, to stop drawing everyone's attention.

Speaking at a barely reduced volume, he objected to the way Hannah made out that Elsie was some kind of saint before Zeide's death. Even as a little girl she'd had a stubborn side, he insisted, and had always made trouble at school. 'It all comes from the transmutation of senseless events into linear narrative. Elsie's life is not a sequel to Zeide's. That's marketing, that's bullshit. Elsie's life is like anyone else's. It's chaotic and messy, and it doesn't fit into three acts.'

We left the canal path now to walk into Port Meadow. At the far side of the green, where you hit the Thames, a group of cows had gathered by the riverside, standing in the sun, chewing at the grass. I asked Tovyah what Elsie made of the whole thing. He said he'd be able to ask her in person the following weekend: she was coming to visit.

'She is? That's wonderful!' I said.

'Yes, well, she always makes an effort for my birthday.'

His birthday? I had no idea. Hurt by the casual way he'd slipped it into the conversation, I asked when it was.

'Next Saturday, if you're that interested. I'm sure Hannah's furious she's coming.'

That, apparently, was the most important thing to him; Elsie's visit would be a major victory in the war against his parents. What did they have planned? Not much, apparently. They'd walk around the colleges, visit museums, maybe catch a film.

'Surely we can do better than that,' I said. 'We should throw a party.'

'With who?' Tovyah said.

'It doesn't have to be big. Even if it's just the three of—'

'There is no "three of us". Look, I hate to say this. But I think it might be good if you gave us a little space.'

'Sorry?'

'With everything going on, I don't want her to feel that people are ogling her, like some curiosity.'

I felt a burning sensation behind my eyes. How could he act like I was just one of the crowd, trying to catch sight of the famous witch?

'But it's your birthday!'

'What do you want? I can't be dealing with this, Kate. Not now.'

I was at a loss. 'Dealing with what?'

'I thought I'd made things pretty clear. Looks like I overestimated your ability to take a hint. Me and you, it would never have worked. We're just not the same. I'm sorry if I've hurt you, but there it is. *Fini.*'

Fishing in my bag, I withdrew a cigarette, which I then struggled to light. When the flame took hold, I inhaled greedily. Tovyah, seeming not to notice, had walked on a few steps. I felt lightheaded, and it seemed a long time since I'd had a glass of water.

'I'd like to speak to Elsie, actually,' I said. 'I saw something, the night of the Schultz lecture. You saw him too.'

'What are you on about now?'

'Your grandfather. In his funeral robes. I *saw* him.'

Tovyah sighed. When he spoke again, he was talking to himself. 'Is no one in this world sane?'

We walked on, not speaking. A football, knocked off course from a nearby game of five-a-side, came rolling in our direction. Rather than stop it with his foot, Tovyah stepped over the ball, and let it drop into the river. As one of the players jogged passed to retrieve it, I apologised. The ball was drifting out into the centre of the river. The footballer asked what Tovyah's problem was. He said he wasn't anyone's ball boy.

'You can be a total shit, you know,' I said.

'We're all flawed,' he said. 'I have no illusions about that.'

'Just because you've spent your life reading books, you think you know everything. But there are things you know nothing about.'

'Undoubtedly. I suppose you're going to furnish me with an example,' he said.

'I've been dating someone.'

'Oh?'

'A boy from Christ Church. We met at the faculty library. He's on the university running team, and he plays the drums. Super smart guy, very quick. You might get on with him, actually, if you gave him a chance.'

Tovyah rolled his eyes. 'Somehow, Kate, I fucking doubt it.'

Behind us, the footballer was now lying down at the riverbank, stretched over the surface of the water, trying to reach the ball with a twig clutched in his outthrust arm.

Chapter Seventeen

Elsie got in on the Friday at noon, and Tovyah went to the station to meet her. I had a seminar at one of the colleges in town, so was not in when he brought her back. Later, while I skimmed an essay on post-structuralism for ideas I could lift for my essay that week, I heard them talking through the wall, though the words were inaudible. His professorial baritone gave way to her breathy alto.

I couldn't sleep that night. Still furious, I found myself tallying up the favours I'd done Tovyah, whenever I'd defended his obnoxious behaviour, or got him invited to events where no one wanted him. I also tallied his litany of insults, the times he'd called me stupid, craven, trivial. Why had I put up with it all? Prying open the slats in my blinds, I looked out into the moonless sky, and thought I could see a few shapes way off in the gardens, students who'd snuck out after the gates closed to drink spirits under the stars. Carefree souls, not yet spurned by false friends. I decided to make myself a cup of herbal tea in the kitchen. I opened my bedroom door carefully, not wanting to wake my neighbours. With the overhead light off, it took a moment to see the figure standing before me in the darkness a few inches from my face. Like walking up to an open doorway and realising at the last second it's a mirror you've approached, and there's your eerie double, striding to meet you. In another moment, I'd have smashed straight into her.

I screamed.

'Shh, shhh! Haha! Shhhh. Sorry, I am sorry, I didn't mean to scare you, haha. We must be quiet, people are sleeping.'

Even before I'd adjusted to the dark, I knew who it was.

'What are you doing out here?'

'I thought I heard you stirring. I didn't want to knock in case you were asleep. I am sorry, I had no idea you'd yelp like that. It's Kate, right? We met last term. I know all sorts of things about you now. And you're not Jewish. I only need a tiny favour. Please help me, oh please do.'

'What do you want?'

'Oh, you are wonderful, thank you, thank you.'

As she walked backwards out of the shadows, her hand gripping my sleeve, I realised the moment to point out that I hadn't agreed to anything had passed.

'The thing is I couldn't sleep, and so I thought I'd read in the kitchen. I'm a dreadful insomniac, always have been. Can't stop those blasted thoughts whizzing about.'

Though I knew Elsie was now twenty-three, she looked much younger in the semi-darkness of the corridor, perhaps only fifteen or sixteen. Especially when she flashed that broad, innocent smile.

'You wanted something,' I said.

'The lights. I can't turn them on.'

'The switch is on the left. It's lower down on the wall than you'd expect but you'll find it if you feel around.'

'No, no, you don't understand. I *can't* use the light switch. You have to do it.'

I was puzzled.

'It's forbidden!'

Tonight was the Sabbath. So here it was, the fundamentalist religiosity that Tovyah had been casting off ever since he left home. Encountering this obedience in Elsie disarmed me; Tovyah had made it sound as though she shared his rebellious attitude. After I'd done what she asked, we stood under the dangling bulb and looked at each other. Her skin was wrapped tightly around her bony face.

'You're all set,' I said. 'Though for the record, I'm Jewish too.'

'Not your mother, though,' she corrected.

The roles we're assigned as off-stage characters in other people's lives always sound implausible, and when she'd said Tovyah had told her about me, I thought she was being polite. What else did she know?

'Don't worry about turning out the light,' I said. 'People leave them on all the time.'

'Wait up a moment, will you?'

She had her hand on my sleeve again.

'What for?'

'Don't be *naughty*!' she said. I felt myself blushing. 'Nothing wicked, I just want to talk to you. You see, I'm such a fool, I came here to read but I left my book in Tuvs's room.'

'*Tuvs*?'

'Yes, and I daren't go back in, he might wake up.'

Although I'd been eager to spend time with Elsie during her visit, now that the opportunity presented itself, I hesitated. Something about her frightened me. A jumpiness. At any given moment, you had no idea what she was about to do.

'Oh, do stay up! Just twenty minutes or so. Please. Tuvs hasn't let me meet *any* of his friends, and I'm dying to hear about his life here.'

Her hand had now progressed from my sleeve to my fingers, which she stroked. In the harsher light, she no longer looked like a teenager.

'You wanted to meet Tovyah's friends?' I said. 'Plural?'

I agreed to stay for twenty minutes but added that I'd need a drink. Having retrieved a couple of G&Ts from the fridge, I snapped open the first and handed it to her. 'You can *drink* on the Sabbath, can't you?'

Elsie handed it back, shaking her head.

'Better not,' she said. Then added, lightly, 'Doctor's orders.'

I had just offered booze to an alcoholic – thank God she was not in a more self-destructive mood.

Elsie said she was awfully glad I had agreed to keep her company.

'You won't regret it,' she went on. 'I'm quite famous, you know. Mummy's written a book about me, made me out as the wicked witch of North London! It's all bunk, of course, but people are taking it *seriously*.'

'You mean you don't mind?'

'Mind? I think it's hysterical.'

It was the appropriate word, but not the way Elsie had used it. I didn't say that I'd read the book, though my copy was hidden in a drawer, not ten metres from where we now sat.

'And you don't feel betrayed?' I said.

'Gosh, you're a very serious lady, aren't you.'

While Elsie asked some obvious questions about how I was finding university life, to which I gave uninspired answers, she continued to touch me now and then on my wrist, my forearm. My nerves tingled. Before long, our conversation turned to her brother. She wanted to know what impression

243

he'd made at the college. I told her a modified version of the truth. I said that I admired him, but mostly he kept himself to himself.

'I don't believe you! I bet he's surrounded by girls! Why are you laughing? You two aren't an item, are you?'

'God no. Nothing like that. He's not exactly seeing anyone, as far as I know.'

'You speak like you're a bit afraid of him.'

'Maybe I am. A bit.'

'But that's ridiculous! He's a sweetie, really. And he *adores* you. Why are you making that face?'

It was hard to believe Tovyah would talk about adoring anyone. But who knew? If I was being honest with myself, Elsie's words made me happier than anything I'd heard all term. I'd been out quite a few times with the boy from the library, and though he was easy to get along with, the prospect of another date was somehow exhausting; I didn't need to hear, yet again, who from his year would end up famous, or why he voted Lib Dem. My feelings for Tovyah were of an entirely different order. Which is not to say they were altogether favourable.

'I don't think sweetie is the word many people around here would use,' I said.

Elsie was surprised. Growing up, Tovyah had been the kindest little boy you could imagine. Never had a bad word for anyone, did everything to make his parents, his siblings happy. A little angel, she said.

I asked if he ever lost his temper.

'Not when he was younger, no. The last few years have been . . . difficult for him.'

There was a photo of the family in Hannah's book, where Tovyah must have been about six. They're at the beach; he waves a spade in the air and wears a bucket on his head, squinting in the sunlight.

We were sat now on the kitchen worktop, our heads bent together so we could speak at low volume, our legs touching. Now and then you meet someone and all the difficulties of making yourself understood seem to fall away. Elsie just got it. She could see at once that Oxford could never live up to all the hopes I'd projected onto it, and she seemed to intuit that between leaving home and meeting her brother, I had become somehow unmoored, in ways that even I did not yet appreciate. She said I was looking for something.

'There's a gap, no? Something that needs filling.'

I said I wasn't sure, and she proceeded to tell me her favourite name for God. *Eyn sof*.

'It means endlessness, something utterly unknowable. Nothing like Jehovah, with his big beard and his stern face! No, Jehovah is just one of the emanations, the ways the true God makes Himself known to us. You can't even talk about *Eyn sof* directly, you can only sidle up to it in metaphors. The old sages called it the fog at the centre of a dark flame that is neither black nor white nor red nor green. Colourless itself, the flame gives colour and light to everything that is. Don't you think that's beautiful?'

I agreed it was. Beyond the window, the night sky burned a shade of dull orange. Distant trees shook their branches.

'You said Tovyah's not seeing anyone,' Elsie asked suddenly. 'What about you?'

I weighed my response. 'There's no one just now.'

'Pity, I was hoping for some vicarious living. I haven't had a boyfriend in years and, between you and me, the men I know are beasts.'

Her tone was casual. But knowing what I did of her life – those nights she'd spent sleeping rough – I could guess what she meant by beasts.

She placed her hand on my thigh. 'Kate, this is terribly embarrassing, but I have a confession to make. A confession and a favour. Is that OK?'

Feeling tipsy, now, and a little reckless, I told her to go on.

'It was no accident that I ran into you this evening. I've been meaning to speak to you since I got here, but Tuvs won't let me out of his sight! I'm sure you know about him refusing to talk to Mummy or Daddy. He's entitled to his own opinions, but this really is too much, and it's making them both miserable.'

'You mean you're on *their* side?' I said. I leaned forwards, and she removed her hand.

'Don't be silly, it's not a question of sides. I just want everyone to get along. Whether Tovyah likes them or not, his family are the only people who will ever understand him. Except you, of course.'

She asked if I would help bring about a reconciliation between Tovyah and his parents. She thought I might have more sway over her brother than I realised.

Meaning what?

'Meaning,' she said, 'I think he might be a little in love with you. And after tonight, I can understand why.'

By the time I went to bed, I was dizzy. It wasn't exactly a crush, but it wasn't far off. I kept seeing her face in the shadows, recalling the sound of her voice. I could still feel her curled fingers against my thigh.

*

Over the course of the next two days, I hoped to catch Tovyah alone, if for nothing else than to wish him happy birthday. I had ummed and ahhed over what to get him as a present and was not entirely confident with my choice. But his door remained closed. He and his sister went out early each morning, and I had no idea how they spent their days. Other students were interested in seeing Elsie in the flesh, too, but Tovyah managed to shield her from intrusive eyes.

On Sunday night, I was heading home after several drinks in town with the boy I was still, to my surprise, seeing. It was late, and on the long walk up Woodstock Road I found the streets deserted. A single car drove by, and the headlights blinked, startled by a speed bump. When I came in through the main gates, the college was dark and quiet. Apart from in the library, where the odd lighted window attested to the work of a few tireless students, no one was about, not even the nocturnal smokers you normally passed on the steps up to the great hall. Back on my own corridor, light from Tovyah's room spilled through the crack under his door. My heart thumped. Looking at that sheet of light, I felt I was in the presence of something beyond simple good luck. This is hard to explain. I was overcome with a tremendous sense of peace. Like hovering on the verge of sleep. Woozy, light-headed, perhaps a little sick. The more I looked at it, the more I realised something was off. As I watched, the carpet outside Tovyah's room grew bright, then dim, and then brighter again. Strangest of all was the colour, a sort of dull gold. That doesn't do it justice. It was a colour I had never seen before. I felt a wave of nausea. Then, as if compelled, I got down on my knees and traced the outline of the glow with my finger against the floor. Where the light shone the carpet felt warm to the touch. And I knew then, with absolute certainty, that there is a God who created the universe, a fog at the centre of the flame. Just as I knew that I loved Tovyah and I loved his sister also, that even though one of them was confrontational and difficult and the other I barely knew, I loved them both with a kind of selfless love that would last as long as I lived and perhaps beyond. The way God loves. God who created each and every one of us, who knows all and has always been there, and who watches over everything for ever. Just as I had always known. And Tovyah knew it too. Despite everything, he must. And so, Hannah was dead wrong about her daughter. Elsie had summoned God's light, and her children were celebrating His glory together. I felt a happiness so intense I thought I might pass out.

I heard voices, what sounded like a muted argument. Then a shout. But when I tapped on the door, the voices hushed, the light was extinguished, and all the warmth in the carpet was gone.

Chapter Eighteen

The following day, a little hungover, and already embarrassed by the thoughts that had filled my head the previous night, I emailed Ruth, the rabbi at the liberal synagogue, to ask what she could tell me about Kabbalah. Without guidance, my own investigations had not taken me far, even after I'd swallowed my pride and visited the central libraries. The English versions of the Kabbalistic texts were mostly the work of oddballs and eccentrics, such as Samuel Liddell Mathers, founder of the Order of the Golden Dawn, a man born in Hackney who dressed up as an ancient Egyptian to perform magic ceremonies. I didn't think he had much to tell me about the beliefs of actual Jews.

Ruth said it wasn't her area, though what she understood of the Kabbalah, she admired. It emphasised personal connection with God over the performance of arbitrary rituals, she said, and did much to debunk the vengeful King of Kings depicted in the Old Testament. I liked Ruth, but her well-reasoned answer disappointed me. It was the more occult side of Kabbalism – how the fanatics had read the mystical texts – I wanted to know. The scraps I had picked up, mostly from Hannah's book, did not satisfy me.

Ruth said if I wanted to learn more, I should talk to Rabbi Michael, who ran the Ben-Scholem society. Odd that she should direct me to the very people who believed she had no right to call herself a rabbi in the first place.

Rabbi Michael was not in when I reached the society, but the doorkeeper I'd met previously was there. 'Still working things out?' he asked me.

I left my name and number for the rabbi, and we arranged to meet the following day for a coffee in town. I had the idea he would see this as an opportunity for evangelism and arrived nervous. The rabbi greeted me with a broad smile.

'The girl who never came back!'

'You recognise me?'

'You came once and only once to Shabbat. You looked about as comfortable as the little boy who wandered into the ladies' room.'

It was only now I realised he was American. I apologised for my absence, explaining that I attended a different synagogue these days. He asked which one. When I confessed that I was with the liberals, I expected him to tell me I was on an express train to Hell.

'Think I care about where you pray? It's all Judaism.'

I berated myself. The night of the Schultz lecture, he and his congregation had welcomed me – a total stranger – with a warmth virtually unknown among atheists. Pull up a chair, they said, have something to eat. And when I had coldly and clumsily ignored their friendliness, he'd immediately forgiven me. No wonder Ruth had a genuine respect for him, despite theological differences. I asked if he remembered Tovyah, another student who used to go to his services.

'Of course. Interesting boy. Interesting family! I suppose you're worried about what he's going through. To tell the truth, me too.'

I asked if the rabbi had read Hannah's book, and he said no, he didn't care to.

'That girl has issues,' he said, 'but she's no witch.'

When I asked if witches exist, he laughed. I said what about golems or dybbuks, and he laughed again. 'What is this? Been neglecting your studies, yes, spending too long in the cinema?'

'But doesn't it mention witches in the Torah?'

'Wandering through the desert, the Israelites were frightened by an army of giants. Are such things true? It is true that there are some very tall men, and a tall man is a giant. To me, Michael Jordan is a giant, no? And guess what. I wouldn't fancy my chances in a fight with the guy!'

'So you don't take the book seriously.'

'Between you and me, Hannah Rosenthal should stick to politics. On Israel, she makes a lot of sense. On the nature of miracles, less so.'

We didn't end up talking about Kabbalah. I suspected that Rabbi Michael would tell me much the same as Ruth, that the mystical books were not mainstream Judaism, but perhaps held a certain wisdom if you were patient enough to go looking.

Instead, we discussed Tovyah. He hadn't been to a Friday dinner all term. The rabbi urged me to bring him along some time.

'You know Tovyah's an atheist, don't you?' I said.

'Poor boy. There is no pain worse than the absence of God.'

Was that so? I thought of Tovyah's door, a crack of light at the base. And I wondered again if the belligerent non-believer stuff was all a front.

When we'd shown up at the café, the rabbi had ordered a peanut butter brownie, confiding that these were his 'great weakness'. He now dunked his brownie into his coffee and took a bite. I asked him about the biblical figure of Jephthah. This was the story Elsie rewrote for class, the story which got her worried teacher to send her to therapy, all those years back. The episode is the inciting incident of Hannah's narrative.

'That's not a very nice story,' The rabbi said.

I explained that it was connected to an essay I had to write.

'The first time I heard about Jephthah I was twelve. My bar mitzvah was coming up. At that time, I was really thinking about what it is to be a Jew. Why were we so different from everybody else anyway? "The chosen people". Chosen for what? As you can see, I was a real teacher's pet, and I did a lot of reading on my own. And one night in my bedroom I read this awful tale. I was so upset, I ran to my parents and I said, "It's off! I'm not becoming bar mitzvah!" I thought my father was going to beat me black and blue.' The rabbi gave a sad smile, presumably remembering the old man, either dead or on the far side of an ocean, with no more violence left in him.

'Why were you so disturbed?'

'You mean you don't know the story?'

According to the Book of Judges, Jephthah was born east of the River Jordan in the ancient mountains of Gilead and he rose from destitution to preside over his people. This was long after the death of Moses, but before the coronation of Saul. A difficult period for the Israelites. They lived in houses built rapidly from stone and slime, and families banded together under flimsy coalitions, not so much a nation as an assembly of vagrants, ragged men and women who argued over the price of livestock and cursed one another for their misfortunes. For hundreds of years, they'd been imprisoned first by one hostile neighbour and then by another, recalling the slavery in Egypt and Pharaoh's whips. This was the blood-soaked world into which Jephthah was born, himself the progeny of sin – his mother was a harlot. Sorry, Kate, that's not my word, and I don't like saying it. But it tells you what they thought of her. Her name, I'm afraid, is lost.

Bastard is another word I don't like, but it's apposite. Again, forgive me. There must have been many bastards born in those chaotic years between the death of one Judge and the emergence of a successor, when so many Israelites had forgotten their Torah and had fallen to serving Baalim, or as the Christians call him, Beelzebub. Not all were treated as harshly as Jephthah, though, cast out of Gilead by his legitimate brothers, assured he would not inherit a thing from his lecherous father. He fled to the edges of Canaan, far from his kin and from life as he had always known it. He settled in Tob. Whether he stood in exile, gazing over the low sands, and whispered to himself that Hashem had other plans for him than this, is not told.

Out in the strange land of Tob, mentioned nowhere else in the vast biblical narrative, Jephthah thrived. Endangered sons often see their luck turn around in the old tales – think of Daniel and the lions, think of Joseph winning first his freedom and then untold riches.

You know those stories, at least? I'm kidding. Gentiles know those ones.

In exile, Jephthah made friends. He grew strong, fell in love, got hitched. He worked in the sweat of his brow, nurturing the land, and when he went to bed at night his sleep was unbroken by worries or regret. In time his wife gave birth to a daughter, the couple's only child. Often the day's end found Jephthah eating fruit in the shade of an olive tree, and bouncing the little girl on his knee as she babbled her enchanted baby-talk. If he hadn't been marked by God as one of his people's deliverers, Jephthah might have had a really happy life. You can't say the same for Moses or Samson, murderers both, whose inability to contain the hurricane of passions they were born with always excluded them from the ordinary joys. Unlike them, when Jephthah first spoke to Hashem, he had everything to lose.

Now we come to the moment Jephthah's destiny was sealed. Years passed and a day came when enemies from the East, the Ammonites, once again made war with leaderless Israel. And the elders of Gilead, the same men who once spat in Jephthah's face and called him bastard, came to him for help. Somehow they knew it was this harlot's son who would help them defeat their invading neighbours. 'But you guys hate me, you kicked me out of town,' Jephthah said. 'Why do you come now, just when you're in trouble?' A reasonable question that contains its own answer.

Despite the resentment Jephthah felt towards those who had cast him out and cut him off, and despite the nameless dread now rising in his chest, he consented to lead the fight against the sons of Ammon. On one condition. He wanted to be made sovereign over all the people of Gilead. A high price, you'll think, but it was a great deed he was being asked to perform, and the deal was struck.

Poor Jep. Why did he have to look for a higher station than the one that had contented him so long? The resentment of the bastard son, punished for the sins of his father, dies hard. And so, when Jephthah was called upon to serve his people, the people of his God, he bargained for his own interest. This arrogance, this self-centredness did not go unremarked by Hashem, in whose book the words and acts of all the men and women on Earth are set down in ink so dark that even He is powerless to wipe it clean.

Don't forget that, Kate. You can say you're sorry, but there are no fresh starts. You want to start over, become a Christian.

On the eve of the battle with the Ammonites, the Spirit of God came to Jephthah and a second bargain was made. Don't misunderstand. Hashem did not appear to our boy in the way He once appeared to Moses atop Mount Sinai. Nor did Hashem speak. So how did Jephthah know He was there? The scriptures don't say. I like to think he noticed the swaying of a candle flame on a windless night, or a tremor along his back. Regardless, Jephthah asked what generals have always asked their gods at such times: give me victory over my enemies, let me dance in the streets with all my conquering brothers. And in return he offered up an oath to Hashem, who had not forgotten how this bastard son likes to barter with destiny. 'If you put those Ammonites under my sword,' Jephthah vowed, 'then when I get back from battle, whatever comes out of the house first is yours.'

Animal sacrifices were common then. Had been since Cain and Abel – apparently our forefathers believed Hashem was pleased to see his lesser creatures set alight. Feel OK, Kate? You're not vegetarian, I hope.

At daybreak, the red sun was low and massive on the horizon. The Israelite army, if you can give that name to the unorganised rabble, to the crowd gone mad, swelled over the plains and through the towns and hamlets. By the afternoon, blood ran through the streets of Aeror and Minnith and

255

twenty cities besides. Jephthah stood in the thick of the battle, hacking at his enemies, half sick with the smell of gore. So many corpses festering in the heat, grown men crying for their mothers at the gate of death. When the sun sank into the sea that evening and the moon rose, the victory Jephthah had prayed for was his. Look how the bastard had risen: now he was not only leader of his people, he was a war hero, marked out for special favour by invincible Hashem. With a prayer in his heart, he knelt down, grabbed a fistful of earth, and brought it to his lips.

And then he made his way back home. You're a smart kid, you see where this is going.

At the long day's end, he reached the village of Mizpah in Gilead. With aching limbs, he trod the familiar road until his own house appeared, and there, rushing through the open door to meet him, her arms open, her lips stretched in a smile, was his only daughter. For a single ecstatic moment, he forgot his vow. And then, he remembered. 'What's wrong?' his daughter asked when she saw how his face fell. The news of the battle had carried, and she was looking forward to a celebration.

'I have opened my mouth to God.'

Jephthah hardly dared hope that Hashem might show him the same leniency that was extended to Abraham when he raised the knife to Isaac's neck. After all, Jephthah made the vow of his own free will. But if not Hashem, perhaps his daughter would tell him what he wanted to hear, that he didn't have to keep his word, that men before him had broken their oaths and lived. The young girl didn't even ask what he'd sworn. Here was her father before her, the best man she ever knew, letting tears fall into the dust without even wiping his eyes. The tone she now used, whether it was bitter, resigned, defiant, ironic, or pious is unrecorded. 'If you opened your mouth to God, then you must do as you have sworn.'

The girl's mother, if she lived to witness this conversation, is not mentioned in the texts. Perhaps death spared her that horror. The girl, meanwhile, asked a favour. She wanted a reprieve of two months, to climb the mountains of Gilead and lament her virginity. She had no children, no one to carry on the line. Never has anyone wanted the sun to halt in its revolutions more than Jephthah did those two months. Each night he prayed that time would cease its march into the future, that the whole world would be suspended, that the morning would never break, and that every living thing would be stuck fast in its place forever. But Hashem was deaf to Jep's pleading now, and the days continued to grind down as they always had. Soon the eight weeks were up, and the obedient daughter returned from the mountains.

The rabbis have observed that human sacrifice was explicitly forbidden by Mosaic law and so we should not take what is written at face value. Hashem would never allow it. Between you and me, I find this interpretation a convenient sidestep. It is known that these were dark years for the Israelites; brutalised by slavery and warfare, they had all but forgotten the law handed down at Sinai. Besides, Jephthah would hardly be the only man in history to convince himself of a relationship with God that never existed. Who knows if he could even tell the difference any more between Hashem, Jupiter, Vishnu, or Beelzebub? All we are told is that whichever god's name he believed he was acting in, Jephthah did with his daughter 'according to his vow which he had vowed'.

The rabbi was done speaking. As though others besides me had been listening, a hush descended on the café. I asked what the story meant.

'When I first read it, there was no meaning. None that didn't demean both human beings and God. Perhaps the idea is that when you go to war, you must be ready to bury your own children. Or perhaps it's a warning about ambition. What do you think?'

I said it was a horrible story, whichever way you looked at it. But I wasn't really thinking about biblical exegesis, or what it meant for Jewish worship. I was thinking about Tovyah's sister, aged thirteen, reading this same story. *Writing* this story. Reading what she'd written.

*

Elsie stayed five days in all. On the morning she was due to catch her train home, she came to my room while her brother was in the shower. 'I just wanted to say how lovely it was meeting you again,' she said. Her eyes scanned my room and came to rest on the window. Something in the garden beyond seemed to take her interest.

'I know you've read it, by the way. Please don't get the wrong idea. Mummy knows how to sell a book, but she doesn't know the first thing about Kabbalah. It's not some secret magical sect, nothing ridiculous like that.'

I said I didn't know what she was talking about.

'Not much of a liar, are you?'

She told me not to forget what we'd spoken about, the planned reconciliation. After she'd gone, Tovyah himself emerged from the bathroom with his dark fringe flattened against his forehead and a thick towel around his waist. I was still standing in my doorway, but his glasses were all steamed up and he managed to walk past without seeing me.

We next spoke at dusk, after he returned from walking Elsie to the train station. He sought me out, and was in a good mood, for once. He told me of what he'd been up to with Elsie, how they'd sat together in cafés and in libraries, him at his studies, she with a novel, followed by long strolls in the university parks, only turning back each evening when the light began to fail.

'It's funny,' he concluded. 'You'd think that with that crazy book coming out, things would be worse than ever. Don't get me wrong, she's as furious with Hannah as I am, but I think having something to rail against has done her good.'

Furious with Hannah, was she?

I asked why he had made such a thing of keeping me away from her. He apologised and put it down to misplaced insecurities. Then he told me about his birthday, his first outside the family home. It had been very simple, and absolutely perfect. They'd had dinner at the Randolph Hotel, then he'd taken her on a tour of the city, visiting the old haunts of some famous alumni. Back in his room, they'd played several rounds of chess before screening *La Règle du jeu* on his laptop and falling asleep halfway through. For an evening, at least, the years ahead shone with possibility.

'I got you something, by the way,' I said. I went over to my wardrobe and fetched the loosely wrapped parcel.

When I turned around, he asked, 'What is it?'

'Open it!' I said, throwing it in his direction.

He did as instructed, carefully peeling back the Sellotape and unfolding the paper to reveal a faded denim jacket. Tovyah held it before him with his arms at full stretch. As far as I knew, he'd never owned anything like it.

'I know it's not your usual thing,' I said. 'But I thought it'd suit you.'

'Why?'

'Because you're not fifty, Tovyah. You're twenty.'

Placing his gift on my bed, he removed his blazer and put it over the back of the chair at my desk. He then threaded his arms into his new jacket and popped the collar in the mirror.

'You like it?' I asked.

'It's . . . magnificent.'

I walked up behind him and straightened the shoulders, so it hung properly.

'How's the boy from Christ Church?' Tovyah asked.

'Just like your degree,' I said, milking the pause. 'History.'

'Ho-ho,' Tovyah said.

I put my chin on his shoulder, and my arms around his waist. 'And what about us?'

Tovyah nodded, slowly. 'I do love you, Kate. But not like that. What happened last term was – I don't know what that was.'

Uncoupling my arms, I took a step away, and my double in the mirror backed away from his. 'Just friends, then,' I said.

'Not *just* friends. You're the only friend I've got.'

He turned around and we embraced. As he gripped my shoulder blade, I flooded with longing. For a time, we just stood there, holding each other. Then our mouths met and we were pulling off clothes. I was surprised by both his strength and his certainty. As he pressed into me, I told him to slow down, slow down, then pulled him towards my bed. Soon, he was rubbing between my legs, and as I grew wet he eased his fingers inside, first one then two.

I held him close, felt his tongue on my neck. Every corner of the room glowed with soft, inexplicable light. My body shivered, rippled, unfurled, collapsed.

Afterwards, we sat up against my pillow, eating pitted olives straight from the can, feeding them to one other, licking the salty brine from our fingers.

We slept in one another's arms, our limbs coiled.

Come the morning, he told me he was planning to go home to his parents the following weekend for Sabbath. Elsie wanted the two of them to confront Hannah together. Mussing up his hair, I said it sounded like the right thing to do – he couldn't simply ignore them for the rest of his life. Then he asked me to come with him. Without me there, he said, he didn't know if he could do it.

There was a silence. 'Are you coming?' he said at last.

As I kissed him, the fear of rejection fled from his face.

Chapter Nineteen

The house was so much as Hannah described it that arrival felt like a homecoming. The front garden throbbed in the heat of the day, colours migrating from one flower to the next. I hadn't realised how secluded it was. On either side, the houses were separated by footpaths that led out into alleyways, and both had prominent for-sale signs. I'd arrived with Tovyah, and Hannah greeted us at the door. Her face lit up when she saw her son. 'Tuvs! How handsome you look!' She threw her arms around him. Tovyah let himself be held for a moment before pulling away. After fussing over her son, Hannah's attention fell on me.

'Lovely to see you again, Bridget,' she said.

'Actually, it's—'

'Kate. I know. How nice that Tovyah brought you along.'

On the threshold, Tovyah reached up distractedly to touch the mezuzah, and I copied the gesture. Hannah offered to brew a pot of tea, but Tovyah said no for both of us. Hannah wished her son a happy birthday and presented him with a perfectly wrapped box, tied with green ribbon. Inside was a pair of cufflinks, which Tovyah regarded coolly.

'The word is thank you,' Hannah said. 'Those weren't cheap, you know.'

'My shirts all have buttoned sleeves.'

'They're for dress shirts. Your friends will be turning twenty-one soon, you'll need something nice to wear. Now, if you're done being ungrateful, your father wants a word. He's in his study.'

'Can it wait?' Tovyah said. 'I just got here.'

Something silent passed between them. Tovyah said fine, and wandered upstairs, leaving me alone with his mother. The last time we'd stood this close, she'd insulted me, perhaps not knowing I could hear. But if she felt as uncomfortable as I did now, she didn't let on.

'Don't stand on ceremony. I imagine you want to look around. Go ahead! You might find some interesting things in this house. Be warned, we're not the most attentive hosts. Sometimes we get people over then everyone forgets they're here. One time, a friend of Gideon's told me he'd been living with us a week! It generally works out, as long as you're happy to grab breakfast for yourself, find your own towels. Pluck with a free hand, dear – nothing's precious.'

I thanked her and asked where I was sleeping.

'Hang on.' She moved to the foot of the stairs. 'Elsie? ELSIE! Tovyah's little friend is here. She'll be down in a minute. ELSIE!'

Unlike her mother, Elsie was subdued when she appeared. Her eyes kept wandering to the corners of rooms, as though checking for dust, and I got the uncomfortable sense that she didn't recognise me. As I followed her upstairs, she didn't attempt conversation.

On the landing, I said, 'So, how are things looking? Still think we can play happy families?'

Elsie said nothing and proceeded to open a door.

'This is Gideon's old room. Excuse the clutter.'

A few model aircraft sat on a table in the corner, and some magazines were stuffed under the bed, but it was far from messy. The window overlooked the back garden, giving a view of the town beyond, with roofs and chimneys stretching out for half a mile at least. 'Mum's just next door,' Elsie said. 'Knock if you need anything. I'd better change for the Sabbath.'

'Oh. Should I have brought something smarter?'

My current outfit consisted of a pair of black jeans and a floral blouse. In my bag, I had only some clean underwear, a change of shirt, and a light jacket.

Elsie looked me over. 'You'll do fine.' Before she left me, she said, 'Don't try sneaking over to Tovyah's room in the night. If Mummy catches you, you're dead.'

I'd been looking forward to seeing Elsie again and was unsettled by this coolness. Still, I was glad to be in the house where Tovyah had grown up, and I hoped that meeting the rest of the family would help me get my head round his mother's extraordinary convictions.

I wondered when Tovyah would be done with his father and come find me.

After dropping my bag, I shut the door to Gideon's room with the feeling that I was barricading myself in, then lay down on the bed. I must have slept badly the previous night, and I soon fell into darkness. I dreamt there was a room in the house that no one had ever noticed. It was right there, just behind that door in the study. And inside that room—

When I woke, there was a young man at the foot of the bed, squinting down at me. He had a lantern jaw and a broad physique, and he was dressed in a navy-blue suit, though he'd removed his tie and unbuttoned his collar.

'Who the hell are you and what are you doing in my bed?'

For a second, I had no idea where I was.

'Sorry. You must be Gideon.'

'You'd have thought so, yes. We haven't had the pleasure.'

He did not talk like his siblings. He had neither Elsie's seductive charm nor Tovyah's solemn cadences. And as I would soon learn, flippancy was his default mode of conversation.

'There must have been some kind of mix-up,' I said.

'Obviously.'

'Elsie said you weren't going to be home this weekend.'

'Oh, you're a friend of *hers,* are you?'

'No, we've met, but I'm not exactly—'

'Not exactly a friend? Curiouser and curiouser! Well, in case you've got it on your mind to have a go, let me tell you something for free. Not worth it. She's mad as a bucket of frogs that girl.'

Was everyone in this family going to comment on my sex life?

'Actually, I was trying to say that Tovyah invited me. Not Elsie.'

'Tovyah? Hang on, yes, I know who you are.' Gideon suddenly looked very pleased with himself. He sat down on the end of the bed, wrapped his hand around my foot and said, 'You're the Sabbath goy! And here to broker the peace, am I right? Come on then, Kissinger.'

There are few things more subtly distressing than a stranger watching you sleep. The fact that he was still holding my foot compounded the humiliation. I withdrew my leg and sat up.

'Don't you live in Tel Aviv?'

He shrugged.

'What's it like?'

'You're not a lefty, are you? Of course, you are. Friend of Tovyah's, University of Oxford, thank you very much. I suppose you think I'm a nasty imperialist warrior.'

I could smell Gideon's aftershave – bold, faintly balsamic.

'I only meant I wasn't expecting you'd be here. Is there somewhere else I should go?'

'Oh God, ha, you look terrified. Poor girl. Where are my manners? Yes, yes, I just flew in yesterday, and I *was* going to stay with some friends this weekend but turns out Sony's preggers and Winston is going dry *out of sympathy*, the whole nine months, so there's not a lick of booze in the house. Well, sod that, why not come home and observe the Sabbath with dear old Hannah and Eric? Good for the soul, I hear. I'd forgotten Tovyah was going to be around, let alone . . . Anyway, yes, yes, you can have my grandfather's room.'

'Are you sure?'

'I don't suppose Zeide will mind.'

'Why do you speak like that?'

'Like what?'

'Like you find everything funny. Are you trying to impress me?'

Gideon let out a short bark of laughter. 'Darling, I hate to disappoint, but I gave up on impressing girls like you *years* ago. Don't look so frightened. And before you ask, no, they don't know, so don't tell them. That's not even true. They do know, *of course they do*, but they like pretending they don't.'

Now that I had met all three of the Rosenthal children, I was able to triangulate certain of their mannerisms. Those clipped accents, for instance. Only two generations back, the Rosenthals spoke a broken English, a language formed as much in the ghetto and in the *lager* as it was in the streets of London. Here were the third generation of rising immigrants, whose place in this (or any) country has always seemed historically precarious. Children who from a young age had been corrected by both parents into pronouncing their words immaculately; there were no glottal stops, no dropped Hs here. At Oxford, I'd met public school boys with mockney accents. The Rosenthals, by contrast, sounded like aristocrats from a bygone era.

'Are you sure your parents won't mind?'

'Mind what?'

'The room. Your grandfather's.'

'Eric and Hannah? They won't even notice. I suppose I should ask if there's anything I can get for you. I believe that's what hosts do.'

I asked him if I could have a cup of tea, earl grey if they had it, a splash of milk.

'Tea? You know it's gone six, right? You're not a bloody Mormon, are you?'

I had slept much longer than I realised. The daylight beyond the window had not yet started to drain.

'Mormons don't drink tea,' I said, sulking.

'Do they not? And coffee neither? Wow. Imagine if you lived your whole life being good, helping old ladies cross the road, and then you get to Heaven and they don't let you in because the fucking Mormons were right. Too many cappuccinos, mate, now off to hell.'

Gideon was rooting for something in his pocket. I got the impression he was someone who was never quite still, an odd quality for an ex-soldier.

'What are you drinking then?' I asked.

'Wine. And I'm opening a bottle so you may as well have a glass. Don't bother saying no thank you just to be polite.'

'I'm not polite on purpose,' I said. 'It's how I was brought up.'

'Was that a dig? I knew you had some spirit in you, behind those dull manners.'

He crossed to the wardrobe and began pulling out various bedclothes, cushions, and several shoe boxes closed with elastic bands. Eventually, after making quite a pile on the bedroom floor, he produced a dusty bottle of Pinot Noir.

'Knew it was in here! Last of his brothers, mind, saw each one taken off by the cruel hand of chance. Bit like Odysseus and the Cyclops, ha ha, except this time the Cyclops wins.'

He worked open the cork with an attachment on his key fob.

'You have to keep everything hidden in this house, especially booze. All my family are drinkers and thieves. Even little Tovyah. Where is he by the way? Shouldn't he be looking after you?'

The glass Gideon handed to me, which came from a cupboard by the side of the bed, had been neglected as long as the bottle itself. When he poured out the wine, particles of dirt floated on the inky surface.

'Well then. *L'chaim*!' he cried. After his first extravagant gulp, his front teeth were already dark purple.

My new accommodation was spotless. I don't just mean it was tidy; aside from the bed there was nothing in it. The closets were empty and even the bedside lamp had no bulb. Nor were there any prints on the wall, no photographs, nothing. Just an armchair to one side, a place to sit and read. I wondered if they were planning to redecorate and had only got round to clearing everything out. Someone must have come here for a quiet cigarette, now and then, as the walls carried the smell of smoke. I opened the windows a crack, before lighting one myself. I distrusted all that emptiness. It reminded me of a corner in a furniture store where a bed has been made up and a desk drawn near, giving the impression of a room where no room exists.

It was Tovyah who eventually came to summon me downstairs. When I asked what he'd been doing for the last two hours, he said he'd been reading, mostly. He had changed into a white shirt, freshly ironed, and was wearing the cuffs from his mother. The shirt was the gift from his father, he explained; Hannah and Eric had coordinated.

I told him he looked good and, when he did not return the compliment, asked if he was still planning to confront Hannah for what she had done. This, after all, was why he was here.

Tovyah shook his head. 'I don't think, with the state she's in now, Elsie could take it. She gets into these funks, it's like you can't even talk to her. There's no one *there*.'

When Eric had called for Tovyah earlier, it was not simply to present him with a new shirt. He needed to tell his son that Elsie was seriously not in good way. She'd been hitting the booze and was now in withdrawal. Just the day before, father and daughter had gone for a stroll around the block, just to get some air. And when they were out, they heard someone screaming obscenities, kicking bins. They looked up to see a woman on the far side of the road, dragging a bin-liner behind her, clinking with bottles. She was shouting at herself, shouting at the whole world. 'You think all these people are going to heaven?' she cried, gesturing at no one. 'Welcome to hell!' Protectively, Eric drew Elsie towards himself, but he couldn't get her to look away from the woman. As they walked parallel to her, she was still screaming.

Then, after throwing a spent bottle at a nearby pigeon, she squatted down beside the smashed glass, pulled down her knickers, and pissed in the street.

Back home, Elsie was distraught. Eric assured her that the woman, though obviously troubled, was no real harm; they were never in danger. But Elsie wouldn't stop crying. 'Don't you see?' she said at last. 'That's me.'

Eric told his daughter she was nothing like that woman. The poor vagrant had been addling her mind with substances for decades. And who knows what trauma she'd suffered, what underlying—

'No, Dad,' Elsie said. 'That's how I *feel*.'

Eric nodded his head slowly. 'All the time?' he asked.

'All the time,' Elsie confirmed. Then she corrected herself. 'All the time, *unless I'm buzzed*.'

Now that Tovyah had finished speaking, I said something didn't sound right. In Oxford, Elsie had seemed so upbeat. He said so himself.

'You don't get it,' he said. 'She was drinking then. And right after, she crashed.'

I remembered how she had turned down my offer of a gin and tonic. 'Are you sure?'

'Who knows? Whatever's going on, I think what she needs right now is peace.'

'So what's the plan, we just give up?'

Tovyah shrugged, then indicated it was time to go downstairs. As we descended, I took in the photos on the wall. Family portraits spanning generations. An old sepia print of someone's wedding, in what I assumed was pre-war Poland. The three children, aged about seven, ten, and fifteen, posed on a white sofa. Gideon on his bar mitzvah, cutting cake in his tallit. Zeide being honoured in synagogue, reading from the Torah scroll, the silver pointer clutched in his stubby fingers. Tovyah's matriculation at Oxford. Hannah and Eric in their youth, toasting something. And at the bottom of the winding staircase: Elsie as a small girl, her hair still blonde, a shy hand raised to cover her face.

Chapter Twenty

In the centre of the table was something wholly unexpected in this religious household. A large Roman vase, empty of flowers, depicting huntsmen spearing a doomed stag. Was this not a relic of pagan culture, celebrating practices that were certainly not kosher? I was reminded of a conversation I'd had with Tovyah around the time we met. He'd told me his parents attempted to mingle Orthodox tradition with a bourgeois appreciation of *les beaux arts*. Here, I supposed, was the evidence.

Eric caught me looking. 'You like it? The genuine article, I'm told. Third century. A gift of course – my wife has some illustrious friends.'

He sat at the head of the table, large and imperious, with the great dome of his belly rising behind his plate. At the other end was Hannah, dressed in lime green, now waving away her husband's flattering words, though she did not look displeased. In her ears were ruby studs, and from her neck hung a small golden pendant, the Hebrew word *Chai*. She invited me to take the seat to her left, opposite an empty space that would later be filled by Elsie. Tovyah took the seat beside mine, and Gideon sat on the far side of the table. There was no wine glass before Elsie's place, but the rest of us had one for red and one for white and a champagne flute besides. Gideon was refilling his red wine when we came in.

'So,' Eric said, once we were seated, 'are you going to tell us about yourself?'

Whether because he was protecting me, or because he feared what I might say, Tovyah tried to derail the conversation.

'Let her settle down first.'

But I said it was fine. 'What would you like to know?'

'For starters, why don't you tell us if you've been to Shabbos before.'

I glanced at Tovyah.

'This is my first time.'

'Nervous?'

'Should I be?'

Here Gideon interrupted. 'But you've heard about the human sacrifices, right?'

Eric tried to take back the conversation. 'Gideon I—'

'You must know how we make bread with blood of Christian children.'

'What a thing to say!'

Gideon caught my eye. 'She's not an idiot. She knows I'm joking.'

Eric scowled. 'But who's laughing?'

I could see that Gideon had played the family comedian his whole life, and everyone, especially his father, was tired of the act. Eric turned to me and spoke confidentially.

'Ignore him. You're going to have a wonderful evening. The Sabbath is a lovely time, the holiest part of the week.'

Now it was Tovyah's turn to contradict the patriarch.

'Eric, she's not religious.'

'I know, I know. But she likes weekends. You like weekends, don't you? Did you know that it was the Jews who invented the weekend? This is what we're celebrating now. It's all in the Torah.'

'Darling,' Hannah said, smoothing down the tablecloth and speaking more softly than anyone else, 'I think you might be boring our guest.'

This admonition from his wife succeeded where his sons had failed. Eric held up his hands, indicating that he would be silent for the next few minutes. I swore that I hadn't been at all bored, and everyone laughed. Even Tovyah. Upending all my expectations, here was a warm, good-humoured family, and tonight I was going to have fun.

'I like this one,' Eric said. 'So polite.'

Gideon said, 'Don't give her too much credit. It's not on purpose, she told me earlier. Just a knee-jerk reaction to weirdos like us.'

'Nobody thinks we're weirdos,' Hannah said.

In the hush that followed, Gideon asked me what I was planning to do after graduation. I wasn't sure.

'What did you say you studied? English? No money in that, I'm afraid. Tell you what, you're a bright girl, I don't think you'd make a bad consultant.'

I knew Tovyah thought his brother's chosen profession ridiculous. 'Based on what?' he said. 'You don't even know her!'

'She's got that hungry look. There, you see? She's got good manners, sure, and she's charming enough, but I think there's some ambition lurking down there. Would you say so, Hannah?'

'To be honest,' I said, 'I'm not even sure what consultants do.'

'Nothing to it. Just bullshitting.'

'Gideon! Don't swear. It's Shabbos.'

He apologised to his mother, and then went on. 'I'm serious. It's only a question of language, of codes really. How do you think bankers make their money? They know how to talk to other bankers. Lawyers know how to talk to other lawyers. Sorry, Eric.'

Eric moved in his chair, which squeaked under the weight. 'I try to talk about scripture, and I'm told I'm being boring. And this, *this* is interesting!'

'Anyway, Gideon,' his mother chipped in, 'you shouldn't be talking shop on Shabbos.'

'You're right, you're right, I forget myself. Always hustling, that's my problem. But won't you look at that, the sun's about to go down. We should get started. Who wants fizz?'

'We can't get started,' Tovyah said. 'Elsie hasn't come down yet.'

'If we wait for her, we'll be eating at midnight.'

Gideon was already fiddling with the top of the champagne bottle, which flew off with a satisfying *fthunk*. There followed a small eruption of foam. He went round the table from glass to glass and suggested that his mother start lighting the candles.

'Let's give her ten minutes,' Hannah said. 'Compromise.'

'Oh come on, you know what she's like. She only does it for the attention, especially with a new audience. She'll be hours.'

'I'm right here.'

Elsie had crept down the stairs in silence and was now standing in the doorway. She had changed for dinner as she said she would, but not how I'd imagined. The bright summer dress was gone, replaced by pyjama bottoms and a baggy jumper. Her parents exchanged a look and said nothing.

Gideon wasn't so reticent. 'How nice, Elz, you dressed up.'

Hannah spoke next. 'Come on, love. Let's do the lights.'

Elsie went about lighting candles with a burning match pinched between her thumb and forefinger while Hannah recited the Hebrew prayer. *Baruch ata Adonai, Eloheinu Melech ha'olam* . . . I had witnessed similar rituals on a few occasions, and the foreign words were starting to sound familiar, but I had not seen this. The passion and intensity of the Rosenthals hinted a depth of feeling beyond anything you'd get in Oxford's liberal synagogue. Something primordial was taking place here, something fundamental, not so different, really, from how they ushered in Friday nights in the ancient Kingdoms of Israel and Judea, centuries before the birth of Christ, when after the week's struggle families would gather around their fires to thank Hashem that they were still here, had food to eat, and had earned another brief respite from the toil of existence.

Once the candles were all lit and the prayer was finished, I became aware that Gideon was hovering by my elbow. He brought his lips to my ear and whispered.

'Now *your* work begins.'

I had no idea what he meant.

'Tovyah! Phones away. Let's do this properly,' Eric said. '*L'kavod Shabbos.*'

Without apologising, Tovyah pocketed his device. The twenty-four-hour moratorium on all forms of work, creation, and trade had begun. Electronic appliances could not be used. Even writing was out. I felt my phone vibrating against my thigh but didn't dare reach for it.

That evening, we ate like kings. I'd been bracing myself for mushy fish balls, dried crackers, and that nasty mixture of beetroot and horseradish I'd encountered on previous Friday nights. In fact, we were treated to rich pâtés spread across slices of bread still warm from the oven, silvery-pink cuts of gravlax that trailed off into mysterious weeds, endless wine, fine meats, all accompanied by various dips, spreads, and sauces. Barely could I finish a glass before someone – usually Eric – was leaning over to top me up. Gideon's appetite was indefatigable. Again and again, he piled up his plate with food, only to devour the mountainous stack in not many minutes and with obvious delight. It was only after I saw him eat that I realised just how pudgy he was around the face. He was in his twenties then and if he carried on like this, he'd have a paunch before he made thirty-five. More than once I complimented the meal. Each time, Gideon said I deserved nothing less, it being my last. It seemed that when people didn't laugh at his jokes, he only took it as a challenge to repeat them, with ever more enthusiasm.

At dinner, the Rosenthals could pass for a normal family. Almost. Gideon, Eric, and Hannah were friendly hosts, who enjoyed each other's company. They gossiped about old friends, exchanged news from their respective lives, asked interested questions. Eric took it on himself to explain to me, resident outsider, the significance of the Sabbath.

'Work without cessation isn't a life. It's why slavery is an abomination. The Sabbath breaks the chain. How long are you with us? If you're around tomorrow evening, you'll be here for the Havdalah. It's worth seeing.'

Looking at Tovyah, I said I wasn't sure – I might need to head off early.

'Oh, you must stay,' Hannah said. 'We have a very special visitor coming.'

'A *second* special visitor,' Eric corrected.

'Rabbi Grossman is honouring us with his presence,' Hannah went on. 'Now there's a man you want to meet.'

Tovyah looked up from his food. 'What does he want?'

'What do you think?' said Gideon. 'He's doing an exorcism on witchy over here. The ultimate showdown: white magic versus black magic.'

'You're not serious,' Tovyah said.

Eric exhaled. 'Emmanuel Grossman is not Max von Sydow. Kate, I must apologise for my two sons, a pair of imbeciles. The rabbi is coming to observe the Havdalah with old friends. That is all.'

'Brilliant,' Tovyah said. 'I look forward to being bowled over by wisdom.' Elsie had said nothing during the whole exchange.

Clearly wanting to move the conversation on, Eric ignored Tovyah's irreverence and changed the subject. It turned out we had common ground – he was a fellow Eli Schultz reader. His works on the Shoah, Eric opined, were second to none.

'I met him once,' Hannah said. 'We were both reading at the same event. I hate to say it, but I'm pretty sure he was flirting with me.'

'A man of taste,' said Eric, blowing her a kiss.

He took back the reins of the conversation. Thanks to his profession, he had a decent store of anecdotes to parcel out. Most of his stories concerned brainless policemen and corrupt barristers who only saw the error of their ways after he, Eric, staged an intervention. 'I know guys who won't let their clients plead. If there's no trial, it cuts the pay cheque in half. And when the dope lands a heftier sentence, so what? It's not their funeral.'

Gideon reminded his father that they weren't supposed to be talking shop.

'This is a parable! An illustration of human folly!'

Still he ceded the floor to his wife, who said the problem with the English legal system was that in defamation cases, it always favoured the plaintiff, regardless of evidence. Hence, she had been stung for describing a famous singer as utterly talentless, various MPs as homicidal, and a certain well-known nun as a Godless charlatan.

'Would that be talking shop,' I asked, 'or would that count as another parable of human folly?' Both Gideon and Eric roared. Remarkably enough, in this strangest of families, I was a hit.

All the while, Elsie had sat there moodily, saying nothing. And at this great familial dinner, she'd hardly eaten. I only saw her put one slice of bread on her plate all evening. She buttered it, sprinkled a little salt on top, and then cut it into thin strips, no more than a finger's width. Slowly, avoiding all eye contact, she ate the strips one at a time.

Hannah put her hand on her daughter's shoulder and asked if everything was all right.

'I'm fine,' she said.

'Sure? Is there anything else you'd like? There's plenty more food.'

'I wouldn't mind a glass of wine.' She spoke loudly enough to break off other conversations.

'Now, now, Elz,' Gideon said, 'behave yourself.'

As I looked across the table at Elsie, I saw she wasn't the same girl I met in Oxford. She lacked all buoyancy: if you dropped her in a lake she'd sink faster than a pound coin. She had no spark of life in her, no humour, no personality even. It was as if the shy girl in the photo on the landing, with her hand covering her face, had died long ago – in her place, this empty husk. No wonder she wanted to blot everything out with whatever drink she could get her hands on. I felt my phone vibrating again. Almost forgetting, I reached into my pocket, but stopped myself.

'I don't know about you lot,' Gideon said, scraping up the last of his dessert onto his spoon, 'but I'd love a cup of coffee.'

There was something provocative in his tone.

Elsie spoke again. 'Everyone else gets to have wine. Even Tovyah and his guest. What are they, like twelve? I just want one glass.'

I suspect this was not the first dinner she'd made such requests; silence was the agreed response.

'There's some iced coffee in the fridge,' Hannah said. 'I thought we might want it tomorrow morning, but you're welcome to have yours now.'

'I know, mother dear, but I like my coffee *hot*.'

'Gideon, don't be ridiculous,' Tovyah said. He'd cottoned on before anyone else, bristling with indignation as he looked at his brother. And then I realised too. Hot coffee required turning on the kettle, an act now forbidden.

'But I'm *not* being ridiculous. After all, this is no ordinary Friday night. Tonight, *Baruch hashem*, we have a Gentile among us. A shiksa! I'm sure, if we ask her nicely, she'll run along to the kitchen. Won't you now? The Sabbath goy strikes the match.'

I was tempted to point out that I was Jewish too but didn't want another lecture on mixed blood. Besides, I was not superstitious and didn't believe in these ancient strictures. If it would shut him up, I'd boil a kettle.

'Don't call our guest a shiksa,' Hannah said. 'It's not nice.'

'Please can I have one half glass of wine?'

Eric said, 'You don't have to make the coffee. He's only teasing you.'

'But I'd be happy to.'

Tovyah scraped his chair back. '*I'll* do it.'

'No, no, little brother, that won't do, even if you are a heathen these days.'

'I don't understand,' Elsie said. 'Can you lot hear me? I would like a little wine, please.'

Tovyah was glaring at his brother. 'You're being a prick.'

'Tovyah. It's Sabbath.'

Elsie slapped herself, hard, and everyone shut up. It was Eric, who had so indulged his daughter as a little girl, that took her part now. 'OK, why not? I don't suppose one glass will do much harm. As long as you promise.'

'Are you fucking kidding me?' Tovyah burst out.

The exhalation was forceful enough to blow out one of the candles. This was not a table at which people said 'fuck' lightly. Hannah rested her hands in her lap. Elsie looked at the floor.

'Apologise to your father, Tovyah,' Hannah said.

'*Me?* You heard him, didn't you? This is insane. Elsie doesn't do just one glass of wine.'

'I want you to apologise, now.'

'I'm not the one in the wrong here.'

'TOVYAH!'

The noise from Eric's mouth was impressive, the blare of a trumpet up close. Tovyah sank in his chair and said nothing.

Eric spoke next. 'We can't have one night together as a family. One night. Apologise now, and we'll draw a line under it.'

'Fine,' Tovyah said. 'I'll say I'm sorry. Just as soon as she apologises for writing that fucking book.'

Eric's face shone.

'Here we go,' said Gideon.

When no one else spoke, Tovyah continued.

'I'm not joking. I'd like to hear her say sorry.' He turned to his mother. 'You want Elsie to go to Oxford, right? Get a good job, meet a nice husband. Who's going to give her a job when they know her life story? You think that's a picture of a stable employee you've painted? Everywhere she goes, for the rest of her life, people will stop what they are doing, and they will look at her. There she is, *that poor girl*. Such a sad story! But you never thought about that.'

Now even Elsie begged him to stop his accusations. 'Tovyah, I can have one glass you know. I've done it before.'

Hannah spoke next. 'Everything is my fault, you see, Kate. Go on, Tovyah, why don't you tell us again? You do it so well. Perhaps you could tell us about being a parent while you're at it. You don't want to know what sort of house your father grew up in. You lot have it easy. The life we've provided for the three of you. The holidays you've had, the education. Elsie knows we love her. Who do you think feeds her, clothes her, puts a roof over her head? Who pays for everything she's stolen over the years? Who pleaded with teachers, doctors, *police officers*, on her behalf? Your father and I, no one else. While you're swanning about in Oxford, who do you think is stuck here, doing the work with your sister? So go on. Let's hear what tyrants we are.'

'Spare me the handwringing, Mum.'

'Always the same. Once he gets going, no one else is allowed to speak.'

'But why are we even here?'

'Excuse me? It's Shabbos.'

'I mean here! In this situation! Why is Elsie how she is? You have three children, you put straightjackets on the lot of us, and look what's happened! Gideon moved to the other side of the world to shoot Arabs, Elsie's sick in the head, and as for me, I'm the worst of the pack. Everyone thinks I'm a fucking psycho!'

281

Gideon looked at me. 'Got siblings?' he asked.

Elsie, meanwhile, was saying something. 'You shouldn't talk like that. Really, Tuvs, you don't know everything. I'm not sick, and it isn't their fault.'

'Can I just say, I've never actually shot anyone.'

'Of course it's their fault! Who else? We were the children, and they were the adults. They made our lives for us. Why do we never speak about things honestly? Why can't we say what's right in front of us? Even she can see it.' He was pointing at me.

When Gideon spoke again, all levity was gone from his voice. 'No more, Tovyah. We're done now.'

'No more? I've hardly even *begun*.'

'Tovyah—'

'You tell me how it is then. Captain bigshot. What are you *doing* in Israel? What's there, aside from the greatest possible distance you can put between you and this nut house?'

'It's a beautiful country.'

'*Italy* is a beautiful country, and it doesn't have barbed wire round the edges. Spain is a beautiful country! You wanted to get the hell away from our magnificent, back-breaking parents, and you went somewhere you could actually save the Jews. A big man, just like the biblical Gideon, the great deliverer! You felt so ashamed of what Zeide got up to in Poland, all those years ago, it's the only thing you could think of. You were sick of your idiot friends telling you how your grandfather helped the Nazis shovel Jews into the ovens. Which he did, by the way, *he did*, so why don't we talk about that? Oh no, let's do what healthy families do, shall we, let's just keep silent while Hannah publishes her trashy book and tells the whole world what she never would have told her own children! I bet you were thrilled when you figured him for a collaborator. Just think of the sales!'

'He was never a collaborator,' Eric said.

'*Wasn't* he? He asked her to destroy the tapes, burn the manuscript. Begged her! Did you ever think, maybe if you'd let Zeide be, if you hadn't sold his life-story to the highest bidder in a literal auction, your oldest son would still live in Western Europe?'

Hannah said, 'Zeide did nothing we should be ashamed of.'

'Not the way you wrote it. How do you think Elsie felt? She adored the man. And you made him a monster! You—'

No doubt Tovyah would have gone on speaking, but Elsie let out a noise then like nothing in this world, a tremendous wail that contained both rumbles and shrieks. Her eyes rolled back in her head, and her outstretched fingers scratched at the tablecloth. A loud popping noise arose and, in the centre of the table, the vase cracked and fell into two clean pieces. Open mouthed, Hannah stared at the spot where it had once stood. Elsie rose from her seat. In a low, growling voice, not her own, she said, '*Voss is doss?* Who collects this rubbish?'

No one answered. Elsie wilted to one side, then folded down to the floor, muttering to herself. She reached a hand towards her mother, who recoiled in her seat. At last Gideon went to his sister, dragged her up, then half-carried, half-walked her out of the room.

Eric's voice emerged from the shattered silence. 'Are you happy?' he said. 'We've trodden all over the Sabbath, now.'

With nothing else to do, Tovyah suggested that we go and make that coffee after all.

Hannah picked up the two halves of the vase, as though wondering if they could be reattached.

Chapter Twenty-One

In the kitchen, Tovyah filled the stove-top kettle, and left the tap running. When I tried to spark the gas ring, it clicked a few times without catching, so I used my cigarette lighter. A stream of gas flared out into wide orange flames for a moment, then pulled back into a tight blue ring.

'Tovyah, what happened back there. That vase!'

Apart from the light of the stove, we were in total darkness.

'It went, just on its own.'

He thought about something. 'They're infectious.'

'And I can't help thinking about some of the stuff your mother's book. I—'

'My family's infectious. You only have to come near them to go straight out of your mind.'

'Don't shut this down. Your grandfather was there, at the lecture. And just last week, when Elsie was staying, there was this strange light bleeding under your door.'

'Listen to yourself, Kate. The things you are saying don't make sense.'

'Then tell me. How do you make sense of all this?'

'Hannah pulled the tablecloth and it tipped it over.'

'It didn't tip, it exploded! You don't smash an antique for a cheap stunt!'

Tovyah shook his head and told me had more important things to worry about. He was planning a prison break. Tonight: it couldn't wait any longer. This was no life for someone with Elsie's troubles, mocked by Gideon, and regarded as a sorceress by her parents. 'Who knows what's really going on with Grossman's visit tomorrow? There are no reliable narrators in this house.'

All through Tovyah's gap year, he explained, he'd worked in a hotel. He hadn't travelled, hadn't done anything, just folded towels, checked in guests, and put the money away. On top of that, he had savings. Whatever else you could accuse his parents of, they weren't tight-fisted. They'd put money into an account on his birthday every year of his life. Twenty princely deposits.

'I have enough to rent a place for the two of us, outside London, somewhere we can figure out what she'll do with her life. She can have another go at A Levels if she wants, she's so clever. I'll help. Or she can get a job. As long as she's away from all this.'

'And when your savings run out?'

'I can make money.'

He didn't say anything about his studies, but I understood he meant to drop out.

'What about Oxford? You're just going to quit?'

'Oxford? I'm afraid to say, Oxford has been one of the great disappointments of my life.'

His face took on a ruminative look. He might have been thinking of all that had gone wrong in the last year. But if I had to bet, I'd say he was recollecting the hope that smouldered inside the seventeen-year-old he once was, knocking at Oxford's door, so unprepared for this first encounter with the outside world.

'And us?' I said.

He couldn't meet my eye.

'You could help me break her loose,' he said. 'If you stay the night, distract my parents in the morning—'

'That's not what I was asking.'

He said nothing.

'You could be free of all this,' I said. 'Your mother didn't drag you back here, you know. You reinserted yourself – it's like you have to prove something to them, you can't just leave them be.' I paused, weighing my words. 'You don't have to keep being unhappy.'

'What do you want of me, Kate?'

'Just to see where this goes. You and me. This is your chance to forge your own life, to give up this obsession with hating your family. Finish your degree, let your parents take care of Elsie. They do love her, you know.'

'That's the stupidest thing I've ever heard you say. Love her? They're *killing* her.'

I was determined that I would not cry. Not now.

'So are you going to help me or what?' he said.

I couldn't speak.

'Guess that's a no then. Can I at least count on you to stay silent?'

'This isn't my fight.'

'Careful there, Kate. Sometimes when people do nothing, it ends up counting as something, and they regret it.'

His mouth was taut with anger, but at the same time there was pleasure in his eyes. I suspected a part of him had enjoyed that horrendous display at the dinner table. And he was enjoying this too, the conspiracy, the argument, the whispers. I wondered, for the hundredth time, what we were to each other.

'It's a fantasy,' I said. 'There's no way you can provide the help she needs. The moment you're out that door, it's hopeless.'

Finally, after all those nights spent hashing things out, I had said something that punctured through all Tovyah's conceit; disappointment swept across his face. I think at that moment he hated me. At last, he told me to go to hell.

'I'd like to go home now, actually,' I said.

'No one's stopping you.'

The kettle whistled. Tovyah killed the gas, scooped coffee grounds into a large cafetiere, and poured over boiling water. 'You can have one, by the way.'

'Sorry?'

'Your cigarettes. You've been reaching for them all evening. The door to the garden's right behind you. I only wish you'd lit one up at the table. *That* would have made an impression.'

I stood on the lawn with my back to the house, smoking by the weak light of the moon and stars, willing myself to calm down. My surroundings were murky, and I felt the darkness pressing in against my skin. When I moved my head too quickly, the world tilted on its axis. A low voice sounded behind me. 'Well if you're having one, I might as well have one.'

It was Gideon. When I turned around, he held up his index and middle fingers to his lips.

'I thought you don't make fire on the Sabbath,' I said, passing him a cigarette.

'Do you know how many of those damn rules there are? Follow every single one, you'll go crazy. Lighter please.'

I handed it over.

'Apologies, by the way, if I gave the wrong impression earlier, about the Sabbath goy and that. I was only messing around. And sorry about my family. They love each other really, but God they're nuts.'

'So you agree with Tovyah?'

'I half-agree with him. Hannah's books are a little reckless, sure, but they're not bad parents.'

I brought up some of the things Tovyah had told me about Hannah and Eric. That when Elsie went missing, Eric's response was to fast. Or that later, when her problems really started heaping up, her parents commissioned a new mezuzah.

'You don't know the one about the prize fighter's mother,' Gideon said. 'He's got this big fight coming up, biggest of his career. The guy he's up against is a monster, Mohammed Ali and Genghis Khan rolled into one. So the mother says to her rabbi, "Will you pray? Pray that my son wins?" The rabbi looks at the leviathan in the far corner, and he says, "Sure, I'll pray for your boy. But it'll help if he can punch." One of Eric's favourite jokes. They never prayed instead of being parents. They prayed *on top* of being parents.'

I said that's not what Tovyah thinks, and Gideon said he knew. When Tovyah has an opinion, he doesn't just say it the one time.

'What about Elsie? Was tonight . . . normal for her?'

Here Gideon paused. This was not a subject he could navigate on autopilot.

'That girl left normal behind a long time ago. Sometimes she's sullen and unreachable. Tonight, you saw a mild version. At least, up until Tovyah kicked off.'

'What's the not-mild version?'

'Won't leave her room for weeks on end. Starves herself half to death. Or she slips away, no one knows where. The police won't take it seriously. She'll come back sooner or later. An adult daughter running away from her parents is no crime. And then other times, she seems perfectly normal. She's talkative, funny, even charming. In a way, that's the most painful bit of all. Because every time—' his breath caught in his throat '—sorry, how embarrassing.'

'How do you cope?'

'Were you not paying attention? We *don't*.'

I asked him why he thought Elsie ran away in the first place. That seemed to be at the beginning of so much.

'Tovyah would blame it on Hannah and Eric, no doubt. Too much pressure, pushed her away. And Hannah, as you know, thought it was all to do with Zeide's death. She had to go searching for his spirit, or whatever. All that Kabbalah shit.'

'But what do you think?'

'Maybe I'm just projecting what I was like at that age. But I always wondered if there was a boy in it.'

'She'd have been very young,' I said.

'Elsie stopped being young all at once. I don't think it's supposed to happen like that.' Gideon stopped talking, looked over his shoulder. We were quite alone. I was getting used to the light now and could see more of the garden. Raised flower beds, little gnomes standing guard round the edge of a pond.

'But you're OK, right? You look all shook up.'

Lines from the fight I'd just had with Tovyah were running through my head. Trying to supress them, I told Gideon that I was a little thrown by what happened at dinner, but basically OK.

Gideon ran his hand through his hair, assessing. 'I think you could use a drink.'

'I should go,' I said. 'I need to get back.'

'Don't be ridiculous. The last train's gone, and you're among friends here. Besides, it's Shabbos. The Shekinah is with us, God's light is filling up the house. I'm gonna pour you that drink.'

'What does it look like?' I said.

'Sorry?'

'You said God's light is in the house. Can you see it?'

Gideon smiled, bemused, and I grew shy.

'You know Tovyah doesn't believe in any of it,' I said.

'Why do you think he gets so angry?'

Gideon led me back into the kitchen, where he doled out a couple of glugs of whisky into two stubby glasses.

'*L'chaim*!' He raised his drink. When I repeated the toast, he asked if I knew what it meant.

'To life.'

'Very good. To life. Goes on, doesn't it. As the rabbis say, however bloody awful it gets, it still goes on.'

'Which rabbis?'

Gideon laughed. 'A turn of phrase.'

Speaking sensibly, more alcohol was the last thing I needed. I was a touch unsteady on my feet as it was and had trouble following the train of my own thoughts. But there was no one there to speak sensibly. Just Gideon with his strong arms and his heavy pour, the functional alcoholic that was fewer steps than he realised from becoming, like his sister, a dysfunctional one.

We each knocked back a stinging gulp.

'It's not true, by the way. What Tuvs said, about me flying to Israel to become this great hero. My parents like to believe I have a saviour complex. And Tovyah, who thinks he knows best about everything, is a total dupe. You want the real story? I spent a week in Tel Aviv when I was nineteen.

And I met this boy. A sabra – that's what they call the ones who were born there. Spoke good English. And he had the most beautiful skin. He told me the thing about Israel is everyone knows they're on the brink of a terrible war that kills everyone they've ever met, so no one gives a fuck. You see? They don't give a fuck about embarrassing themselves, or saying the wrong thing, or what strangers think, or any of that English bullshit. They live their lives at a million miles an hour and they party like bastards. And I thought, this, this is what I want. I want this boy. These mountains. These nights. I want to party like a bastard. I want this life, and nothing but this life, until I die.'

As if to punctuate this little speech, he topped up our drinks. The square glasses were now brimming with amber liquor.

'Are you still together?' I said. 'You and this guy?'

'No.'

'And what about the life? Is it what you wanted.'

Now he laughed again. 'It's not for everyone.'

Gideon said he'd better go check on Elsie and bade me good night. I decided to head outside for one last smoke before turning in. I tripped on the step and found myself taking a few steps to recover my balance. When I reached into my back pocket, cigarette dangling from lower lip, I realised with some annoyance that Gideon had taken my lighter with him.

Chapter Twenty-Two

I only learned what happened next the following day, when Tovyah, ashen-faced, ran feverishly through the whole sequence of events. At some point in the night, while the rest of us slept, Tovyah wandered across the first-floor landing, treading lightly so as not to wake his parents, and tapped with a fingernail on his sister's door, an act he'd performed countless times in childhood and had not repeated in years. Now was the time for definitive action, he told himself. No more deferments. A quiet voice ushered him in. The lamp that hung from the ceiling was dead. Elsie was sitting on her bed with legs crossed, back against the wall, arms drooped in her lap.

For a while neither of them said anything. They had known each other so long, had spent so much time probing each other's thoughts. Years earlier, on the day when Elsie had slipped and broken her tooth at the public swimming pool, while everyone else was fretting over the girl, trying to staunch the bleeding, little Tovyah had taken it upon himself to find the fragment of tooth, the small white shard that was camouflaged somewhere against the paving stones. He found it too. And when he did, though it was smaller than he expected, disappointingly small, in fact, barely worth the trouble, he presented it to his sister, believing in his innocence that it might be glued back on.

'Why do you pretend to be Zeide?' Tovyah said at last. 'Just another way of lashing out?'

Elsie stared blankly. 'You never thought Mum might be right? That I'm possessed by an evil spirit, and it'll take a holy man to drive it away.'

'You're unwell.'

'You've said that already tonight.'

Tovyah looked at his sister, who now lay down on her bed. She wore only a cotton vest, and it was impossible to ignore how thin she was. Almost skeletal.

'Did you ever wonder why Zeide wanted to be cremated anyway?' she asked.

'Does it matter? To be honest, I figured Hannah probably made that up.'

'No, no, if anything, she played it down. He told me himself. That man knew his mind, right to the end.'

Tovyah was struggling to mask his irritation. He hadn't come here to talk about what happened ten years ago. But Elsie had always controlled the conversations between them.

'I suppose you're going to tell me he felt guilty,' Tovyah said.

'No, not just *guilty*. I wish you weren't always so sarcastic these days. You end up reducing everything. Eli Schultz, Dad's favourite, wrote that by fleeing Europe at the time of the Shoah, he felt he'd somehow missed his date with destiny. He knew it was an appalling thing to say, but that's how he felt.'

'Who cares? Eli Schultz is a windbag. There is no destiny. This is what's real, Elz, this right here.'

He was on his knees beside the bed. It was only then he knew that what he'd come to suggest was impossible. He couldn't spring her from this place. It had all been going on so long. He couldn't even spring himself.

'What do you want?' she said.

'I want you to get better.'

Elsie nodded, agreeing perhaps, perhaps just considering. 'I don't suppose you could pop downstairs and fetch me a nightcap?'

'No. You know I can't.'

'Pity,' she said. Then she sat up. 'What if I don't want to get better? Ever think of that? What if I'm not ill and I'm not possessed, this is just how I am. Maybe I like everyone running around shit scared. All the attention, the total lack of responsibilities.'

Tovyah stood and took a step away from his sister. Like a cat, she followed him with her eyes.

'I'm not an idiot,' she said. 'I do know what I'm doing. Even when I was a little girl, if I wanted a day off, all I had to do was play sick for my Mummy. Always worked.'

'It's not possible.' He put his hand on the corner of the bookshelf by the wall, and no longer kept his voice lowered. 'It isn't possible,' he said again.

Elsie laughed.

'Oh, Tuvs. Come back here. Didn't you know? Everything's possible.'

She was still laughing when he pushed the door shut behind him, as if to muffle the sound. At the foot of the stairs to the attic, I'd like to think Tovyah hesitated. I'd like to believe he stood there for a moment, wondering if he could still patch things up with me.

*

Someone must have gone up to the room at the top of the house after I came down for dinner, because the windows had been closed again. Although it was my room only for the night, I resented the intrusion and now the air was thick with heat. Before going to bed, I pushed them wide open, letting in a faint breeze.

I was a fool not to be on the bus home. Here I was, friendless in this old house, trapped in this creepy room until morning. Not even able to smoke. The walls swayed a little as I got into bed. I had lost count of how many glasses of wine I'd drunk, not to mention the whisky. And I couldn't stop thinking about that vase. The noise Elsie had made. Growing up, losing my mind seemed worse than anything else that could happen, worse than blindness or paralysis. The continual revelations that what you had thought solid and reliable was a phantom, and that nothing could be trusted, neither your friends, nor your senses, nor even your own memories. Is that what life was like for Elsie? You could sense all the accumulated sadness of that place. It dripped from the walls.

For a while I drifted in and out of sleep. The course of the evening now seemed blurred and uncertain. Had Tovyah really picked that awful fight with his parents? I tried to picture the members of the family, but their features eluded me. It was as though I'd sat at the table with mannequins, wooden creatures with faces smoothed into blank surfaces. All except Tovyah, whose drooping eyes glared at me as clearly as ever. And I remembered what he was planning. To remove Elsie from the influence of her parents forever. Like something out of a fairy tale.

At one point in the night, I sat up and thought I could see a figure standing in the room, his long robes trailing to the floor. Straining my ears, I heard a faint wheezing sound, someone struggling for breath. I said hello, and a face turned in my direction. Even in my dream, it was not so much terrifying as repulsive. Yes, there was something obscene about the dead man refusing to give up the room he'd lived in, like seeing someone's chest unzipped by a surgeon, the fleshy heart pulsing in plain view. As he approached, he held up his hands towards me. One held a candle, the other was empty, beckoning. He wanted a match, I thought, but I had nothing to offer. Then the curtains lifted on a gust of air, and in the light from the street I saw that I was alone.

Some time later, I was woken by voices tearing through the silence of the house. Another terrible argument.

I rushed from the room. There was no sign of anyone in the corridor, and the voices rose from below, more animated now. A weird glow climbed through the house, spilling upwards through the stairwells and bouncing off the walls. It was the same colour as the light I had seen emanating from under Tovyah's door earlier that term. As I took to the stairs, I missed a step, and realised with a bump that I was still drunk.

On the first floor, Gideon's door was shut. But the one leading to his parents' bedroom was ajar. I could hear a low voice within. Eric's, I thought. There came a heavy sound of weight redistributed, then the groan of an ancient floorboard. Not wanting to be seen, I darted into the room on the other side of Eric and Hannah's, hoping it was unoccupied. The window gaped open, and there was plenty of light filtering in from outside. In the centre of the room was a bed that had been slept in and abandoned. Against the wardrobe, a stack of books piled up. I gathered this was Elsie's room. So where was Elsie?

Eric's voice now boomed through the house. 'Why are all the lights on? Is nothing Holy?'

I heard him thumping down the stairs and after a careful pause, left Elsie's room. As I stepped out, Gideon appeared on the landing, wrapped in a dressing gown, rubbing his eyes, yawning.

'You know anything about this?' he said.

Together we stumbled downstairs. With each step, the weird light grew brighter, until I could feel its warmth. Only when I reached the bottom did I smell burning. We trod carefully to avoid broken glass. The mirror that stood opposite the coat stand was cracked neatly down the middle. The face that met me was viciously torn.

In the sitting room Eric stood gazing out through the windows, his stony face all lit up. The curtains had been ripped from the rail, revealing the front garden, blindingly bright. 'Oh my God, oh my God, oh my God . . .' Eric was saying to himself.

Gideon darted to the kitchen sink, found a large bowl, and turned on the tap. As he waited for the bowl to fill, he yelled at me. 'Do something!' At that moment, everything seemed to slow down. Perhaps, as well as drunk, I was still half asleep. Finally, I saw what Gideon had seen, what had sent him rushing to the kitchen, the sight that had reduced his father to a catatonic stance. In the centre of the patio outside stood Elsie, bolt upright with her hands raised to the sky. She was dressed entirely in white with an empty canister at her feet. Nearby, leaning closer, then backing away, were Tovyah and Hannah. They were trying to wrap her in a rug or a blanket but the heat was too much. Across the street, a few of the neighbours were framed by high windows, backlit and silhouetted inside their bedrooms, or standing outside their own front doors, looking on. Elsie's entire body, to the tips of her fingers, was encased in flames. Fire swayed and rippled over her limbs, her head. Blue, red, orange, and white. Yet she didn't move. And the expression on her face was tranquil.

She tossed something to the ground beneath her. Without having to go and check, I knew it was the neon pink lighter that had been taken from me by her brother, earlier that evening.

Then Gideon charged through the front door, sloshing water as he went. But the hurled contents of the bowl did little to kill the flames that were now starting to change both the colour and shape of Elsie's face. It was like she was being peeled open by unearthly fingers. Only a sound as atrocious as what I then heard could have turned my head. A deep, masculine howl. Eric was now kneeling by the side of the couch. He had both fists buried in his thick, greying hair. When he yanked them out, the crying grew louder. He opened his hands, and clumps of hair fluttered to the carpet. Howling still, he reached for another fistful.

Chapter Twenty-Three

I only saw Tovyah once more. Years later, long after he'd dropped out of Oxford, moved to Berlin, and cut ties with everyone, me included. Between stable academic jobs, I was on a research trip, riding trains across central Europe. At a station whose name I forget, I spotted him in the waiting room, sipping from a Styrofoam cup, glancing irritably at the announcements. He'd barely changed. Was still clean-shaven, and with the same gawky-adolescent body. He even dressed the same, in a scruffy shirt and badly fitting blazer. Seeing him there was so perfectly unexpected, that for a moment, I almost believed we'd arranged to meet.

His face jerked upwards as I approached, then looked away.

I do not remember the neighbour who finally doused the flames with his garden hose. Or the ambulance whose arrival came much too late. The paramedics with nothing to say or do. I do not remember the charred corpse. I read about them all later, of course, but I cannot remember them.

I remember Elsie. Elsie wrapped in terrible light, her back ramrod straight. Who was she then? The biblical daughter, burnt on the pyre of her mother's ambition? Or the fervent young believer, the girl who strayed too far? Or was she the impatient, heaven-bound soul, casting off the shell of the body before her time? Tovyah would say that was nonsense, the lot of it. What happened, happened, the facts were all laid out. Her family had driven her insane.

Once the coroner's report had been filed and the police concluded there was no investigation to pursue – Elsie had taken her own life – Gideon returned to Israel, where he got fat and adopted children with the husband he married in Amsterdam. Hannah wrote her inevitable sequel to *Daughters of Endor*, the first book in which she herself was the protagonist. Its title, which I suspect was thrust upon her by the publishing house, was simply *The Mother*. It told the whole story from her perspective. Five hundred pages long and frighteningly unmaternal, the book is no more than an unself-reflecting grab for the world's pity. Personally, I didn't have the stomach for it, and left my unfinished copy at the free-books stand outside Arsenal Station.

After that summer, I was in no state to sit my end of year exams, and I took some time off from my studies. When I returned a year later, I joined a new cohort of students, fresh faces, people who'd never met Tovyah Rosenthal, though soon every one of them knew his name. I found it difficult to relate to old friends – so much had happened in my absence – but had little interest in making new ones. As a result, I spent my final two years of university very much on my own, for the most part buried in my books. I was awarded a first-class degree and a full scholarship to pursue a master's programme, accolades that by all rights should have been Tovyah's. I felt as if I had become his shadow, living the life he'd abandoned. Perhaps that spurred me on.

When I tapped on his knee in that European train station, he affected not to know me.

'Tovyah,' I said, 'it's me.'

He shook his head and muttered in German, too low for me to catch the words. There was a mole to one side of his chin that I did not remember, and amidst his dark hair were a few grey strands. There was so much we needed to talk about. He continued to act as though he had no idea who I was. But when he looked at me, I could see the recognition in his eyes. Recognition and something else, something darker. Regret? Loss? No. The emotion I saw, kindling in the rich darkness of his pupils, was fear.

'I'm so sorry,' I said, standing to leave. 'I took you for someone else.'

Then he said, still in German, but now with slow careful diction, 'Good luck. Good luck finding your Tovyah.'

*

Just recently, I visited Oxford, and among the friends I called on was Ruth, my very first rabbi, who remains a frequent correspondent and moral guide. She told me there was once a sage who preached that God's goodness can be found in everything, even in atheism. His reasoning went like this. The believer can say the world's problems are not my fault, they're God's, *He* should sort them out. But the atheist forces us to take responsibility; there's no one else to blame.

'You know what the name Tovyah means, right?' Ruth asked me. I did. God is good.

We spoke about Elsie too, that brilliant girl, with whom I spent one unforgettable evening, half in love, maybe, and filled with all the yearnings and possibilities of youth. The girl we all failed, some of us in ways more mysterious and roundabout than others. When I think of her brief tenure in this world, I am reminded of the writings of the Talmud. Life is a passing shadow, say the Scriptures. The shadow of a tower or a tree; the shadow which prevails for a time? No; even as the shadow of a bird in its flight, it passes from our sight, and neither bird nor shadow remains.

Epilogue

Along the clifftop, shrubs long menaced by the sea wind
grew at fierce angles, their gnarled limbs groping madly
inland. The girl's shadow lengthened beside her. Soon it
would be nightfall then night another cold clump of hours
and prickling dark. How long had she trawled this path?
When did she last eat? Time was all stretched and squashed.
A purple bruise ruining the peach green as you look closer
white fur already sprouting. A few metres out to sea a gull
flapped its wings to hover in place. She lowered her eyes and
watched her feet. Traced the cracks in the soil as though
reading a foreign script. The ground beneath her teemed
with life. Earthworms butterflies ants spiders grass weeds
thistles dandelions. Teemed with death too. Dead flowers.
Crushed beetles. Stalks flattened underfoot. The body of a
crow its guts open for the world to see the wound smoth-
ered by insects. Look at you now arrogant bird once shining
and black and hurtling. The Norfolk coast then. Not where
she'd choose but there was no choice. Carried along with
the tide. On the edge of her vision an old windmill white
against the dimming sky. Beyond, the coastal path must go
on and on. She could keep walking forever. Would come past

this very spot eventually if she just followed the coastline all the way round. Would she remember it? Shudder at the second visit. Every soul has lived before has lived in Heaven and also down here on earth maybe hundreds of times. Déjà vu the faint recollection of an erased memory. Not erased just misted over. She fixed her eyes on the windmill. That was her destination now just keep walking until I reach the windmill I'm not tired and I don't feel pain one foot in front of the other and the windmill must spring up before me. If the light holds. Someone up the path no two of them two men. Nowhere to hide out here. More Carls. The world was full of Carls. That one yesterday with the Toyota. His hands on her his tongue in her mouth the hardness between his legs. Get off me! Leave! Go! And now these two. Whispering as they came. *You all right darling?* Who was darling. *You sure? We've got a car just up the way, could give you a lift somewhere. Do you have a phone? Use mine, call anyone. Suit yourself.* She wouldn't look over her shoulder to see them go. They knew nothing. She could push them over the cliff-edge if she chose. Bone-splintering death at the end of a shoulder barge. She kept walking, the path unfurled. There was no one else in the world just her. Just her and this. Just the dark and silence and peace and cold and the openhearted vastness of everything. The chill wind and the endless sea. Stars like eyes. Ariel wasn't here. She'd been all over and she knew he wasn't anywhere. She was sure if only she tore off on her own she would find him and he would sit down with her and tell her everything unlock the buried secrets of eternity. A thousand doors cracking open at once. A lightning bolt to her soul. But it was stupid all so stupid. The boy wasn't here, he was out at sea or up among the stars if he was anywhere. How far had she come now? One hundred two hundred miles. Zeide told her that the ancient mystics calculated the size of God. His feet were thirty million parasangs long. And a parasang was a long way maybe three or four miles. As a point of comparison that's a hundred times the circumference of the sun. Not that he'd use a word like circumference. So if you thought you couldn't see Him that's why. It's like the world. Every schoolkid knows that the world is shaped like a marble, no? A little ball. Blue bits here, green bits here. But look down, look at the ground under you. Do you see a ball? Do you see a pattern of blue and green? You don't see nothing. It's too big, you're too close. So if God was closer than your shirt to your back, and if just His feet were a hundred times bigger than the sun, how do you expect to see anything? Lucky too. Look on His face and you will not live. But if the skies parted for an instant. If the sun turned black and the moon broke and the skies ripped away and the oceans poured into the heavens and there He was beautiful colossal terrifying older than a line of mountains come out from beyond time ancient and infinite wouldn't that be worth seeing. Worth dying for. The boy might know, if only she could find him. That sad sad boy. Plucked from the pages of the Bible. How could anyone not believe in God? Zeide said in the *lager* there were times when he was so cold, so hungry, in so much pain, that he stopped existing in his body. The whole thing just fell away. Numb. Like I was dead. And I tell you it wasn't a bad thing. Being dead was OK. The windmill wasn't getting any closer. Why not admit it? She was in agony. No pain like this her whole life. Her feet her stomach her head her fingertips her lungs her everything everything everything burned. Like when she held a match too long the flame kissed her thumb. No numbness here no escape from the physical. No relief

305

anywhere. And she'd done it all to herself. How could she? An evil child. A wicked child. A child, no woman, a child. Stupid, stupid, stupid, but evil. As she walked on towards an eternal recession and the world darkened around her she was sure that this was it she would die out here. The final revelation. But that was OK too. Being dead was OK.

She lay down to rest. The grass under her was spongy and a little wet. This would do. Way out to sea a blinking light bobbed on the horizon. *Eyn sof*. אֵין סוֹף. The fog at the centre of a dark flame that is neither black nor white nor red nor green. Colourless itself the flame gives colour and light to everything that is. This light was nothing she'd seen before. She let go, allowed herself to drift into the abysmal dark, and the darkness swallowed her.

Acknowledgements

A novel has one parent but innumerable aunts, uncles, godparents, and unexpected well-wishers. A few words of gratitude are in order.

Firstly, I'd like to thank my agent, Becky Thomas, who has masterfully guided me through the strange journey from Word doc to hardback. Along the way, I've been lucky enough to have two incomparable editors, Federico Andornino and Lauren Wein, who have held me to higher standards than I held myself. Thanks also to Holly Knox and the rest of the Sceptre team, to Amy Guay and the Avid Reader team, to Saliann St-Clair at Lewinsohn Literary Agency, and to James Pusey and Nicole Etherington at Blake Friedmann.

For the belief that *Fervour* might find a readership in multiple languages, thanks to Tiffany Gassouk, Sabine Schultz, Anni Moilanen, and Varya Gornostaeva.

During the composition of the novel, the staff at Morocco Bound, Elsa and Cal especially, made me innumerable coffees and sold me very few books. Thank you, and I promise to buy more reading matter on my next visit.

Huge thanks to my parents and to my brother, Jacob, who have put up with so much over so many years, and have never told me to stop. Mercifully, their portraits are nowhere in this novel, but next time they may not be so lucky. As they have always known.

Thanks to early readers, commentors, and enthusiasts: Ben Dalton, Eli Lee, Ann Kaiser, Alex Burrows, and Alice Chappell. An encouraging word goes a long way. Thanks also to Richard Gallagher, whose friendship and advice came at just the right age.

A special debt is owed to Clarissa Pabi, who has always championed my writing in general and this novel in particular.

I couldn't hope for a better and more tireless reader than Dave Wingrave, whose intolerance of sub-standard writing is his best (and most annoying) quality.

And lastly Zoey, to whom this book is dedicated. Thank you for suggesting my title and for a thousand other things.

Notes

Chapter Four: The story recounted by Eli Schultz is a retelling of a supposed Hassidic legend found in Elie Wiesel's *Somewhere a Master* (1982).

Chapter Twelve: Tovyah's Napoleonic narrative is a retelling of a legend found in Elie Wiesel's *Somewhere a Master* and also in Martin Buber's *Tales of the Hassidim* (1947).

Chapter Fifteen: Different versions of the tale Hannah reads can be found in Meyer Levin's *Classic Hassidic Tales* (1931) and also in Martin Buber's *Tales of the Hassidim*. The testimony of the fifteenth-century Tzaddik is loosely based on an account given in Gershom Scholem's *Major Trends in Jewish Mysticism* (1946).

Chapter Seventeen: Elsie's understanding of *Eyn Sof* is derived from Gershom Scholem's translation of selections from the Zohar (1949).

Chapter Eighteen: Rabbi Michael's telling of the story draws a few direction quotations from the King James Bible rendering of Judges.